CW01521421

SHADOWS

Alex Hunter is the *nom-de-plume* of a well-known business school academic and author based in Brussels. He is married with two grown-up children, a dog and 5,000 square metres of unkempt Belgian countryside, which he refers to as a wildlife garden. Alex Hunter has written three best-selling management books under his 'real' name and *Shadows* is his first thriller.

SHADOWS

ALEX HUNTER

WHITE &
MACLEAN
PUBLISHING

First published in Belgium as a paperback original
in 2009 by White & MacLean Publishing

Copyright ©Alex Hunter, 2009

The moral right of the author has been asserted.

All rights reserved.
No part of this publications may be reproduced,
stored in a retrieval system, or transmitted, in
any form or by any means without the prior
written permission of the publisher, nor be
otherwise circulated in any form of binding or
cover other than that in which it is published
and without a similar condition being
imposed on the subsequent purchaser.

ISBN: 978-2-930583-00-6

Cover Design: Arati Devasher
Designed and Typeset in Adobe Garamond Pro by
Arati Devasher
www.aratidevasher.com

Printed and bound in Great Britain by
CPI Antony Rowe, Chippenham and Eastbourne

White & MacLean Publishing
La Houlette 3
B-1470 Baisy-Thy
Belgium
www.whiteandmaclean.eu

To Fiona, Riba and Siobhán

All authors rely on the help and encouragement of numerous people and I would particularly like to express my thanks to Amanda Scott, the American historical novelist, who was unstinting in her support and assistance, and who gave me a Master Class on writing a novel. My thanks also to Antony Lawson-Smith for his technical help and being there to talk about plot ideas over several good lunches. I am also grateful to Paul Müller, who assisted in the editing and preparation of the manuscript, and Fiona White, who copy-edited the manuscript numerous times without complaint. Of course, any errors or omissions are entirely mine.

Alex Hunter
Belgium

As this book is a work of fiction, the characters, incidents and dialogue are drawn from the author's imagination and are not to be construed as real. Any resemblance to actual events or persons, living or dead, is purely coincidental.

PROLOGUE

Cîme de Caron, Val Thorens, France

The French Ski Patrol brought the body down the mountain.

The wind drove the falling snow in swirls through the gathering dusk. The cable cars had ceased operating and most of the skiers were off the slopes.

At the *téléphérique* station below the Cîme de Caron a small group watched the ski-patrol manhandle the sledge, with its orange nylon bag strapped to it, down the treacherous Combe de Caron: the Devil's Chasm.

Three in the waiting group wore the blue ski suits of the Val Thorens *police municipale*, while others were in the green outfits of resort employees. A radio crackled and one of the police officers spoke briefly before silence returned.

A break in the falling snow revealed two other figures high on the slope, one in police blue and the other in the darker blue of the *pompiers* paramedics. They were descending swiftly, sliding to a stop in a spray of snow.

"Dead for hours," said the paramedic. "A few broken bones but you'll have to await the autopsy for cause of death."

The man with the radio nodded.

The policeman drove his sticks into the snow and waved a hand back towards the mountain. "No sign of where she went off, sir, but it looks like an accident."

Two hundred metres away, the killer put his binoculars back in his jacket, pulled on his goggles and skied down to the village out of sight by way of the back slope.

CHAPTER ONE

Twenty-four hours after the discovery of the dead girl, Luc Hansen walked into the small police station in Val Thorens, stamped his feet to dislodge the snow and approached the counter.

"Inspector Maillot, please," he said quietly.

"Is he expecting you?" the sergeant asked.

"Yes. I'm Luc Hansen of the DER," he replied, referring to the *Département de Enquête et Recherche*, the European Union's intelligence and security service.

The sergeant nodded, turned and walked off down a corridor that led further into the building.

As he waited, Hansen contemplated the events of the last few hours. The telephone call from Maillot had come in at eight that morning and had galvanised the DER into a frenzy of activity. He had been pulled from his current cases and sent from Brussels, via a quickly arranged military flight to a French

3

airfield near Albertville and a rather unpleasant sixty-kilometre car ride through the snow to Val Thorens.

The sergeant returned, accompanied by a well-built, middle-aged man who immediately held out his hand.

"*Monsieur* Hansen, I'm Henri Maillot." The men shook hands, rapidly assessing each other. "You got here quickly. I hadn't expected you until the morning."

Hansen shrugged, "The Director said it was urgent."

"I suppose it is…I suppose it is. Not the best of facilities but we have some good coffee." Maillot led the way through to his small office.

Hansen took off his thick parka, looked around in vain for somewhere to hang it and dropped it on the floor. Maillot gestured at a chair.

"Take a seat. Have you been briefed on developments so far?"

"All I know is you've got a dead body, a probable identity as Emma Darbly from her ski pass and you asked us to help." Hansen handed over his warrant card, which Maillot glanced at and handed back.

"Inspector…why did you contact us?"

"I didn't," replied Maillot stiffly. "I called the Belgian international police liaison office. They put me through to you. I guess there must have been a flag on her name."

Luc replied noncommittally, "Ah, I see. Do we have anything on how she died?"

"The medical examiner reckons her neck was broken before she went off the mountain."

"So it's murder?"

"We're proceeding on that assumption."

"But an autopsy hasn't been done?"

Maillot shook his head. "No. We need a positive ID and a next-of-kin release."

"I checked around in Brussels before coming down. It appears Emma Darbly, of the European Press Bureau, is on a week's skiing holiday. We should have an address by morning. This is a recent picture of her." Hansen handed over a print.

"Yes, that's her. *Mon dieu*, you lot work fast."

"We aim to please." Hansen's smile flashed white teeth in sharp contrast to the olive-brown skin of his face. He ran his hand across his short-cropped black hair and noted that the other man relaxed.

"Mind you, the journey down wasn't much fun. How about some of that coffee?"

Maillot nodded and went out. Hansen looked round at the piles of papers, forms and files that were so typical of a provincial French police office. He had seen many such over the years — and not always as a welcome guest.

Maillot returned with two steaming mugs. "And something to keep out the cold." He took a bottle of brandy from a drawer and poured a shot into each mug. The coffee was as good as Maillot had promised and the brandy was welcome.

Maillot asked abruptly, "Why is the DER involved in a murder inquiry? I thought you were *s'occupé* with organised crime, terrorist threats, international fraud and intelligence work…"

Hansen considered the question and decided that, for once, the truth might serve him best.

"We have a particular interest in Gerald Darbly, Emma's father. He's a Member of the European Parliament so we have a file on him. Emma's a well-known journalist and her murder raises all sorts of questions."

Maillot asked suspiciously, "Oh, I see. Are you going to take over the case then?"

"No. The case is yours. I'm just here to help."

Hansen knew full well that Maillot would want it. A high-profile murder is always good to have on one's record but he did not have the resources that the DER could make available.

"*D'accord*. So what is the next step?"

"I'll look around on my own and let you know what I find."

He looked steadily at Maillot. The DER, under its charter, took precedence over national police forces in terms of authority and could act independently. He did not need Maillot's permission, and he knew that Maillot knew that, but a cordial working relationship was better than an antagonistic one.

"And you'll keep me informed?"

"Absolutely." Hansen smiled and stretched, easing the stiffness in his shoulders. When he saw Maillot's eyes flicker towards his wrist, he casually pulled his sleeve down to cover the tattoo.

Maillot said, "*La Légion*, huh?"

Hansen nodded but said nothing and knew that Maillot would not ask. Legionnaires did not talk about themselves. He had joined the French Foreign Legion straight from university instead of doing his Belgian National Service. After serving in the Legion's paratroop regiment, the elite 2nd REP, in Europe and in the jungles and deserts of Africa, he had left at the end of his second four-year contract.

"How long have we got before contacting the family?" He changed the subject to Maillot's evident disappointment.

The policeman glanced at the clock. "It's now, what... eighteen hundred hours on Tuesday. I can give you until Thursday afternoon...that's when I have to tell the Investigating Magistrate what we've got. If she's satisfied with our ID, we tell the family then. We only get seventy-two hours before the system kicks in."

"How can I contact you direct?"

Maillot took out a card and handed it to him. "This is my mobile number. We've pretty good coverage up here. They even work on the slopes."

The après-ski drinking sessions were in full swing, the bars teeming with people, as Hansen made his way through the town. He had not told the policeman the complete truth: he already knew the address where Emma Darbly was supposed to be staying. The sharp air of the mountains felt good and the walk eased his travel-stiffness.

The apartment block was not easy to find and Hansen almost missed the entrance. A security lamp flicked on as he approached the door. Finding it unlocked, he made his way to the second floor. The door of the apartment stood open and he could hear female voices. Risking a quick look, he saw a redhead and a blond, both of whom seemed to be speaking at the same time to a third person beyond his view. The girls in the apartment appeared to be about to go out for the evening. He listened for a while longer and then returned to the ground floor.

Twenty minutes passed before the three girls left the building. Hansen let them get about thirty metres ahead of him and then followed. They walked arm in arm, showing no sign of stress or concern at the fact that they had not seen their friend for more than twenty-four hours. That intrigued Hansen. They entered a bar and sat down.

Hansen chose a table next to where the three girls were now drinking hot chocolate. He ordered a *café noir*, paid for it and listened to the conversation at the next table: clothes, skiing, what runs they would do the following day, clothes again, their plans for the rest of the evening — all the normal conversation of friends on holiday. The girls talked on and the build-up of noise in the bar became a distraction. As a result, he almost missed it.

It was the redhead speaking: "...after all, she's *your* friend, Gillian, and I think it a bit much not telling us where she was going."

The blond said, "Emma may be my friend, but you know how she's always secretive if there's a new man about."

The third girl, a plump brunette, joined in. "I bet she's shacked up with a ski bum and doesn't want to share him."

"And I bet he has a tight little arse," the redhead said and they all laughed.

The brunette said, "She'll turn up tomorrow all innocent-like and we'll have to beat it out of her."

"You just want to know the gory details," replied the blond as they put some money on the table and left the bar.

Hansen followed at a distance. He had a problem if they went straight back to the apartment, but if they went off to eat he could search their rooms before they returned. The three girls went through the sports centre, up past the swimming pool and then headed for the upper part of town. Hansen watched them enter a crowded restaurant where they were immediately surrounded by a group of attentive young men.

Hansen went straight to their apartment. In the dim corridor he pulled out a flat wallet and unzipped it to reveal a set of picklocks. Thirty seconds later he pushed the door open and stepped inside.

The balcony door was open. He crossed the room and looked outside. There were plenty of footprints of various sizes but no sign of anyone.

He switched on the lights, shrugged at the disorder and started his search. It had been ransacked: clothes were scattered, cushions and magazines strewn about. It was the same story in the double bedroom. The next room was a single and, according to letters on the bedside table, occupied by the girl called Gillian. It was also in a state of disorder. Hansen considered: it was either made by a common burglar — there were enough of them around in a place like this — or it was a professional wanting it to look like a burglary. Then he thought that perhaps he had disturbed the intruder, explaining the open door to the balcony.

The final room was tidier but looked as though it had not been used for a couple of days. Hansen searched it methodically. The cupboard and dresser revealed nothing. The bedside table, however, produced a bunch of keys and a wallet containing large denomination euro notes, two credit cards and a driver's licence in the name of Emma Darbly. Jackpot!

Hansen opened the small cupboard beneath the drawer to reveal some books, a bottle of mineral water and a BlackBerry smartphone. He reasoned that there had to be a computer somewhere — journalists always had the tools of their trade with them. And the most likely place would be...yes...there it was under the bed. He reached under and pulled out the bag. Inside was an Apple laptop along with various cables and some blank CDs.

Hansen carried the computer into the main living area and sat down at the table. He switched it on and, after a few moments, a login dialogue box appeared. He swore quietly and switched off. He would have to take it with him.

It was the same with the BlackBerry. He put the equipment back in the bag, picked up the bunch of keys and, certain that he had left no evidence of his presence in the apartment, switched off the lights.

Wednesday 5 February, Val Thorens

The morning air was brisk and maintenance crews were still servicing the cable cars as Hansen walked down to the big covered car park at the bottom of the town. His earlier enquiries had given him the make and number of Emma Darbly's car and revealed that it was not at her home in Brussels. He wanted to see if it was in Val Thorens.

The car park was huge and about ninety percent full. He started at the top, checked each floor and had almost completed his search when he saw it. The Renault Clio was parked in a corner, covered in the same fine white dust that lay on all the vehicles. There was no one around so he took a closer look.

Judging by the thickness of the dust it had been there for a few days. He noticed disturbances around the door handles, the boot-lid and a rippled pattern of dust on the windows as if someone had recently entered the vehicle and then slammed the door. He looked through the windows without moving the dust but could see nothing. He walked round the Renault and saw no sign of forced entry. He wiped a window and took another look inside. Nothing out of the ordinary, but the rippling still bothered him.

He checked the dust on nearby cars but it was smooth and undisturbed.

He knelt down and looked under the car but saw nothing suspicious. He took out a small flashlight, lay down on his back and eased himself partially underneath the vehicle. The neat package of *plastique* with a trembler switch rested on the drive shaft, ready to explode when the engine started.

Merde! Hansen cursed as he carefully eased himself from beneath the car and away from the vehicle. This was very messy. He took out his mobile phone and dialled Maillot's number. The Frenchman was not going to like this.

Thursday 6 February, Brussels, Belgium

Karel Vandenhove, *Chef de Cabinet* to the European Union Commissioner for Foreign Affairs, looked at his watch and tried to hide his irritation. Why did these Thursday meetings have to take so damned long? He looked across the large table at the Commissioner for Foreign Affairs and tried to will him to get things moving. They needed an official position on aid to Iraq for next week's meeting of the full Commission and yet the pompous ass had only covered the first couple of items on the agenda. But Commissioner François de Foucaud seemed impervious to time constraints or subtle hints. Vandenhove sighed.

"Have you something you wish to contribute, my dear Karel?" de Foucaud asked sarcastically, his voice grating on Vandenhove's nerves.

"Commissioner, given the pressing urgency of the current situation and the escalation of violence in Iraq, we need to press ahead and establish a position on aid to the Kurds sooner rather than later."

De Foucaud flushed at the implied rebuke, "Quite, quite, Karel. You are absolutely right, of course."

Vandenhove was not concerned with the Commissioner's finer feelings or the minuet of protocol; if de Foucaud didn't like being told to get on then he shouldn't spend so much time on the unimportant. Damn but the man was a waste of space.

"May I propose, Commissioner, that we move directly to item six on the agenda?" Vandenhove spoke calmly and with a deference that fooled nobody in the room.

"Of course, Karel, if you feel we must."

After the general shuffling of papers had subsided, Vandenhove said, "Commissioner, let me be blunt. I firmly believe that we must take the position that the American and British approach on aid to Iraq is counterproductive. The European Union should take the lead in sending in aid." Vandenhove tried to hide his frustration. All he needed was for the Commission to take a position, any position, so he could tailor his plans accordingly.

There was a general murmuring of agreement and fifteen minutes later, a position had been established: the European Union should commence aid shipments immediately — starting with aid to the Kurds in the north.

Hiding his smile of satisfaction, Vandenhove excused himself from the meeting. It would probably go on for another couple of hours but it could do so without him.

Back in his slightly smaller but no less sumptuous office down the corridor from the Commissioner's large and lavishly appointed one on the eighth floor of the Bâtiment Breydel, Vandenhove picked up the list of incoming telephone messages and scanned it. Near the bottom was the name Gärtner followed by a mobile phone number. He would have to make that call.

Vandenhove reached for his mobile telephone.

A man answered on the third ring. "*Mit* Gärtner."

"You speak with Karel Vandenhove."

"*Ach*! And how is the Commission this week?" The German accent was pronounced.

"As always. Now, what's the problem?"

"*Mein Herr*, calm yourself. I never call unless it is important."

That was true enough, thought Vandenhove. Dieter Gärtner, Head of Security at Groupe Franco Belge, never called anyone unless he wanted something.

"So tell me what is so important that you call me here."

"I need more information. The girl knew nothing but was suspicious of my interest. She met with a fatal skiing accident on Monday."

"That is indeed unfortunate, and potentially dangerous. She was well connected here in Brussels."

"I do what I have to do." Gärtner's voice contained no emotion.

Vandenhove sighed, "The park, 18.00 hours." He hung up.

Two hours later Vandenhove left the Breydel, crossed to the Cinquantenaire Park and started walking towards the ghostly, floodlit triumphal arch that dominated the skyline. The constant drizzle made the tree-lined path an unpleasant route but the sodden grass beside it was not an option. He had gone less than fifty yards when he sensed someone beside him. He turned and found himself looking at a tall, muscular man in his late thirties, with watery blue eyes and dark hair, which Vandenhove knew was dyed. A deep knife scar was clearly visible against the pale skin of his right cheek, which was covered in neatly trimmed stubble.

"Gärtner, why did you kill the girl?"

"I told you. She became suspicious." Gärtner shrugged. "It's not important..."

Vandenhove snapped. "It *is* important. You're not being paid to kill people, you're being paid to protect our interests."

"I do what is necessary."

"Then do it more discreetly. Killing people attracts attention and we don't want attention. Understand?"

"*Herr* Vandenhove, I need more information. I know where the Darbly girl worked and where she lived, but I need more if I'm to find how much damage she's done."

"Very well. I'll call you on Monday."

Friday 7 February, Brussels

Alan Radcliffe, the 58-year-old Director of the DER, had a rather distracted professorial air despite having been in the security services all his working life. The 7 a.m. Friday morning team meeting — an institution in the DER — had just finished and he was now sitting at the large conference table in his office peering at Luc Hansen over his half-moon reading glasses. "You were unusually silent in the meeting, Luc. What's on your mind?"

"Emma Darbly. Her death seems so bizarre," Hansen replied.

"Do you want to tell me why?" While waiting for a response, he regarded the 35-year-old ex-Legionnaire, his most outstanding find for the DER. At one metre seventy-five and extremely fit, Luc Hansen was a serious young man with outstanding military skills, a superb investigator, an excellent linguist and an exceptional agent who specialised in authorised but deniable operations. It came at a price, of course: he was a bit of a maverick and had to be reigned in occasionally, but was one of those priceless men who are both dependable and absolutely trustworthy.

Hansen glanced down at his notes. "According to the French pathologist at yesterday's post-mortem, she was killed by a left-handed rotation of the neck delivered from behind — clearly a real professional killing — then thrown over the edge to make it look like an accident."

Radcliffe said nothing.

"So, why plant a bomb in her car if you intend to kill the victim somewhere else? That's just overkill."

"And your conclusion?"

"Perhaps the killer wasn't sure of getting her, or he was sending a message, or..."

"Are you sure the killer is a man?" Radcliffe asked.

"Yes, sir," replied Hansen emphatically. "The girl was tall and strong, so the killer had to be around one metre eighty-five and powerful. Definitely a male, and left-handed at that."

"So, not a casual killing?"

"No, sir. I think the killer was also after her computer and ran off when I broke into the flat. That's why I took it.

The local police were not happy but I think they understood, especially when I told them about the bomb under the girl's car."

"And what was in her computer that would get her killed?"

Hansen shrugged, "I don't know…yet. She was a journalist who wrote some really in-depth exposés so maybe she got too close to something."

"And you want to run with it?"

"Yes, sir."

"Very well. I'll reassign your other cases, but Claudia Chalon has the Gerald Darbly file, so liaise with her." Radcliffe waited until Hansen nodded agreement and then said, "Right, you'd better get on with it."

Despite the slow moving traffic, the yellow BMW 1100 GS was making good progress around the Brussels inner ring road, its throaty exhaust hammering at the inside of the tunnels. The rider handled the big bike with confidence, correcting expertly as the rear wheel momentarily lost traction on a patch of oil, before powering up the slope from the Porte de Hal Tunnel and then down to the railway viaduct. Pausing for a moment at the lights, the rider turned left towards the Gare du Midi, the Brussels South station, and then accelerated hard under the railway, across the tram tracks and down the steep slope into the underground car park.

Ten minutes later, the rider strode across the reception area of the DER while removing the bright yellow helmet to reveal the smiling face and short black hair of a female in her late twenties.

The security guard looked up and said, "Morning, Miss Donnelly."

"Hi, Marty!" Her voice was light and tinged with an Irish lilt.

The guard opened the barrier and Joanna Donnelly went down the corridor to the office she shared with Luc Hansen.

"*Merde*! What are you doing here? The boss said you'd pulled an all-nighter." Luc sat back and lit a cigarette.

Joanna pointed her right index finger at him in a simulated handgun fist. "I thought you were quitting the weed."

"And I thought you were dealing with security attacks on the Commission's computers at the Breydel." He ignored her comment.

"Done and dusted. So what have we got?" She dumped her rucksack beside her desk.

"A dead girl, a computer and a BlackBerry."

"Sounds fun. Let me get out of this lot and you can tell me all about it."

She started to remove the protective clothes, knowing Luc was watching. Conscious of her own good looks, she was used to male attention, but didn't trade on it as a matter of taste.

"You can take your eyes off a girl while she's undressing…"

She and Luc had been operational partners for two years and while Luc did what she called 'the action man stuff', she was responsible for the team's communications and technical support, and deployed a range of computer skills that he did not begin to understand.

Joanna ran her hands through her hair and sat down.

"Who was the girl?"

"Emma Darbly, daughter of Gerald Darbly, MEP."

Joanna whistled in surprise. "How did she die?"

"Someone broke her neck and threw her off a mountain." He pushed Emma Darbly's computer and BlackBerry across the table. "We need to know what's hidden inside these."

"I assume these are hers," Joanna said neutrally.

"Yes."

"And did we get them legally, Luc, or did you just take them?"

"Who me?" he asked innocently.

"Jeezus, Luc, the boss is not going to be pleased."

"You're one suspicious *poule*, Jo Donnelly. I've already told the Director, so there." He pushed a bar of chocolate across the desk with a smile.

Joanna shook her head in mock exasperation. Luc was right, of course. She was suspicious, but the DER had procedures and he did not always follow them. She knew he had run-ins with the Director from time to time but usually got away with them. He was the team leader so there was not much she could do about it.

She nibbled the chocolate, then picked up the BlackBerry, opened her laptop computer, took a multi-format cable out of her desk drawer and connected the two. A few keystrokes later, she scribbled two numbers on a pad of paper and handed the phone and paper across.

"The first is the four-digit basic PIN, but she had a second one of eight digits, the master PIN number." She yawned. "God! I'm knackered. I'll take the computer with me and get you the passwords and answers over the weekend. Okay?"

"She was obviously into security. You anticipate any problems?"

"If I hit a wall I'll come in Sunday night and run *CrackIt* on the main computer."

"Monday will do. Get some sleep."

"What are you going to do?"

"Check out Emma Darbly's apartment this afternoon before the police start walking all over it." He picked up the paper with the PIN numbers.

Emma Darbly's top floor apartment was located in a *fin de siècle* townhouse at the end of a cul-de-sac off a quiet, narrow street near the lakes in the Ixelles neighbourhood. The house itself was vaguely art nouveau but the panel of bell pushes was very modern, as was the combination lock panel to the right of the front door. A discrete sign in etched plastic next to it provided instructions in a dozen European languages and Arabic:

> The Occupant may have given
> you a one-time four-digit code.
> Enter that code and press the
> talk-key for that apartment.
> Otherwise ring for Reception.

Luc scratched behind his ear. It seemed obvious that apartment key-holders would use the same keypad for their own entry. From memory, he tried Emma Darbly's birthday in both European and American orderings, the subgroups of four-digit pairs in her phone numbers, both fixed and mobile, her birth year forward and backward. No luck. He fingered the useless picklocks in his jacket pocket.

An elegantly dressed but elderly woman approached the door and Luc stepped aside courteously. He watched her enter an eight-digit number and the door clicked open. As the door closed behind the woman he turned away and thought for a while. Would the system have individual combinations for each flat? It seemed likely.

Luc turned to the keypad and entered, '12481632'. The door clicked open and he entered a well-lit hallway, grateful for his ability to remember numbers after seeing them only once.

He ran silently up the stairs. A hall light clicked on as he reached the right apartment. He pulled on a pair of surgical gloves, selected a key from the bunch he had found with Emma's things and opened the door.

The apartment was a surprise. One large dining-come-sitting room with an open fire, a small but functional kitchen, a bathroom and a bedroom with a king-size bed. The whole place was obsessively tidy and organised. Luc inventoried the bathroom: female toiletries, no lurking razor and aftershave: no sign of a resident male. He checked the bedroom: tidy, overly so. Beside the bed was a pile of novels: Jilly Cooper, Anaïs Nin, Simone de Beauvoir, Catherine Cookson, Amanda Scott. The dressing table echoed the same obsessive neatness. Perhaps she was just a well-organised young woman.

The sitting room had a desk positioned against one wall with a fax-answerphone, space for a computer, a printer and a range of dictionaries.

But something was not right.

Then it came to him. He had not touched anything but now ran his finger across the bookshelf in front of the dictionaries, then squatted down to look obliquely across several flat surfaces that were backlit by the windows. There was no sign of dust on any of them. He would easily have spotted the inevitable fluff even after a day's absence, never mind a week. The place was spotlessly clean as though someone had very recently wiped it down. Was there a super cleaning lady in the picture, or...had a professional already searched the apartment?

Luc took out his wallet of picklocks, extracted a dentist's mirror and a small pencil flashlight. Then, cautiously, he opened the desk drawer a short way and peered inside with the aid of the mirror. Nothing of interest. The first drawer of the small filing cabinet gave nothing more: mainly private papers, bank statements and proof copies, presumably from some of her published articles. He had already determined that she had a good income and paid the rent regularly. No obvious outstanding debts.

He inserted the mirror into the second file drawer and switched on the flashlight. Wires led from a lever switch to the back of the drawer…it had been rigged.

Very carefully, he removed the mirror, put it away and reached for his mobile telephone.

Two hours later, Jacques Legrand, the DER scene-of-crime officer, a tall, thin man with small gold-framed glasses, closed his notebook and nodded to his forensics colleague, Dr Monique Verhagen, who showed Luc the explosive device.

"*Plastique*. Probably military stock C4 but we'll check. Simple lever detonator. You were very lucky," she said.

"So it seems. Can you find out where it came from?"

"Possibly, but it'll take time. This stuff needs an End User Certificate and it's closely controlled. I'll let you know."

Luc nodded his thanks and turned back to Legrand.

"Is there anything else you can tell me, Jacques?"

"No fingerprints. Your guy also uses surgical gloves. Very professional. The answer phone had seven messages plus a number of connections that didn't leave a message." He referred to his notebook: "Six messages from people wishing her a good holiday and one from her father earlier today."

"Saying what?"

"'Emma, where are you? This is your father. Call me. We need to talk.' Then he rang off."

"Interesting! I wonder why no one has told him she's dead."

CHAPTER TWO

It was raining heavily as Quentin Morgan, a junior project manager at EBRD, the European Bank for Reconstruction and Development, eased his silver-grey Porsche slowly forward in the morning London rush-hour traffic. This was the worst part of the day: the slow grind into work in the marble and over-lavish offices of the EBRD — not that we do much reconstruction and development, thought Morgan. In the five years he had been there, he had watched with amazement as the management had built the organisation a fabulous headquarters but had blatantly failed to disburse the development funds for which they were responsible. So far, the bank had not been a model of modern efficiency.

The traffic lurched forward. He could now see Tower Bridge, so twenty minutes to go at this rate. He was going to be late… again! Fuck it! He had to be careful. He had to avoid attracting attention at this stage.

He looked to his right and saw the lights of the St Catherine Dock development. In another few months he would have enough money for a deposit on a nice flat there overlooking the harbour and the river — Emma would like that — Emma of the long legs and insatiable sex drive. He let the thought wash over him.

Suddenly he was past the Tower and five minutes later he was in the car park. A short walk took him across Bishopsgate and into Exchange Square and the luxurious headquarters of the EBRD. It was 7.41 a.m., only eleven minutes late.

A detour via the coffee machine brought Morgan to his desk at 7.58 a.m. and he logged onto the computer network at 8 a.m. precisely. Mrs Kirkpatrick, the department chief, or 'the old biddy' as Morgan called her, had not been in her office as he slipped past and if she checked her records, she'd find he had logged in by the correct time. He called up the email program: nothing from Emma. Where could she be? She should be back from skiing by now. There was another message from Vandenhove at the Commission in Brussels.

Morgan ran his hand through his wavy blond hair. The girls in the section said he looked like a young Robert Redford and indicated he could 'audition' them anytime. He hit the compose button and wrote a quick message to young Anna, the gorgeous Swede in transmissions, proposing a film and bed (in that order). That sent, he opened the message from Brussels. Another transfer to make and that meant more money into the Morgan bank account. He smirked in satisfaction.

Monday 10 February, Brussels

In the DER offices overlooking Brussels Midi Station, Luc lit a cigarette and poured some coffee. It was a little after 9.30 but he was satisfied that he had retrieved all the data from Emma Darbly's mobile phone.

The phone's memory had forty-seven numbers listed. Luc had copied them out on a pad. Eight were numbers in the Commission offices (he recognised the Brussels 295 area code) including, he was surprised to see, the number of the DER. A further twenty numbers covered Belgium, Luxembourg, France, Germany and the Netherlands. The last nine numbers, however, all had country codes he did not recognise. These he put aside for more detailed analysis.

He had checked the most recently called numbers. There were eight and they all matched numbers from the memory. One of the calls had been placed to the DER. There were no stored text messages.

"I wonder who she was calling here," he said aloud as he called up the internal DER directory on the computer and entered the number. "Mark Anderson in Central Records. Interesting!"

The telephone on his desk rang and he picked up.

"Luc, it's Jo. I'll be there in about twenty minutes. In the mean time, I've asked her service provider, ProxiStar, for Emma's calls for the last three months. They're emailing you the record right now."

"Great. Any luck with the rest?"

"Yes. I've got all the passwords and stuff. It's not very exciting but no doubt you'll tell me why I'm doing all this."

"The minute you arrive." He hung up and went back to his analysis.

By the time Joanna arrived, Luc had constructed a spreadsheet that correlated the telephone numbers in the dead girl's mobile telephone and the recently called numbers with names and addresses and frequency of calls. He had also checked the 'recently received calls' list and added them to the spreadsheet. As a result, he had sixty numbers and had identified fifty-five.

"Why are we interested in a simple murder?" asked Joanna as she sat down.

"Because we're interested in the father," replied Luc.

"But isn't Claudia Chalon running that case?"

"Yes, but we're keeping this one until we find a link."

Joanna looked askance for a moment but Luc said nothing.

"Luc…"

"What?"

"Claudia is not going to like this. You know how prickly she gets."

"Tough. The boss wants us to run with this for the time being. Now, what have you got?"

Joanna referred to her notes. "There are a total of fifty-four files and three databases from the two machines." She slid a list across the desk. "Three spreadsheets covering her business expenses, private expenses — well organised girl, this one — and a diary. Expenses are normal, nothing out of the ordinary, and the diary gives no real information. The fourth spreadsheet is interesting though. It's a series of movements, probably money, but I'm not certain. The headings are some sort of code. The numbers are small but could represent much larger ones."

Luc made a note.

Joanna continued, "The fifty remaining files are all in MS Word. Forty are articles she's written dating back to the beginning of last year, all of them with publication dates. She's good, by the way. I read a couple of her pieces." She picked up Luc's cigarettes and shook one out.

"I thought you'd quit smoking," he said with a wry smile. She quickly put the cigarette back and reached for the chocolate instead.

"Okay, there are some form letters, a list of information sources and two files that could be important."

"Why?" prompted Luc.

"One file is a series of dated entries of information, meetings and ideas. It's full of acronyms, jargon and initials. And the other is the beginning of an article. It's only about three hundred words long and is the start of a second draft according to the file name."

"What's it about?"

"That's what's so interesting. It's about an international aid project and how the money is being misspent."

"That's not odd. That's what journalists write about."

"Yes, but she suggests that this is a European Union aid project to Iraq. I checked…there are no authorised EU aid projects to Iraq!"

"Now that *is* interesting." Luc made another note. "Are there any names mentioned?"

"No."

"What about the databases?"

"Names and addresses and telephone numbers; she kept two on the laptop and one on the BlackBerry. There is a certain amount of overlap."

"Email?"

"Now that is real interesting. She had an email account with Skynet and a second one with AOL," said Joanna, naming the local Belgian service and the biggest of the US suppliers in Europe. "I checked the files. There's nothing."

"Nothing? You mean she didn't save any of the messages?" Luc looked incredulous.

Joanna nodded. "I'm running a recovery program for deleted files to see what turns up. What have you got from the GSM?" she added, using the acronym for the Global System for Mobile communications that most people in Europe use when referring to their mobile telephones.

Luc sent his spreadsheet analysis to her computer via the network. "Nothing unusual, except for one number in London. It turns out to be the European Bank for Reconstruction and Development, the EBRD. And there are five I haven't identified yet."

"And one inside the DER," said Joanna pointing at the entry. She leant forward and read the notes. "Mark Anderson…that's interesting. Why would Emma Darbly be calling someone in DER Central Records on a regular basis?"

"What else do you know about Mark Anderson?"

"Personally or professionally speaking?" Joanna leaned back and bit into some chocolate.

"Both," said Luc as he reached for his packet of Gauloise Bleu. Meeting her look of reproof, he sighed, adding, "It's damned hard to quit after twenty years."

She smiled sympathetically and then said, "Anderson is about 30, good looking, a sporty type, into bodybuilding and squash, but a bit of a loner. I think he's been with the DER for about two years. Very professional." She accessed the DER server and Anderson's data came up on the screen along with a recent photograph. "Not married, no known girlfriends…or boyfriends. Lives alone in a flat on Avenue Winston Churchill. Nothing unusual."

"Except that Emma Darbly called him at least every other day for the last two months from her mobile." Luc's increasing concern was evident. "The record shows they talked for about five minutes each time. What's his home phone number?"

Joanna gave it and Luc checked the records again and said, "Yep, she called him regularly at home as well."

"Isn't he in charge of the data team at Central? Do you think he's leaking information to her?"

"It's possible." Luc regarded her thoughtfully.

"What?"

"This has happened in the past and it puts us all at risk. I'll have to take this to the Director after we've checked a bit more."

Joanna tapped the screen, "Okay, these are Anderson's outgoing calls from the office." Luc came round and scanned the list over her shoulder. Anderson had made very few calls from his own extension and they were all routine stuff: members of the DER, various data centres with which he worked and the occasional call to a restaurant. Joanna scrolled the page bringing up the call activity for the last two weeks.

"Will you look at that?" Joanna pointed. "His call rate has trebled in the last few days. At least three per day to the European Press Bureau…"

"…and just as many to Emma's mobile." He looked at Joanna. "Any chance you can get a record of calls from his mobile and home numbers?"

Joanna immediately entered some code and after a few moments said, "This lot's his mobile…nothing unusual. He's getting through to her flat but that's about it. Ah, now we have his home phone. Yep, similar pattern. He's desperate to talk to her."

"Obviously doesn't know she's dead. If he was leaking information to her then we've got a real problem. I think we'd better check this out."

Mark Anderson was seriously worried. He had failed to make contact with Emma for over a week and it was unlike her to be out of touch for so long. She should have been back on Saturday. He had important information for her but he couldn't leave it on her answering machine and he certainly couldn't tell anyone at her office. No, it was too personal for that. If he was quick, he could get to her flat and back during his lunch break.

He looked at the rain, sighed and picked up his coat.

Anderson walked through the foyer and out towards the Metro. No point in taking the car as there was never anywhere to park. The Metro and tram would be just as quick. He hoped he wasn't making a fool of himself and panicking, but he had to see her. He had so much to tell her.

Fifteen minutes later he reached the building in which Emma Darbly lived. His heart was beginning to pound but he'd come this far so there was no point in turning back. Please let her be at home.

He entered a one-time code and pressed the bell for her apartment. He had been here a few times but never during the day. Emma had said she had nosy neighbours and didn't want to arouse suspicion. He rang again. Still no answer. There was silence. He felt his heart rate rise. Shit, where was she? He had to see her.

"Damn, damn, damn." He pressed the bell again. "Oh fuck it."

She wasn't there. He wished he had her main access code and a key but she wouldn't give them to him, although she had a key to his place. He turned away and started down the street. He'd call her office and see if they knew where she was.

But it was just after 4.15 p.m. before he finally had the chance to call Emma's office. The data centre had been busy when he got back from her flat and he had been called into a meeting, which had only just finished. But there were a few minutes to spare so…

He identified himself to the receptionist at the European Press Bureau and was put through to the manager.

"It's Mark Anderson, is Emma back yet?"

He felt himself go cold as he listened to the woman at the other end of the line. It couldn't be true! There must have been a mistake! She couldn't be dead! He dropped the phone and cradled his head.

"No," he muttered and then sat up. "No!" he screamed.

He could see his colleagues looking at him. He swept the telephone off his desk.

"Impossible!"

Now he could see a security guard coming towards him. She was talking on her radio. Another person was approaching.

"What's the matter? Mark?"

"She's dead," he shouted.

"Who's dead?"

"Emma. Oh my god!" Tears were streaming down his face and he flung them away, angry with himself that he could not control his emotions.

A glass of clear liquid was placed in his hand and an authoritative voice told him to drink. He did so without thinking. He suddenly felt calmer and a great lassitude welled up inside him. He relaxed and closed his eyes.

A hand on his shoulder was shaking him gently. He opened his eyes, recognised Joanna Donnelly and smiled weakly.

"Hello, Mark. What happened?" Joanna's Irish lilt softening the request.

There was someone else with her. Mark tried to focus and then realised that Luc Hansen was there as well. His brain started to function again.

Hesitantly, he began to explain that he had just learned that his girlfriend was dead.

"How did you find out?" Joanna asked.

"I called her office. They told me she had died in a skiing accident."

"Who was she?"

"Emma Darbly." He noticed Joanna glance at her colleague. There was something about this that bothered him but he was too wound up to work it out.

"How did you meet her?"

"At a party last year and we started seeing each other after that." He paused. "I knew she was a journalist but we talked about books more than anything else."

Luc asked, "Did she know what you do?"

"I guess so. She used to ring me here every day. We never talked about my work and I didn't ask about hers either. It was easier that way. I didn't want to have to lie."

"Why would you have had to lie, Mark?" said Joanna.

"Come on, Jo. This is a classified job with a high security clearance. If I'd opened my mouth about it I'd have lost my job."

"So what *did* you talk about?" Luc's scepticism apparent in his voice.

"Food and drink. Travel. Us. That sort of thing."

"Did you visit her flat?"

"Not often. I picked her up there occasionally. She used to come and stay at my place most weekends. I even gave her a key." He slumped forward. "Oh, God, she's dead. She's really dead."

He gradually pulled himself together and sat up.

"Why didn't you go skiing with her?" Luc continued.

"I couldn't get leave. Anyway she was going with a bunch of girlfriends."

"Did you go to her flat today?"

"Yes. That's when I got really concerned. I thought she was coming back on Saturday. I rang her office earlier this morning and they said she hadn't come in but they expected her today. I went to her flat at lunchtime, but she wasn't there. I called her office again and that's when they told me she'd been killed in a skiing accident. Oh, hell!" Tears ran down his cheeks and he sniffed loudly.

Joanna patted him on his shoulder. "It's okay, Mark. Look, it's well after five. Go home, get some rest and we'll talk again tomorrow."

He nodded and managed to walk to the door reasonably steadily. He'd go home and have a drink.

"He's not telling the whole truth," said Luc turning to Joanna as the door closed behind Anderson.

"I think you're wrong," she replied.

Dieter Gärtner was annoyed. He had already searched Emma Darbly's flat but had found nothing of interest. Her office was a problem that would have to wait. He was sure she had been on to something and he needed to know what, and quickly.

Gärtner reread the paper Vandenhove had given him that morning. The fat man clearly had sources that he did not know about. Obviously, he had bribed someone, or threatened them into revealing information. Probably got his current job that way as well — although why anyone with a successful commercial business that had made him rich would want to work for the European Commission was beyond him. If you could bribe the bastards, why bother working for them?

He checked the information again. Emma Darbly had a boyfriend called Mark Anderson who worked for the DER. If those bastards were involved, he would have to work fast. The paper contained not only Anderson's address but also a telephone number. He took out his mobile telephone.

It took three attempts before a voice said, "Mark Anderson, can I help you?"

"Mr Anderson, I'm a friend of Emma's and…"

"She's dead." The voice was flat, lifeless, the speaker in a state of shock.

"I know, I saw her in Val Thorens just before she had the accident." That at least was true, he thought. He put as much sympathy as he could into his voice. "It was terrible shock. The police asked me to bring some of her stuff back but I don't know where to deliver it. Her flat is empty and it doesn't seem right to leave it at the office."

"You can bring it here, I suppose. I'll get it back to her mother." Anderson's voice was hardly above a whisper.

"I really don't want to bother you but…"

Tuesday 11 February, Brussels

"*Merde*! What a fucking mess," said Luc as he surveyed the inside of the apartment.

"I suppose that's one way of putting it," replied Benoît Montegnie with a tight grin. At one metre eighty, he was slightly taller than Luc and was dressed in faded jeans and a black leather jacket and had his long brown hair roughly combed into a pigtail.

"All right, Benny, talk to me," said Luc.

"Nothing much to say. We got here as instructed. Rang the bell but there was no answer, so I sprang the lock, found this and called you." Benoît shrugged and watched as Luc contemplated the body of Mark Anderson.

"Luc, are you going to tell me what this is about?"

Luc and Benoît had been Legionnaires together and when Benoît had finally left the Legion, Luc had arranged for him to be taken on by EFL Security, the DER cover operation that handled surveillance and a whole range of tactical support activities. When Anderson had failed to show up for work, Luc had asked Benoît to find out why.

Jacques Legrand, the DER scene-of-crime officer, entered the room accompanied by Dr Monique Verhagen.

Legrand gestured at the body, "Dead bodies this time, Luc? Good to have a bit of a change, huh?"

"Hi, Jacques. Yes, but watch out for more booby traps," he said as he crossed the room to squat beside the forensics specialist as she studied the body.

"Monique, How was he killed?"

She looked up. "His neck's been broken very expertly. No fight, just a quick twist and that's that."

"From the back or front?" Luc asked thoughtfully.

Dr Verhagen studied the body more closely and then looked round the crime scene. Finally, she looked at Luc.

"From the back, most probably. A left-hand rotation. The autopsy will tell us more. Why?"

"Because this is probably linked to Emma Darbly's murder," Luc replied.

"I'll need to see the other autopsy report to confirm similarity and likelihood of it being the same killer. Can you let me have it?"

"I'll get it to you. When was he killed?"

"Best estimate…dead for about fifteen hours."

"Thanks, Monique."

Luc regarded the body. Emma Darbly and her boyfriend murdered in the same way was too much of a coincidence. There had to be a strong link.

He turned to Legrand. "Any sign of forced entry?"

"No. He must have let the killer in."

An hour later, Radcliffe considered the information Luc had given him. "Was Anderson leaking information to the dead girl?"

"There's no evidence of that, sir, but the data team are checking. I've asked Benny to act as liaison. He knows what we're looking for."

"And your conclusion?"

"The killer is still looking for her files."

Radcliffe grunted. "Shouldn't you have put a guard on Anderson?"

"No reason to, sir," Luc replied calmly.

Radcliffe replied tartly, "Well, *someone* knew he was seeing the Darbly girl and knew where to find him and we still don't know for sure what the killer is looking for."

"I might have a lead on that, boss," said Joanna as she entered the room.

"Well?"

"I've found a couple of partially retrievable files. The first one contains notes about the EU aid project to Iraq we found earlier and gives us the project number ZX.98.02.02.04."

Radcliffe turned to regard her in some impatience. "What type of project is it?"

"A multi-country, multi-sector, multi-year aid project into Eastern Europe that started in 1998. Just why she thought it had anything to do with Iraq, I have no idea."

"Then you'll just have to find out, won't you," he replied.

"And the second file, Jo?" Luc prompted.

"I can't recover the file contents, Luc, but she burnt it to a CD entitled, 'Journal for Mark' and it is dated early on the Monday she was killed."

"Good work, Jo. I'll get on to Maillot in France and see if the CD has turned up there and I'll get Benny to see if he can locate it this end."

Luc led the way back to their office and watched as Joanna opened the web browser on her computer and logged onto the European Commission's website. All EuropeAid projects were listed in a dedicated section and after a few moments, she had the list on the screen. She quickly scrolled down to ZX 98 and found the link she wanted. Luc started to read over her shoulder.

The programme supported the development of the telecoms infrastructure within the Czech Republic, Slovakia and Hungary and would run for six years. The Programme Management Unit or PMU was headquartered in Prague. The funds came from the European Union's development budget and the European Bank for Reconstruction and Development (the EBRD) in London.

"I can't find the full financials. There's only a summary here," said Joanna.

She checked the file again and did another search. "They're not here. We'll have to get them from the EuropeAid office."

"You go. I think we need to find out if Darbly *père* is somehow involved in all this so I need to do some research."

As Joanna left the office, Luc accessed the main DER database. Gerald Darbly was the subject of an existing investigation and Luc wanted to read the whole file, which he had not had time to do before going down to France. The oldest entry covered the DER investigation undertaken when Darbly took on the Chairmanship of the Audit Oversight Committee in the European Parliament. It was all routine stuff but was linked to a second and third file that were both access-restricted, indicating an ongoing inquiry. He would have to talk to the case officer: Claudia Chalon.

She was alone when Luc entered her office. An attractive 40 year-old with auburn hair, Claudia had joined the DER at about the same time as Luc, but he knew she concentrated mostly on political cases. She waved him to a chair.

"What do you want to know?"

"Just about anything you can tell me on Gerald Darbly."

Chalon leant back and gazed at the ceiling. "I assume you've read all the stuff about his background."

"Yes, he made a lot of money as a consultant advising on Eastern Europe and some of the deals he was involved in were not entirely kosher. He entered the European Parliament in 1998 or thereabouts. But what's the current investigation about?"

Chalon responded cautiously, "Well, we're looking into some of his other activities at the moment because of the company he keeps."

"Like who?"

"Like Svetlana Nikolaevna. She's his mistress, but she's on the European Parliament payroll as his personal assistant. Nothing unusual about that, except she's a Russian."

"But why is that of interest to the DER? There are plenty of Russian émigrés on the EU payroll."

"Not ones whose brothers are arms dealers. She travels with Darbly and most of his journeys don't fit with his duties either as a MEP or as head of the Audit Oversight Committee. He goes to some really strange places and all at the expense of the EU budget."

Luc regarded Chalon thoughtfully. Darbly was certainly a very interesting character but what was the link to his daughter's death? And why was Chalon so protective of the case files?

"Luc, what is your real interest in Gerald Darbly?"

"He's incidental to a case I'm working on and I want to see if there's a link," replied Luc smoothly.

Chalon pursed her lips and then, after a moment, looked at him thoughtfully. "I'll do a deal…you can access the dossier if you promise to let me know of any developments concerning Darbly."

Chalon's straight look conveyed another message that Luc understood all too well. She was afraid Luc would muscle in on her investigation. *C'est la vie!*

"Claudia, I promise to let you know if anything comes up, but the boss wants us to cooperate…"

Luc had finished reading the Darbly dossier by the time Joanna arrived back looking frustrated and angry.

"What a bloody waste of time that was," she announced angrily.

"Why?" Luc looked up in amusement.

"Because the financials are not in the files there either." Joanna scowled, picked up Luc's coffee and took a drink. "And to make matters worse, it's bloody raining again."

Luc laughed. "So buy a car."

"And give up the freedom of the open road? Not a chance."

Radcliffe walked in and took a seat. "Frankly, as expected, your activities have ruffled some feathers. I've just had a call from the EuropeAid office asking why we were interested in a six-year-old programme. I wasn't able to help them. The question is: should I be able to help them?"

"Hang on a minute," Luc interrupted sharply. "How did anyone know we were interested? Jo checked the website and she uses a normal access card when visiting the Commission's buildings. Unless she was seen by someone who knew her connection with us, there is no way they'd know of our interest."

"Unless they've got a web tracer running on that file," Joanna replied thoughtfully.

"And what, exactly, is a web tracer?" Radcliffe looked at them over the top of his glasses.

"A small program that sits on the website server and interrogates the visiting browser for its address and other identification details. They usually have an associated database so that they know who visits and how often. Our system tells us when a 'cookie' is being set and allows us to disable it, but it wouldn't pick up a tracer."

"So, we have two dead people who are linked, among other things, to a EuropeAid programme with unconventional security monitoring it. And that's all we know?" Radcliffe spoke caustically. "Well, you two had better find out fast."

When they were alone again, Joanna asked, "What did you get from Claudia?"

"Well, papa Darbly was in Strasbourg for a parliamentary committee meeting when Emma was killed, then went to Prague and back to Luxembourg for meetings at the Commission."

"And did he really attend them?"

"Yes."

"What's he up to in Prague?"

"Darbly has an apartment there which he shares with Svetlana Nikolaevna, his personal assistant. But he was in Luxembourg when he called Emma's flat on Friday."

Joanna was accessing her computer records, "What's his number?" Luc gave it to her.

After a few minutes Joanna said, "Okay, it's a Luxembourg number registered to Gerald Darbly at an address in Luxembourg. Emma called him on it but not frequently and not at all in the last month." She typed in a command. "And take a look at this, Darbly has used his phone from the Czech Republic, Romania, Hungary, Luxembourg, the Republic of Georgia and Turkey, all within the last three weeks."

"I wonder where he is now." Luc wondered out loud.

"Turkey. He used the phone from Ankara earlier today."

"Good work, Jo."

Wednesday 12 February, Ankara, Turkey

"We need guns, ammunition, explosives and good radios." The speaker, an intense young man dressed in jeans, sweatshirt and trainers, hardly looked like the representative of a significant fighting force but looks in this case were deceptive. His name was Kosaran and he was one of the most effective leaders of the Kurdish People's Defence Force, the PKK. He operated in northern Iraq and was the one thought most likely to achieve significant success.

The man he was talking to sighed. "There is no way the Americans or the Turks will allow shipments of arms to your people."

"So be it, Mr Darbly," Kosaran shrugged. "Then we'll just go to the black market."

"That costs a lot of money — money you don't have." The depleted state of the PKK finances was no secret.

"Then we'll just rob a few more banks!"

Gerald Darbly studied Kosaran for a moment, weighing the comment. Was it merely bravado? Darbly decided that robbing banks was well within the man's capability if the news reports were correct.

"There is another way. There is a man…he's here in Ankara at the moment…and I think he can help."

"Don't mess me about, Darbly. Exactly who is he and how much will it cost?"

For Gerald Darbly, supplying the arms was not a problem, but doing it without the Americans knowing was something else. He had a shipment going into Iraq to what used to be al-Zarqawi's Sunni militia and he could increase the quantity, split out the excess, get it to the PKK and satisfy two customers in one go. Good for him too if he charged the Iraqis for all the weapons and gained leverage from supplying the PKK's share.

"No names. For security reasons you'll deal only with me. We will need to have some direct discussions with the PKK leadership."

"About what?" Kosaran demanded, suspiciously.

"About business with the Kurdish people when the current situation has been stabilised."

"Yes, I see," replied Kosaran.

Darbly elaborated, "Oh, I think that the Americans will be happy to let the Kurds in Iraq run things in the north and that means there will be business opportunities."

"And you want the best of the deals in exchange for weapons."

"Of course! We supply the arms at no cost and, in exchange, we get major contracts when the war is over."

"Who is 'we'?"

"The companies I represent. You'll be dealing with me on this when the time comes."

Kosaran considered the offer and made a decision. "Very well. I'll give you a list of what we need and an introduction to the Ruling Council. Agreed?"

"Agreed. It's a pleasure doing business with you."

"Just deliver the arms!" The young man finished his beer and stood up. "I have some phone calls to make. I'll be in touch tomorrow." He walked quickly out of the bar and into the falling snow.

Wednesday 12 February, Brussels

Joanna arrived at the European Press Bureau just as Helen Carpenter, the manager, was showing a policeman out. Joanna waited patiently for her to return.

"Miss Carpenter…?"

"Who are you?" she replied, warily.

"Joanna Donnelly." She flipped open her DER ID card. "We need to speak in private."

Carpenter examined the ID, handed it back and led the way into a meeting room.

She shut the door. "Why are you here?"

Joanna sat down. "Because the police called us. When did you discover the break-in?"

"Earlier today. I needed to see what Emma had been working on but her computer disk had been erased and her files taken."

"Anything else missing?"

"Not that I can see. Why is the DER involved?"

"If you want me to answer, it must be strictly off the record."

"Understood."

"Because Emma Darbly was working on something that interests us. She was also having an affair with one of our people. She's dead. He's dead. And we want to know why."

"Good God!" Carpenter collapsed back in her chair.

"I've some more bad news for you. Emma and her lover were both murdered, probably by the same man."

"But the police told us she died in a skiing accident."

"That's what we told them to say. However, she was murdered and so was her lover and now this." Joanna carefully watched Carpenter's reactions.

"All right, Miss Donnelly. What do you want?"

"I will need to check the computer to see exactly what was done to it."

"Why?"

"To see if it was tampered with in any way."

"Okay. I'll authorise that. Eric is our computer whiz and will work with you. I can't allow access to everything but we'll cooperate as far as we can."

"Even better. But, Miss Carpenter, this is a police enquiry into a murder and you can't print the story or any of the details until we say so."

"You can't stop us."

"Let me put it this way. If you cooperate with us then you can have the story when we've got what we need."

Carpenter said, "How about we get the story as you go?"

"Then you will have to cooperate. Print *anything* before we're ready and you'll jeopardise the investigation and will end up with a small story…and lots of large problems. Am I clear? What's it to be?"

After a moment, Carpenter nodded. "Okay, deal. By the way, most of us knew Mark but no one knew he was dead."

"That's not surprising, we've not told anyone yet. Nor can you. We need to trap a killer and find out what's going on. Control of information is vital."

"Exclusive?"

"Why not!"

Eric Green turned out to be a tall man in his mid-thirties with the slightly distracted air of an absent-minded scientist. He waved Joanna to a chair and settled himself at his desk in one corner of the large open-plan EPB office. He listened carefully as Joanna explained what she wanted, asked a few pointed questions and set to work.

Eric fingered the keys at warp speed. "Whoever did this thought he knew what he was doing but didn't. Are you sure these people are as sophisticated as you think?"

"Yes, I'm afraid they probably are. Why?"

"Look at this." He quickly opened up a disk and pointed at the displayed files. "These are corrupted but if we do this…then we can recover the data."

"Hold it, Eric. Have you been examining those disks while connected to the server?"

"No. This one isn't in the network. Why?"

"Because they may have set a Trojan Horse or a Time Bomb."

"Good point. Let's see if he got into the server?"

Eric moved to another machine. Directories and sub-directories rolled up the screen. "Things seem normal…what the fuck?" The data on the screen started to dissolve in front of the startled man. Letters started to drop down to the bottom edge and then pile up like rubbish. "The bastard. He's p-p-put a Trojan in here." He stood up and walked to the centre of the office floor.

"Okay, people, listen up. We have a virus attack so please close down everything. Don't bother trying to save, just switch off the machines. Those with laptops that have not been connected to the network in the last week," he turned to Joanna who nodded, "yes, the last week, can safely work with them. All other machines including portables should be left off until I've checked them."

"Bloody hell," Carpenter exclaimed from her desk at the front of the room, but she did not argue.

"Eric…look at this." Joanna pointed at the screen. A large spider sitting on a cartoon bomb appeared and stayed there, glowering malevolently. "Our friend has a sense of humour."

"Let me check the logs." He left the office and returned with a laptop. "This baby is kept in a basement safe. I collected it when we discovered the problem this morning. It contains the backup logs." He switched on and accessed the program.

"You back up every night?" Joanna asked.

"We're supposed to but it doesn't always happen. And we always back up to fresh disks and external drives. Now, let's see. Right, last backup of the whole system was last Friday but the working files were backed up last night."

"And before that?"

"Tuesday. Let's see when the bastard did the damage." Putting the backup machine aside, he plugged his own laptop into the network and went to work. Joanna watched for a few minutes and then walked to a clear area and took out her mobile phone.

It was late and the DER offices were almost empty. The Director had gone shortly after Joanna had left for the European Press Bureau and Luc was on his own. Spread on the table in the conference room was a large map of Europe on which he was painstakingly tracking the movements of Gerald Darbly's telephone calls.

Luc got up and walked round the table. He hated long periods of sitting still. He preferred the rough and tough business of soldiering and sometimes even missed the French Foreign Legion. Those were the days. He picked up the printout of Gerald Darbly's telephone usage.

Ten minutes later, he had a pattern — it was almost too damned easy. Gerald Darbly had called the same five numbers, usually in the same order, every fourth day for three weeks. The other calls did not seem significant: they were mainly hotels, airlines and restaurants.

The first number was in Brussels, then he called Prague, Hungary, Romania and Georgia. He never spoke for more than four and a half minutes to any of the numbers and the timing of the calls put them all in office hours.

Unlike Joanna, Luc was not a computer fanatic but he knew how to interrogate online databases. As he launched the browser application, the telephone rang.

"Luc, It's Jo. What're you doing?"

"Hi. I'm just about to go online."

"Oh, Christ, don't. Remember I said there could be a hidden tracer that we might have picked up from the EuropeAid database. And don't use the network until I've had a look."

"What's the problem?" She sounded unusually agitated.

"Whoever got into the Press Bureau computer really zapped it and my gut reaction is that we might have a destructive Trojan of our own as well…I'll leave the guy here to fix his problem and be back with you in twenty minutes."

The computer guru had spoken. Luc fished his old laptop out of a file drawer, rigged it via its own modem on a secure telephone line, started the browser program and his search.

Thursday 13 February, Brussels

Luc and Joanna were already at their desks when Radcliffe arrived at 7:30 a.m. He knew it was not unusual for the two of them to be in early but it usually betokened interesting developments. Radcliffe nodded a greeting and listened carefully as Joanna started to explain.

"You were here all night?" Radcliffe interrupted.

"It's okay, boss; I had to work that tracer and see if it was in our system." Joanna had not minded losing the night. She had no attachments at the moment and Luc had been good company through the long hours and in a nearby bar for breakfast.

"So tell me the worst."

"The tracer is really sophisticated. It is well hidden and took a long time to find. It tracks any hit on the website that involves that ZX file and then tells someone in the Commission who is accessing it."

"Have you disabled it?"

"No, now we know where it is and we're as certain as we can be that it's not a virus, I thought you should know before we remove it."

"Then do it and let's see who comes out of the woodwork."

Karel Vandenhove was enjoying an early morning coffee when his telephone rang.

"Mr Vandenhove, this is Paul Dukakis." Vandenhove's heart rate shot up. "We've had another hit on the file you asked me to flag. It was the DER again but they've found the tracer program, God knows how, and disabled it. They've also blocked us from placing another."

Carefully controlling his breathing, Vandenhove said, "So how do you know that it was the DER?"

"Because they hit the file, waited until the tracer started and then disabled it on-line, removed the old tracer and forced our machine to accept some blocking code. Very, very clever. They've got a real expert and they did it in such a way as to make sure we knew they knew about the tracer. They're very cool." Admiration was clear in his voice.

Vandenhove couldn't prevent his voice from rising, "Did they get the main financial file?"

"No, it's password protected. They tried for it but backed off as soon as they hit the security barrier I'd put on it locally."

Vandenhove reached a decision. "I want you to remove the data in the financial file but keep monitoring it. If anyone wants the information, they should contact you. I want to know who's interested and why."

High in the DER office block on the other side of town, Joanna was having fun. She was taunting the guy monitoring the ZX file. *I know you're there, and I know you know I know you're there. I also know you're not happy. So why, my friend, have you placed a password on the main financial files?*

She started to hack into the computer system. In theory, and almost certainly in law, this was illegal but the Director wanted to rattle the cages. *So let's see the raw data.*

She was in!

Hah, Master Hacker Donnelly strikes again.

The adrenaline hit was terrific — she was flying.

ENTER PASSWORD> * * * * *
INCORRECT PASSWORD> Retry>

Okay, you clever bastard, try this. She typed in a series of codes and was rewarded with

SELECT FILE>
ZX 98.02.02.04
ACCESS RESTRICTED CONTINUE?>
Yes
CLEARANCE>

This bit would be tricky. Get this wrong and she would be shut out. She typed in some code.

INCORRECT ENTRY. CLEARANCE MUST
BE IN THE FORM OF RECOGNISED
ALPHANUMERIC KEY.>

Oh, it must, must it? Let's try something else. She typed in a high-level security key. The screen faded, a large key symbol appeared and then the file opened.

Got it!

Like all good hackers, and Joanna Donnelly wasn't the only one who classified herself as one of the best, she followed the first and golden rule of hacking: she pressed *Save File As…* typed in 'ZX Financial' and clicked *Save*. The screen flickered again and then stabilised. She started to read. *All the normal guff. Now where…what the hell?* A starburst appeared in the middle of the screen and the data disappeared inwards as though sucked into an electronic black hole. A moment later, the words appeared on the screen:

FOR FINANCIAL INFORMATION PLEASE
CONTACT PAUL DUKAKIS
DG INFORMATION TECHNOLOGY

Okay, smart arse, so you've zapped the file. Let's see if the 'save' worked.

She disconnected from the Commission network and opened the file she had saved.

"Yes! Got it!"

"Got what, Jo?" Radcliffe spoke from the doorway.

Joanna gave a start. How long had he been there? Did he realise what she'd been doing? Shit — better take it straight and hope for the best.

"I got into the main Commission computer to get the financial file and succeeded just before they zapped it." She waited in trepidation.

Radcliffe patted her on the shoulder. "Very good work. Print it." He turned to go and Joanna breathed a silent sigh of relief. "By the by, Jo, hacking is against the law and you are subject to the law. You do understand?"

"Yes, Mr Radcliffe," she replied meekly.

"Good." He walked out concealing a satisfied smile. Behind him, Joanna Donnelly, ex-hacker, tried to force her heart rate down. Damn, that was close, she thought, but she had survived. Maybe Luc is right; if they need it enough you can get away with anything. And hell, this was why they recruited me in the first place.

They had met while Radcliffe was on a fraud case involving Common Agricultural Policy funds and an agrochemical company. She had been hacking into the company's computer for fun, found the fraud and told her boyfriend. The information eventually reached Radcliffe who backtracked to her.

Her name wasn't mentioned to the police, as it could have been. After the case was closed, Radcliffe offered her a job and provided superb training. He extracted a promise that she would not go back to hacking and had never mentioned her illegal activities again. In exchange, Joanna gave him and the DER unswerving loyalty and commitment.

A year later, at her suggestion, the DER set up a covert organisation called JDB Systems and she, with the help of some ex-hacker friends, Dirk Wauters and Bart Jongen, had turned it into a sophisticated computer and communications support operation.

Then, in recognition of her work, Radcliffe offered her an operational role with the chance to work with Luc and she had never looked back. She was not certain if Luc knew about her past but she was now a trusted part of his team and she intended to keep it that way.

CHAPTER THREE

Monday 17 February, morning, Brussels

Luc was convinced Gerald Darbly was connected with his daughter's death but he needed evidence and all he had were the five numbers that Darbly called on a regular basis. It was a thin lead at best, but twenty minutes later he had his answers.

"Very interesting."

Joanna looked at him from over her computer. "What is?"

"Darbly calls the *Chef de Cabinet* in Foreign Affairs, a guy called Karel Vandenhove. He also calls a legitimate arms factory called Schröder-Mannlicher Fegyvergyár near Pécs in Hungary, a senior civil servant in the Ministry of Defence in Prague and a Romanian transport company in Constanta owned by Groupe Franco Belge. The Georgian number didn't answer."

"And who are Groupe Franco Belge?"

"Big engineering company based in Antwerp: originally owned by a French family who sold out to a Belgian industrialist in the 1920s...can't remember the name. They made a fortune in the construction business after both World Wars. The company changed hands at some point in the 1990s but got into the telecom business and they own a telecom engineering company in France called Ligne Verte but, and this is the interesting bit, until about ten years ago they owned a small-arms factory based in Liege."

"Did you say Ligne Verte?"

"Yes. Why?"

"Because Ligne Verte is the contractor for the ZX project."

"*Merde alors!*" Luc sat back and lit a cigarette, blowing smoke towards the ceiling. The picture was coming into focus. He stood up and walked over to the whiteboard on which the operational and information aspects of the investigation were displayed. He drew a diagram and a series of connections. "Groupe Franco Belge, no surprise, is central…they are the parent of the main contractors, but it is clear, I think, that Gerald Darbly is also involved somehow…and *très bizarre*, he's calling up an arms manufacturer on a regular basis!"

Joanna studied the diagram. "The financial file I found on the Commission's server had a link to another server belonging to GFB in Antwerp. I checked it out and it's a more up-to-date version of the spreadsheet we found on Emma's machine."

"Do you think she got the information from there?"

"Could be, but I doubt it." My guess is she had access to a matching source. When I first looked at the data I wondered whether it was a series of transactions, and if so, then there has to be another party and I'd guess Emma got her info there."

Something was bugging Joanna. The arrangement of the files on the Commission's server had been very orderly but extremely well protected. As soon as someone accessed a file, the system notified the fact to a log file or registry. It was a common enough procedure when security was an issue but unusual on an apparently simple EuropeAid programme. Joanna gazed out of the window at the grey winter sky.

"Luc, if you wanted to hide something, where would you put it?"

"Like what?"

"Like sensitive information."

"Where it wouldn't attract attention if seen inadvertently. Why?"

"So far, these guys have put all the files concerning this project on the server but they have unusually stringent security. They blitz the financial file, but it didn't contain anything unusual. We access the files and some *chef de cabinet* starts making waves. To my mind, there is something sensitive in these files."

"Jo, have you looked at the log file you mentioned before?"

"Not yet."

"Just a hunch, but if I wanted to hide something I'd put it where anyone could see it but wouldn't ask questions and then monitor who actually looked at it."

She called up the registry file and opened it as a text document. After a few minutes she said, "Okay. The files linked to the log are the financial summary, the funding dossier and the supplier file."

"Which suggests…?"

"That we need to go back to basics and follow the money. But there's something else we need to know: who is monitoring the information and why."

Tuesday 18 February, Brussels

It was just before midday when Joanna arrived at the office the following day. She looked wet and cold and had a distracted look.

"What's on your mind?" Luc knew that Joanna only became distracted when something was seriously bothering her.

"The log file we found was quite a clever one. It runs a trace on the accessing computer and then sends a message to Paul Dukakis in the IT section with the details. I had a quick peek at Dukakis' email log. He just forwards the information to Karel Vandenhove, the same guy Darbly calls."

Luc said, "I've checked out Vandenhove. He arrived about six years ago. He's Belgian, regarded as a pompous bureaucrat and much disliked by his French colleagues who regard him as a *lèche-cul*, an arse licker." He handed Joanna a picture of a fat man with a self-important air about him.

"So, not too popular…" Joanna studied the photograph.

"You've got it. And what's more, he's a political appointee. He was a big financial supporter of the right wing parties in Flanders and got sent to the Commission as a reward."

"But why would a *fonctionnaire* in the Foreign Affairs Directorate be involved in, or even interested, in an Eastern European telecoms project?"

"I don't know."

Benoît Montegnie knocked on the office door and entered silently.

Luc looked up. "Hi, Benny. What brings you to this part of town?"

"This." He held out a packet.

Luc took it and removed a CD and a letter written in a round, English script.

Mark, I'm frightened and I think I'm in over my head. I've put everything I know on this CD. Please give it to someone with authority in the DER. It's dynamite. I'm not proud of what I've done though and I'm sorry if this will hurt you. Please believe me when I say I love you and I will marry you! Miss you.

Love Em

Luc turned over the packet and saw that it had been posted in France the day that Emma Darbly had died. "Where did you get it?"

"It was in his post box."

"Good work, Benny. Jo, run this please." He pushed the CD across the desk as Benoît left the office.

The CD contained a number of document files. Joanna quickly copied them across to the server and opened the first.

"Jackpot!" she exclaimed at once.

It was a detailed investigative diary, similar to those used in the DER, and recorded Emma Darbly's investigation on the ZX file. It told of how she had heard about it first during her affair the previous year with Quentin Morgan who worked for the EBRD, European Bank for Reconstruction and Development in London and how each step of the way had revealed more and more of the connection between Vandenhove and the project.

"*Merde*!" Luc pointed to an entry dated early December. It showed that Emma had decided to take a close look at Vandenhove himself. Her researches showed that Vandenhove's grandfather had bought Groupe Franco Belge in the 1920s and his father had sold its shares to a Foundation for a nominal 1,000 Belgian Francs in 1990.

"This girl was seriously good," said Joanna admiringly. "Listen to this." She started to read.

GFB has won eight EU contracts in the last five years (see attached). Karel V must have put pressure on the

departments in each case. The Commission's anti-fraud
office investigated them all last year but did nothing.
The investigating officer now drives a brand new 5-series
BMW, which he could never afford on his salary. I don't
believe in coincidences. Karel V must be bribing people
in a big way. Total value of contracts is in excess of 780
million euro. I have enough now to hand this to the
DER. No point in going to the anti-fraud office, they'll
just bury it.

"So Emma finds out about a fraudulent aid project, links it
to Vandenhove who is linked to Groupe Franco Belge. If Franco
Belge found out what she'd been doing, then killing her to protect
themselves would be perfectly logical," observed Luc sadly.

Wednesday 19 February, Brussels

Having submitted an update to the dossier, Luc was unsurprised
at the summons to report to the Director. As he entered his
office, he noted immediately that there were two others present
in addition to Radcliffe. Even from the back Luc recognised
James Ashley, the man with overall control of the DER. James
Ashley was an ex-policeman with a very sharp brain indeed and
Luc knew he had turned down the opportunity to head the
fraud squad at Scotland Yard to accept the appointment to the
Court of Auditors in Luxembourg. Five years later, he had been
given the responsibility of overseeing the development of the
DER as a pan-European intelligence service with his long-time
friend, Radcliffe, as Director.

Luc cared little for politics but he knew that the establishment
of the DER was so politically sensitive within the European

Union that, six years after its founding, it still did not officially exist and ultimate control rested with the Court of Auditors to shield it from political pressure.

"Good afternoon, sir."

"Ah, Luc." Ashley stood up to shake hands. "May I introduce Dr Michelle Robert, one of our senior advisors."

Luc shook hands and wondered exactly what sort of advisor she was.

As Radcliffe waved them all to the conference table Luc saw that each of them had a copy of his dossier and, from the annotations on the tabs stuck between the pages, that each had read it. That would save time.

It was Ashley who broke the silence.

"Before we start, Luc, have there been any further developments since yesterday."

"Yes, sir. We've found that Gerald Darbly is listed as a consultant with Groupe Franco Belge and the Parliament's Register of Members' Interests shows this to have been true for the last six years."

Ashley nodded and Luc waited patiently as the others each made notes.

"It's clear what we *do* know. And it's equally clear that a *carte blanche* to poke and pry is appropriate." Ashley tapped the file and looked thoughtful. "Luc, what are your main priorities now?"

"To find out who killed Emma Darbly and why. I suspect this is linked to her investigation into the GFB contracts. She had also started investigating the ZX programme and my guess is that's what got her killed."

"You think there's a fraud case there as well?" Dr Robert's voice was soft with a distinct French accent.

"Yes, ma'am. Emma Darbly kept a journal, which we've now got. Apparently, there is a fraud going on but she didn't know how it worked or what the purpose was. We've been looking at various scenarios that would fit the facts."

"With what result, Luc?" asked Ashley.

Luc contemplated the man from Luxembourg and then looked at Radcliffe: he had not discussed this with his boss but had spent the last twenty-four hours thinking about little else.

He chose his words carefully. "I think that the money is being used to buy arms but for whom I have no idea as yet."

Ashley looked meaningfully at Dr Robert and Radcliffe who each gave nods of agreement.

"Agreed, Mr Hansen," said Dr Robert. "And if you are right, then this could well bring down the Commission, as well as cause all sorts of other problems."

"In what way, ma'am?" Luc was keenly aware of the increased tension in the room.

It was Ashley who answered. "Luc, the Commission is not the most popular of recent years and is the subject of significant levels of criticism from the national governments. A fraud, perpetrated by a senior Commission *fonctionnaire,* with the money being used to buy arms and linked to the murder of a journalist would be a godsend to the critics."

"Sir, are you saying that this has to be covert?"

"I'm saying, Luc, that this information needs to be kept out of the public domain."

Twenty minutes later, after briefing Joanna fully on the meeting, Luc said, "And that means we're being drawn into another one of those 'authorised but deniable operations'."

"Not again…" Joanna sighed.

Luc shrugged. "*C'est la vie* — that's what the DER is here for, I guess."

"Okay. We've got a *carte blanche*, so what are we going to do with it?"

"The first step is to bug Vandenhove, the second is to follow the money and the third is to find out exactly what daddy Darbly's role is in all this."

"I'll deal with bugging Vandenhove. I'll force his computer to report a fault and then go in and install a Trojan Horse program that'll let us monitor his computer usage. We can halve the time and risk if you come along to bug the phones."

"Can we bug his mobile as well?"

"Not yet, but we're working on it."

Thursday 20 February, Brussels

Like most large organisations, the European Commission has its own fair share of clock-watchers and by six o'clock in the evening the majority of the staff at the Breydel Building had already left for the day. Those still at work were scattered throughout the building but the eighth floor was empty.

Luc and Joanna walked slowly up the corridor towards the corner office occupied by Karel Vandenhove, *Chef de Cabinet* to the Commissioner for Foreign Affairs (Eastern Europe). The surveillance security camera watched unblinkingly as they approached but made no move to follow them as they passed. Moments later they were at the door to the outer office. Without any sign of hurry, they went in.

Luc spoke softly, "Ten minutes maximum."

Joanna then entered Vandenhove's private office. She turned to the computer. Like so many *fonctionnaires,* the *Chef de Cabinet* had failed to close it down properly and it was humming quietly. She placed a CD in the drive and a few keystrokes later had installed a discreet Trojan Horse program.

There were two telephones on the desk. Luc took out a small screwdriver and, within a few minutes, each telephone had a listening device installed.

Taking her mobile phone from her pocket, Joanna dialled a number and spoke quietly for a few moments. Satisfied with the answer, she checked that each of the bugs was functioning and then picked up her tools and left the office. Luc took out a small radio bug detector and swept the room. The two bugs showed up but there were no others.

Friday 21 February, Brussels

Joanna was making progress with the financial file but it was slow work. She had crosschecked to ensure that the data from the file obtained by Emma Darbly matched and she was now in the process of checking the sources of the funds. Luc came in quietly with mugs of coffee.

"Damn but I need that. Thanks." Joanna took a cup and sipped gratefully. She pushed a sheet of paper towards him. "The bugs are working well. According to the intercepts, Vandenhove arrived at 07.45 and immediately used his email to instruct the EBRD in London to make another transfer. He then telephoned Darbly and told him that the funds had been moved."

"Proof positive that Darbly is linked in. Well, I suppose the Director will be pleased."

"Hardly, Luc," said Radcliffe when told a few minutes later. "I was hoping you wouldn't find a link."

"Excuse me, sir, but can you tell me why?"

"Because it would have made the whole thing simpler."

Outside the snow had gone but it was still cold enough to have frosted the cars parked round the Gare du Midi.

The Director asked, "What else has turned up?"

Luc replied, "Immediately after calling Darbly, Vandenhove made a call to a dead number. It seemed odd because it's in Brussels and registered to himself, but there is no such address. We picked up some extra keystrokes and Jo's got our friends running them to see where it leads."

Joanna entered the Director's office. "The telephone people say it's a re-router. The extra keystrokes push it to a number in Antwerp. I'll lay evens that it turns out to be a Groupe Franco Belge number."

Luc asked, "Do we have a record of what was said?"

"Yep, it was short and sweet. He wants to meet with a man called Gärtner at the usual place."

Radcliffe asked, "Do we know who this man Gärtner is?"

Luc replied, "No, his name's never come up before."

"Jo, who was Vandenhove contacting at the EBRD in London?"

"Quentin Morgan."

Luc looked up sharply. "We've seen that name before…in Emma Darbly's journal. He's the guy who told her about the fraud."

Joanna added, "I've checked as far as I can. The only Quentin Morgan at the bank works in the international section handling co-financing. He's listed as being the bank's project manager for our EuropeAid project."

"Then I think we need to talk to this Mr Morgan," said Luc and they all nodded agreement.

On the fourteenth floor of the European Bank for Reconstruction and Development in London, Quentin Morgan was not a happy man. The message he had received from Brussels earlier that morning was going to cause problems. Vandenhove wanted another large transfer paid on the ZX programme. It was out of sequence but they paid him well for this service: a one percent handling fee they called it — but one percent of millions of euro was what paid for the Quentin Morgan lifestyle. He started the transaction.

TRANSACTION DENIED>

What the fuck! He checked the instructions again and it was all correct. He tried again, twice, with the same results. Another attempt would alert the system guardians as only three attempts were allowed before having to take it to a higher authority. Now he was in the shit…he would have to try for direct authorisation that afternoon.

Luc put the telephone down and gazed out over the Brussels skyline. The manager at the EBRD had been most cooperative and had placed a block on all transactions to the ZX programme. She had promised to conduct a full review of the file over the weekend. She and Luc would meet on Monday to see what action should be taken.

Quentin was annoyed. He had gone to the head of transmissions to get a clearance and had been told that all transactions on the project were blocked while Mrs Kirkpatrick was reviewing the file. This was not that unusual, but it was a real pisser in this case since Vandenhove was putting on the pressure.

When he re-entered his office, the message-waiting icon on his computer was flashing. It was from Mrs Kirkpatrick instructing him to come to her office immediately after lunch on Monday.

Damn! He wanted to deal with this before the weekend. Seeing the old biddy last thing on a Friday was not his idea of fun but one percent of 10 million euro was a lot of money and he could see himself in the new flat at St. Catherine Dock.

He walked up to Mrs Kirkpatrick's office.

It was empty.

Shit!

Monday 24 February, London

From his position at the conference table Luc studied the young project manager as he entered Mrs Kirkpatrick's office. The similarity in appearance and build between Quentin Morgan and the dead Mark Anderson was evident, but it ended there. Anderson had been a loner but this guy was full of himself with his slicked-back hair and false tan — Emma Darbly had obviously liked playing a wide field.

Mrs Kirkpatrick introduced them. "Ah, there you are, Quentin, this is Mr Hansen."

Luc nodded a greeting but got nothing in return. Arrogant and rude into the bargain, he thought.

"Please sit down." Mrs Kirkpatrick indicated a chair at the conference table.

Morgan sat down and Luc saw him glance casually at the papers on the table and then look again more intently. The ZX 98 financial file lay open along with various other documents and printouts. Luc saw Morgan's eyes flicker nervously.

"Quentin, Mr Hansen has a few questions for you." The young man turned towards Luc, his eyes wide and alert.

"I'll be down the hall if you need me," said Mrs Kirkpatrick as she headed for the door.

Luc wasted no time on preliminaries. "Mr Morgan, perhaps you can help me to understand this project." He tapped the file gently.

Morgan shrugged and in an unhelpful tone of voice said, "What do you want to know?"

For the next fifteen minutes, Luc asked questions and Morgan answered them but revealed little information. Luc decided to up the pressure

"Look, Mr Morgan, we already know that the funds from this project are being used illegally so a bit more cooperation from you would be the wise choice."

"I don't know what you're talking about. I just manage the transfers in accordance with the protocols. Who are you anyway?"

"I work for the DER."

The blood drained from Morgan's face and he sucked in a shuddering breath.

Luc watched him calmly. Morgan's reaction to the DER was unusual. Not many people had actually heard of the DER and fewer knew what it did, but Morgan clearly knew and was afraid and that was very interesting indeed.

"I need to make a phone call," Morgan's voice was shaking and his composure had shattered.

"Oh I don't think so, Mr Morgan. I have a lot more questions for you before you can do that."

"I want to see my solicitor."

"Why, if you've done nothing wrong?"

Morgan looked round nervously, sweat now visible on his upper lip, a pulse throbbing at his temple.

Luc leant forward. "I'd like to talk to you about your relationship with a young journalist called Emma Darbly."

Morgan stood up and walked to the window.

Luc went on dispassionately. "From the tone of your emails, and of hers, it appears that you and Miss Darbly have been having an affair. Is that correct?"

Morgan did not respond, but he did return to the table.

"Mr Morgan, I have to tell you that Emma has been murdered."

"What the fuck are you saying, man?"

"Sit down." Morgan did so and Luc continued, "I said, Emma Darbly is dead. She was murdered three weeks ago in France. We're investigating her death."

"I don't fucking believe you, man. Anyway, what's this got to do with me?"

"Well, nothing, perhaps, but you were having a sexual relationship with her before she died that must have gone on for, what, six months? And you've been trying to get in touch with her for the last few weeks. What information did you give her about this project?"

"It's a lie! It's a lie!" Morgan stood up and, at a half run, staggered from the office heading for the gents' toilets. Luc followed at a leisurely pace observed by the entire section. He entered the toilets to the sound of retching from one of the cubicles.

After a while the sounds ceased and the distressed figure of Quentin Morgan emerged to the sound of a flushing toilet. He washed his face and drank some tap water.

"When you're ready we must get on." Luc took the young man by the arm and led him back to the office.

"I think we understand each other on this." Luc sounded firm but still friendly. "No matter how distressing, you have to face the facts. Whatever Emma found out about the EuropeAid project got her killed and what she found out she certainly got from you."

"But I didn't do anything."

"Well, I'm afraid you have done something or why else should Groupe Franco Belge, the project money recipient, be sending you thousands of euros after you make each transfer?"

Morgan was silent.

Luc casually slid copies of all the man's personal bank and credit card statements across the table along with a list of all the expensive purchases he had made. Morgan looked down with a stricken look.

"Why not make this easy on yourself, Mr Morgan? Tell us what we need to know and we'll do whatever we can to present mitigating circumstances at your trial."

"What trial?"

"Don't be an ass," Luc snapped. "You've broken any number of laws and obstructed the course of justice. You might even qualify as an accessory to murder."

Luc watched the play of emotions on the young man's face: hope had given way to defeat and then the dawning realisation that his life was over…before it had really begun.

Morgan folded. "What do you want to know?"

It was after midnight before Luc finally let Morgan go. There was no reason to hold him. He had told Luc everything that he knew about the EuropeAid project and he had promised to return in the morning to answer further questions that would be put to him by the Metropolitan Police.

Luc called the bank's security officer and Morgan handed over his access card and promised to surrender his passport the following day. Then the head of security, accompanied by Luc, escorted Morgan from the building.

Luc watched the young man walk across Exchange Square with his head down, a mobile phone clamped to his ear.

The silver grey Porsche was on the centre of Tower Bridge when the bomb went off, killing the driver instantly. The bridge remained closed for the rest of the night and all the following day, increasing the traffic congestion to and from the City to unbearable levels.

CHAPTER FOUR

Wednesday 26 February, Brussels

Back in his Brussels office two days later, Luc considered the implications of what had happened in London. Somewhere, somehow, things had gone wrong. He was certain that Morgan had not had any opportunity to contact anyone during the day of his interrogation. But someone knew that the DER had found him and then made sure that the witness was eliminated.

He angrily stubbed out his cigarette. Perhaps he should have done more, perhaps he should have taken Morgan into custody, but there had been no reason to except a gut feeling that the opposition was closing off loopholes. And Joanna had been monitoring the bugs in Vandenhove's office throughout the time he, Luc, had been in London and had reported nothing. He shook his head in frustration. They had obviously missed something.

Joanna came in with coffee and a sheaf of papers.

"Luc, I've gone over the transcripts again and I can find only one possibility."

"Tell me."

"Someone phoned Vandenhove on his mobile phone at 3.30 p.m. in his office, probably a female from his side of the conversation. Vandenhove then used the mobile to call someone at 3.35 p.m., and I quote: 'We have a problem. We need to meet.' Nothing else. At 4 p.m., he left the office and didn't return. Now, it could have been about anything, but nine hours later Morgan's car was blown away."

"Do we know who he called?" said Luc.

"No, for that we'd need to bug his mobile," replied Joanna.

"Can't we find out from his service provider?"

"I tried, but ProxiStar said it's a pre-paid number and they don't store the data since there's no billing involved."

"*Merde*! All right, let's just assume for a moment that Vandenhove called his tame hit man and then met up with him somewhere locally. Was there time for the hit man to get to London and plant the bomb?"

"Yes. There were no last-minute travellers on the Eurostar or airlines, so I checked the ferries. He could have driven to Calais and caught the 19:30 crossing, which would have got him to London around 10 or 10:30 p.m."

"Did you get anything from the ferry operators?"

"A total of six cars, all driven by single men, turned up on spec for crossings that evening."

"Any security camera footage?"

"I've got Benny going over the tapes. The trouble is we don't know what the hit man looks like."

"You've done well."

"Can we be certain that it was a bomb?" Joanna asked after a moment.

"Yes, the Met have confirmed it, and quite a sophisticated one at that. The bomber used *plastique*, the same type I found on Emma Darbly's car in France and in her apartment here.

Damn! I should have anticipated this. I thought Morgan would try to phone Brussels but someone tipped off Vandenhove anyway. Someone who knew we had found Morgan and knew I had gone to London." Luc paused for some time, holding Joanna's attention and silence with unblinking eye contact. "Someone here is working for the other side!"

"Jeez! Luc. Are you serious?"

"Absolutely. It's the only plausible explanation."

"Bloody hell!"

"I'm going get the boss to deal with that. Our focus must be on the funds. We allowed the last transfer to be cleared. It'll go through today at around 5 p.m. so we trace it. See where the money goes and what happens to it along the way."

Friday 28 February, Brussels

It took Luc and Joanna two days of hard work and a lot of phone calls, but by early Friday morning they had their answers.

Joanna was sitting impatiently in the office waiting for Luc to return with the Director from the weekly meeting. With what they had now, they could really get moving.

Luc and Radcliffe entered the room and sat down.

Radcliffe began, "So, what have you found that you couldn't tell me at the meeting with the others?"

"According to what we got from the Programme Management Unit's financial records, the total payments for this project have been just over 68 million euros so far and it's all accounted for. Jo then checked the *actual* transfers from the EBRD in London, rather than what Morgan's files record, and they're nearly 12 million euros higher."

"And…?" prompted Radcliffe.

"The routing instructions must have a split destination applied to them. The correspondent banks all record that the full amount was transferred, which means the split is being done in the treasury department of the recipient bank in Prague."

Radcliffe nodded. "And Morgan?"

"Frankly, sir, I don't think Morgan was that involved. I think someone has coded the EBRD computer to transfer an increased amount. Morgan just requested the correct amount and the computer factored it up. Jo has asked the bank to check the authorisation codes for this project because she thinks that is where it will be. It's clever and simple, and it would only turn up in a post-project audit. Now I need Jo to talk to the bank in Prague."

"Why Jo?"

"Because she knows exactly what to look for and where it will be in their computers. I've got other leads to follow up."

Tuesday 4 March, Prague, Czech Republic

The Praha Mezistátní Banka AS, one of the Czech Republic's biggest financial institutions, was well established and highly regarded. All the local European Commission aid programme management units had their accounts there and there had been absolutely no complaints about the integrity of the service or security offered. But on this damp and overcast first Tuesday in March, Joanna knew she was about to place that integrity under question.

Joanna had explained in detail what the problem was and the head of the Treasury Department had immediately called in Jiří Novák, the elderly Transfers Manager in the Foreign Currency section, who now regarded him with a shocked look on his wrinkled face.

"But that's absurd, sir. It is impossible for that to have occurred." Novák's voice cracked with scandalised emotion.

"That is as may be, Jiří, but, nonetheless, we will investigate. Miss Donnelly knows what to look for and you will assist her in every way."

"Very well, sir." Jiří Novák walked slowly from the office accompanied by Joanna.

Fifteen minutes later, Novák sat back and pointed at the computer monitor, his incredulous expression rendering words unnecessary. Joanna came round the desk and read over his shoulder.

"So the incoming funds *do* go to two separate accounts," she said.

Novák tapped on the screen. "So it seems. Very unusual. Very unorthodox."

"Who set up the split and who owns the second account?" Joanna asked quietly.

The Czech entered some data and the screen changed. He pushed back his chair. "I'll be back in a moment."

As the banker left the office, Joanna studied the new data on the monitor, whistled silently to herself and quickly made some notes. This was pay dirt.

When Novák returned, Joanna was standing by the window looking out at the *Staré Město* or Old Town of Prague. She had what she needed.

She turned and said, "Mr Novák, you've been very helpful. I am most grateful and will not take up any more of your time." She shook hands with the Czech. "Yes, I really am most grateful."

"I'm glad I could help," Novák replied, clearing the screen.

Luc had accessed Gerald Darbly's Prague apartment with surprising ease. There were no added security precautions, no alarm and the lock on the front door had yielded quickly to his picklocks. A thorough search, however, had revealed nothing of interest and it was clear to him that the place was used infrequently. The only thing he had learned was that the apartment was registered in the name of Svetlana Nikolaevna.

It was time to meet Joanna.

Luc carefully locked the door to the apartment and stood listening. There was complete silence. He walked quietly downstairs and out onto *Na Kampě*.

Twenty minutes later he entered *U Fleků*, a traditional beer hall in the *Nové Město* area. The large, noisy room was filling up quickly and it took him a moment or two to spot Joanna sitting at the end of a long table. As he sat down next to her, a waiter appeared with a tray heavily laden with half-litre beer mugs, two of which he banged down in front of them. Luc took an appreciative sip and then a longer draught.

"What did you get?"

"Everything," replied Joanna.

"You're wonderful. So who owns the account?"

"Schröder-Mannlicher Fegyvergyár."

Luc put his beer down and stared at Joanna. "That's absurd. Schröder-Mannlicher Fegyvergyár is perfectly legit. They make good weaponry and it doesn't foul up. They only sell to clients who can produce the required End User Certificate. Why would they be involved in a fraud?"

Joanna broke the silence that came between them, "What's an End User Certificate?"

"It's a document issued by a government saying the arms are only going to be used by their military. The idea is to avoid military hardware being sold to terrorists and rogue administrations."

"Okay, so how do terrorists and rebels actually get their guns?"

"Either they are supplied by governments direct or someone in a Defence Ministry somewhere issues a false EUC."

"Luc…if the money is going to this arms company then…"

"I know. Someone, almost certainly Vandenhove, is using Commission money to buy arms. Which is exactly what I suggested to Mr Ashley." He lit a cigarette, ignoring her look of reproof. "What we need to know is…"

Joanna remained silent as Luc stared off into space. The waiter put two plates of sausage and dumplings in front of them and, with nothing better to do, Joanna started to eat. A boisterous group of young men in dinner jackets came in and started to sing lustily. A group of tourists crowded around the central table clamouring for the attention of the waiters. Two more beers appeared.

Luke said, "We need to know who Darbly calls regularly in the Czech Defence Ministry."

"Do we have anyone we can ask?"

"Actually, yes. As it happens I've an old *Légion* friend who now works for the Czech security service."

Luc's contact in the Czech security service, the BIS, was still in his office despite it being lunchtime. Luc identified himself, explained what he wanted to know and then waited. A couple of attractive blond girls in cropped tops and tight jeans walked in and Luc looked them over.

Joanna nudged him sharply.

"Down, boy. You've already got a woman with you." She received an amused grimace as an answer.

Luc listened intently for a moment and then terminated the call. "Darbly calls a man in the procurement section called Albert Cerný who is…"

"…just the man who issues these End User Certificates." Joanna finished the sentence for him.

"Exactly."

Luc signalled a waiter, paid the bill and they left the bar. They walked in silence for a few minutes and then Luc said, "Can we get anything from this Dukakis character, the guy who's been monitoring the EuropeAid file?"

"Like what? We've got all the financial data."

"I know, but it's going to be a bugger to prove Vandenhove is behind this. We need more evidence. Is there anything we could leverage with Dukakis?"

"I've already run a security check on him. He's clean. Professionally, he's very good, a well-known expert on hackers and computer security, and a long-time Commission employee. He's not living beyond his means. I don't see him as bent," Joanna concluded.

"There has to be something. We need the guy to talk to us."

"What about a sting?"

"You happy to do that?"

"Sure. What are you going to do?"

"I'm going to Hungary," he replied.

CHAPTER FIVE

Thursday 6 March, near Pécs, Hungary

The Schröder-Mannlicher Fegyvergyár building was, at first sight, something straight out of Albert Speer's Nazi ideal: massive, solid, grey and unadorned 'strength through Teutonic efficiency'. Located about ten kilometres north of the Hungarian town of Pécs, in well-wooded and gently rolling countryside, it was an out-of-time and out-of-place monument to industrial might. Built in the mid 1930s, it had always been an arms factory, and it owed its physical location to the discretion afforded by the woods around it, the proximity of an abundant supply of fresh water and, most importantly, its own spur down to the main rail network at Pécs.

During the Second World War, engineers dedicated to the fine science of building highly efficient small arms such as rifles, pistols and the new machine guns, ran the factory with great efficiency. Originally, the main market had been the Hungarian Army but, by 1939, that had changed and the Schröder family, who owned the factory, with their close connections to Hitler's Third Reich, were soon selling their growing output to the *Wehrmacht*. Trains rumbled up to the factory bringing high-grade steel and slave labour, then rumbled out again with pistols, rifles, machine guns and the ammunition to go with them.

The arrival of the Russians in 1945 looked like a death knell but the ostensibly apolitical Schröders quickly became a preferred supplier to the Russian Army, and the weapons developed and manufactured outside Pécs were used in putting down the 1956 Uprising. The people of the region, if they knew of the existence of the factory, turned a blind eye to it and to the continued use of slave labour shipped in from the vast Gulags of the Soviet Union.

In the period that followed the collapse of communism, local workers replaced the slave labourers causing a mini-economic boom in a depressed post-Soviet region. Serbs became big buyers and Schröder-Mannlicher Fegyvergyár continued to produce at near capacity to supply all sides in the various Balkan Wars that marked the end of the twentieth century. The arms still left by rail, now carried in the ubiquitous forty-foot containers needed for direct transfer to articulated lorries when the need arose.

Now, in the gently falling snow of the late morning, the main gates of the factory that served as both road and rail access were being patrolled by armed guards with Doberman dogs. The watchtowers had gone with the last of the slave labourers. BMWs, Volkswagens and newly manufactured Skodas now occupied the area that, just over two generations previously, had held the vehicles of the Reich and then those of the Soviet military.

From his position in the trees directly across the valley, Luc observed the factory. The overnight journey from Prague had been uneventful, the five hundred-kilometre drive to Budapest accomplished in a little under eight hours despite the snow. There he had met up with Gregor Szabo, the DER man in Hungary. Then, after a few hours rest while Gregor called his contacts, the two had driven the one hundred and ninety kilometres down to Pécs, arriving just before nightfall. This morning Gregor had gone to the factory while Luc took the watching brief.

His mobile phone vibrated. Checking carefully to ensure he was unobserved and out of earshot of any patrolling guards, Luc eased the phone out of his jacket with numbed fingers.

"Yes?"

"Where are you?" Gregor's voice was so familiar that Luc could almost see his ex-*Légionnaire* friend.

"Watching the factory from across the valley."

"Good. I've just heard that they're going to run a second shift today. It'll be lunch break in ten minutes. The lads generally slip out for a beer. There's a bar one kilometre on the left going downhill. See you there."

Luc looked round again cautiously and then trained his binoculars on the car park in front of the factory building. A crowd of men and women emerged and fanned out across it. One man, about one metre eighty-five tall and weighing, Luc guessed, around a hundred and ten kilograms moved away from the main crowd and looked almost directly at him, the face clear and distinct in the powerful glasses. A scar ran from the left eye to the corner of his mouth, a souvenir of a near fatal confrontation with a machete in Rwanda just before Luc had gunned down the Hutu militiaman wielding it. The man raised his left hand and stroked the scar, a natural movement, but one that conveyed a message that Luc fully understood. Gregor Szabo walked to a Skoda and got in.

Luc moved carefully out of his hiding place and crawled deep into the trees before he stood up. He had spotted the bar on his way up and had already worked out the quickest route that avoided the winding road hugging that side of the valley. He shouldered his rucksack and set off. It was good to be out in the open again.

When he entered, the bar was warm, bright and crowded with factory workers. He received a few quizzical looks; it was too early for tourists, but walkers came to the area no matter what the season. He ordered a beer and took it to a table in a corner. He could see Gregor and made eye contact. A group of men carrying mugs of beer and plates of stew surged round the tables and Luc found himself sandwiched between his friend and a huge, unshaven worker who smelt of sweat and gunpowder, machine oil and garlic. The noise level was high and some men in the opposite corner had started to sing lustily.

"Jackpot, Luc." The familiar voice was close to his ear. He felt his arm gripped by a powerful hand, the scarred face close to his for a moment. The room felt warm and close. "Take a piss. There's a door to the back yard. Three minutes."

Luc finished his beer and stood up. He saw the sign for the toilets and headed into the dark corridor, the smell of stale urine and ammonia strong in the air. The corridor was empty when he came out of the stinking toilet. The door to the outside was ajar, which it had not been when he went in. He slid his right hand into the pocket of his parka, checked the Glock 17 automatic he had collected from his BIS contact in Prague and stepped outside.

"Over here." Gregor, accompanied by a small wiry man, was standing by the woodpile smoking a cigarette. Luc looked around, saw no one else and moved away from the building.

"This is Farkas." Gregor indicated the other man. "When you said we needed someone on the inside I contacted him. He's ex-*Légion*. What do you want him to do?"

Luc assessed the situation and accepted it. "All right. I'm interested in a shipment, which should be going out soon. We think the order was cleared for payment this week. We also think it will be going somewhere via Constanta with a shipping company associated with our old friend Groupe Franco Belge."

Gregor looked at Luc sharply, sucked his teeth and said, "Still in the game, are they." He turned to Farkas and changed from French to Hungarian. There was a rapid exchange that Luc could not follow.

"Farkas says there's a consignment going out about two or three weeks from now, towards the end of the month. Small arms, rifles mainly, plus lots of ammunition. There are some rocket-propelled grenade launchers and a lot of grenades, plus some rocket launchers, and rockets. It's all light infantry stuff that can be carried around easily."

"Where's it going?"

"He's not certain. It's being shipped in two containers marked EU Kurdish Aid and the transport orders have it cleared via Belgrade to Constanta. I guess it'll go by sea from there on."

"EU Kurdish Aid!! Jeezus!! That means it's going to Iraq," said Luc incredulously.

Farkas started to speak again but Gregor cut him off. "The container is marked as agricultural machinery and they'll be putting some of that in to disguise the arms."

"Is anyone travelling with it?"

"No, the Russian is to meet it in Constanta."

"What Russian?" Luc was instantly alert.

"The buyer. He turned up here with the Englishman two days ago. Farkas recognised him immediately, unless Gorsky has a double."

"Who's Gorsky?" asked Luc.

"Farkas says it's his *nom de la Légion*."

Luc took his rucksack off, opened it, extracted a small battlefield computer and switched it on. He opened a file containing a clear image of Gerald Darbly.

"Is this the Englishman?" Farkas looked closely, then nodded. He said something in Hungarian.

"Farkas says this man turns up at the factory quite frequently with Gorsky and each time just before a major shipment goes out."

"Do we know anything else about this Gorsky other than he's an arms dealer and an ex-*Légionnaire*?"

Farkas sensed the meaning of the question and spoke rapidly. Gregor acknowledged him, then said, "Farkas says he was a sergeant at Castelnaudary and ran an explosives course, probably about the time you went through the Farm."

"Sorry for not the French speak well ten years since *Légion* no speak French." Farkas spoke apologetically in broken French and then went back to Hungarian. Gregor listened and nodded.

"Right, what do you want Farkas to do?"

Luc took two small black boxes from the rucksack. "These are GPS tracker devices. Can Farkas get them either in with the arms or in the container?"

"No problem." Gregor turned them over. "Magnetic?"

"No, unfortunately. Just slide the recessed switch to activate and they should last ten to fifteen days."

"Luc, are we trying to stop the shipment?"

"No. We simply need to know where it ends up."

"What do you want me to do?"

"Track the arms. Go with them to Constanta. They'll be shipped to somewhere and then flown or trucked to Iraq or near the border. I have to be certain where they're going before we can act. Then I'll need you in Belgium."

"And my assignment here?"

"I'll get the boss to send someone out to take over. Tracking the arms takes priority."

Thursday 6 March, Brussels

Paul Dukakis was a lonely but not unhappy man. A Greek in his mid-thirties and unmarried, he lived and breathed computers, but there was just so much time that one could spend with them. For social contact he had established a routine of going out with colleagues a couple of nights a week, attending a gym for a cardio-vascular workout on a Monday and Thursday after work, and going to the cinema on Fridays. All a bit monotonous but it was better than being entirely on his own. There had been one or two girlfriends but they never lasted long and he had never found any girl who liked computers even half as much as he did.

The gym was near the Place du Châtelain, just off Avenue Louise in Brussels. Dukakis preferred this one since it took him away from the usual haunts of his colleagues and into the more cosmopolitan environment of a better side of town. It was a good place to meet people and there was always the chance to go to one of the local bars to socialise afterwards. Some of his colleagues thought him a bit weird but Dukakis enjoyed this aspect of his life. He was in good shape, he knew, and he never seemed short of people to talk to.

He changed quickly and headed for the bikes. He would warm up for thirty minutes before a serious session on the rowing machine, some time on the steps and then a sauna and shower. There was one bike still free. Not his favourite one, that was in use by an attractive dark-haired girl, but the one next to it. He adjusted the settings and started pedalling. The background music on the speakers was not to his liking so he turned on his iPod MP3 player and retreated into a world of his own.

Twenty minutes later, he ended his warm-up and realised that the dark haired girl was no longer on the bike next to him but was starting a session on the rowing machines. He started to stretch and looked at the girl in the mirror. She was certainly easy to look at. The short, black hair framed an attractive and slightly freckled face, her torso inside the tight tank top was well toned with firm breasts and no signs of fat, the arms were in excellent shape and the legs were muscular without being too heavily developed. "I bet she'd be good in bed," he thought.

Dukakis suddenly became aware that the girl was watching him watching her. He smiled in a 'sorry but you're easy on the eye' way and she smiled back and they stayed in silent communication for a few minutes while Dukakis stretched and the girl rowed gently. The machine next to her became vacant and she nodded at Dukakis indicating he should take it. He nodded back conspiratorially, made the settings and started to row.

They rowed quietly for about ten minutes and then the girl picked up the pace, obviously going for a 'sprint finish' before cooling down. Dukakis kept pace and finished at the same time. It had been a good workout.

"I'm going to take a sauna. What about you?" The voice had an intriguing accent that Dukakis guessed was probably Irish but it was difficult to tell as she had spoken in French. But the greater surprise was that she appeared to want his company.

"I need to stretch some more but I'll be there in a minute." He got off the rowing machine and watched her walk away. He felt good. He would not take too long.

The sauna was unisex and about three metres square. The users normally stripped off their exercise kit and went in wearing swimming costumes. Sometimes a user would be naked but it was not encouraged. The temperature was high when Dukakis, in swimming briefs, entered and the heat hit him like a wall. There was only one other occupant, the dark haired girl. He took a seat at right angles to her. She was certainly attractive.

Five minutes later she stood up and, leaving her towel on the bench, stepped out and across to the shower. After a while, Dukakis was conscious she had returned and was about to put more water on the coals. He stepped past her and showered. He felt good, the tensions of the previous week had eased and his muscles felt supple, the endorphins released by the exercise had kicked in and he felt relaxed and content.

He re-entered the sauna and found the girl lying full length on the bench with her eyes closed. She was wearing a bikini that showed off her figure and Dukakis was able to look at her and savour the image forming in his mind. Was it sexual or simply appreciation of a good looking female form? He sat down and realised that he was mildly aroused. It was a pleasant feeling. Sweat droplets were causing him to blink.

"My name's Jo. What's yours?" Dukakis opened his eyes and realised that the girl was looking at him.

"Paul," he replied and smiled.

"Well, Paul, I've had enough of this and I need a drink."

"Let me buy you one. I'll see you in the bar in, say, ten minutes."

They left the sauna together, entered the showers and allowed the cold water to reduce their body temperatures before heading off to the changing rooms.

Dukakis dressed quickly. He hadn't felt this good in some time. The bar-come-café was fitted out in an ultra-modern style with a lot of polished chrome and light coloured wood. The glass-fronted counter had a light beech top and some tall barstools. The girl entered just as Dukakis sat down. He stood up again.

"What can I get you?"

"Apple juice, please." She took a stool next to his and turned to look at him. Paul Dukakis knew he was no Adonis but he was by no means bad looking. His olive-skinned face glowed beneath shining black hair, his body was trim enough and he knew he had the look of a man in good health. She raised her glass in a silent toast.

"I've seen you here before. What do you do?"

Dukakis put his coffee down slowly. He was a regular here but had not seen her before or, at least, was not conscious of seeing her before. He smiled inwardly at his oversight.

"Commission. I'm on the Information Systems team." This was where it usually went wrong. He was a techie and the sooner it was out the better, but so many girls were simply not interested.

"Hardware or software?"

"Software and security mainly. And you?" So far so good.

"Research mainly." She smiled encouragingly.

"Commission?" That got a shake of the head.

"No. A research organisation. We do a lot of work for the EU Commission, though. Mainly in the funding field you know, locating grants and getting funding for projects." She paused. "But tell me about your…"

Under the gentle probing and encouragement of the girl, Dukakis started talking about his work and he soon realised that he had a receptive audience who actually knew what he was talking about. This encouraged him more as it was so unusual. They finished their drinks and, by mutual consent, left the gym together. They headed for the Italian restaurant on the square where Dukakis paid for the meal and they talked well into the evening. As they left, they agreed to meet again at the gym the following week.

CHAPTER SIX

Luc watched his partner across their office as she explained about her contact with Dukakis the previous week.

"You be damned careful. This caper is getting people killed wholesale and I don't want to add you or Dukakis to that list." Luc failed to conceal the unease in his voice.

Joanna smiled. "I'll be careful but there'll come a point when I will need you to complete the operation."

"When are you meeting him?"

"Tonight."

"*D'accord*. Be careful and keep me informed.

Joanna prepared carefully. Tonight was going to be difficult because she planned on probing to see if Dukakis would reveal more, but at the same time she had to be ready to reveal her connection with the DER and that could panic him. She found the Greek an attractive man and she felt easy in his company: a computer fanatic, certainly, but not a nerd in any way.

At 5 p.m., she left the DER offices, having told Luc what she planned. He had been obviously concerned, which she thought was sweet of him, but had made no attempt to stop her. He would be there for her should she need him. The traffic on the inner ring would be bad at this time on a Wednesday, even on a motorbike, so she took to the back streets, entering the Place du Châtelain from the bottom. It was too risky to go home now, although it was just a block away, in case Dukakis saw her, so she left the bike in the square and walked the last hundred metres.

Dukakis was already there as she entered and had clearly been waiting for her. They checked in and headed for the changing rooms. Their workout followed the same pattern as their previous session and after two hours they were again in the Italian restaurant on the square.

"Paul, you seem tense. Is something bothering you?"

"Just an incident at work, Jo, nothing more."

"Want to tell me about it?" But she could guess what was on his mind. She had spent some time attacking the defences on the ZX file and not hiding the fact that she was probing. Now it all depended on how he would react.

"What do you know about computer security, Jo?"

"Not a lot but I'm familiar with the basics."

Dukakis looked thoughtfully at her and then, with some hesitation, started to explain. Without mentioning any details that could identify the file or the people involved, he explained how he had been approached a couple of years previously by a senior *fonctionnaire* who said he was concerned about an internal fraud in a EuropeAid programme and that he needed a certain file monitored. It wasn't that unusual, Dukakis said, and he'd handled a number of such requests over the last three years but they normally originated in the EU's anti-fraud unit. What was odd about this one was that it came from a department not directly involved in aid programmes. Dukakis had reluctantly complied and then he made a mistake.

"And what was that, Paul?" Joanna sounded sympathetic, but inside she was processing the new information from every angle.

"Strange payments into my bank account started to occur. At first I thought the bank had made an error but, after the third one, I asked them to investigate where the funds were coming from and see if a mistake had been made."

"And what did they say?"

"Apparently the money was coming from the company involved in the aid contract and my bank explained that a standing order had been set up to send me money every month." He stopped speaking and gulped some wine. "The money kept coming. I contacted the company and asked what it was for and they said that it was for consultancy and had been authorised by the Commission. I knew this couldn't be correct and I checked with the *fonctionnaire* but he said it was okay. Stupidly, I didn't take it further and now I've received a total of twenty-four payments." He sounded relieved to be talking about it.

"How much are we talking about, Paul?"

"Two thousand euro a month."

"Jeez, that's a lot of money."

"I know, Jo, especially as I don't do anything for it and I'm not allowed to do outside consultancy. But I don't know how to stop it or what to do about it." He sounded defeated. She smiled in encouragement and sympathy. She reached out and took his hand.

"Have you tried talking to these anti-fraud people you mentioned?"

"No. They're interested in fraud against the Commission but this money was coming from an outside source. All I do is monitor access to a particular file and tell the *fonctionnaire* each time someone accesses it."

"It doesn't seem that you've done anything wrong so why not tell your unit head and arrange to send the money back."

"I would have done, Jo, I really would have but a few weeks ago the file came under scrutiny from the DER and they're a different load of characters, believe me. They investigate criminal activity and work with the anti-fraud unit only when appropriate. They've got someone very good down there, someone who is actually better than I am, and they've defeated the protection I had on the file. If they know what I've done, then I'm in deep shit."

"But all you've done is what this *fonctionnaire* asked you to do."

"Don't you see, Jo, the DER won't believe me. They'll find the payments from the contractor and they'll assume I'm on the take."

Joanna nodded sympathetically. What Dukakis had just said was absolutely true: the DER would certainly think the worst even if she believed him. She squeezed his hand.

"Paul, you've got to tell someone in authority or you'll just get into even more trouble."

He looked round, his confidence gone.

"Jo, I really don't know who to tell. I'll lose my job for sure but if this comes out, I'd never get another job."

"I know someone who could help, Paul. You'd have to be willing to tell him everything but I'm sure he could help." She looked steadily across the table maintaining eye contact with the frightened man and holding his hand reassuringly. It was now or never. "Would you like me to talk to him?"

"Would he really be able to help?"

"Yes," said Joanna, blithely mortgaging her relationship with Luc. "I could phone him now if you like and we could ask him."

Dukakis stayed silent, weighing up the offer and looking fixedly at Joanna his eyes blank. Then, like a drowning man grabbing a life belt, he took a deep breath and said, "Do it."

Slowly, Joanna disengaged her hand, reached into her bag and took out her mobile. She paused. Dukakis nodded absently and she dialled.

"Luc, I have a problem and wonder whether you could help."

Tuesday 11 March, Brussels

Luc thought back to the phone call he had received the previous evening. Dukakis had been with Joanna and she had positioned the relationship with Luc as a friend who could help.

The outcome had been a long meeting late into the night between Luc and a now somewhat relieved Dukakis. Joanna had been present but Luc had been careful not to reveal her connection with the DER. He had explained that he, Luc, worked for the DER. At first Dukakis had been reluctant to talk but, encouraged by Joanna, had finally unburdened himself completely and with startling frankness. Now Dukakis was due to visit the DER offices. This would be the test of his sincerity.

"Luc, you have a visitor, a Mr Dukakis. He says he has an appointment." The Director's secretary was standing in the open doorway of Luc's office.

"Show him in to the conference room please, Sophie." They had won!

Dukakis was standing looking out of the window when Luc entered the room. He turned and Luc had the impression that he looked younger and as though relieved of a great burden.

"Good morning, Paul. Please sit down."

"Luc, can I ask a few questions?"

"Go ahead."

Dukakis sat down, stared at the table for a few moments and then said, "Jo works for you, doesn't she?" It was a statement of fact and not of betrayal.

"Yes, Paul, she does."

There was a long silence before Dukakis spoke again. "Why didn't you just arrest me or something?"

"Because we want your help and, as Jo said, you don't seem to have done anything wrong."

"I've been a fucking idiot, haven't I?"

"Possibly, but no worse than a thousand others would have been in the same circumstances."

"What do you want me to do now?" The conversion was complete.

"I'd like you to work with the person who has been giving you so much grief on the computer." Luc smiled and got a tentative smile in return.

"It's Jo, isn't it?" Dukakis heaved a sigh of relief when Luc nodded. "She's seriously good, you know. I've been doing research on hackers and the like for about four years now: she's damned good." He winked at Luc. "And sexy as well."

Luc nodded absently and then said, "Paul, I'm sorry if she tricked you but this case has become very dangerous and we already have three dead bodies connected with it. We need you safe but we also need your help and we certainly don't want to alert the opposition."

Dukakis nodded in a bewildered way as Luc continued, "Have you told anyone where you are this morning?"

"No. I rang my secretary and told her I was on an on-site inspection. I do four or five a week so she'll ask no questions."

Joanna entered the room, sat down at one end of the table and gave Dukakis an embarrassed smile.

"Hello, Paul." She was visibly nervous.

"Hi, Jo. I suppose I should be all upset with you…no, don't say anything…but I'm not — you were very good and I…and I, well, I'm happy to be working with you."

Thursday 13 March, Brussels

Joanna looked out of the window. It had been a tough few days and, without any chocolate handy, she succumbed and lit a cigarette. It wasn't what she wanted. It was not much fun in the office without Luc to share her thoughts, but he had been summoned to Luxembourg. Damn, she felt sorry for herself.

The telephone rang and she picked it up.

"Jo Donnelly."

"Hi, Jo!"

"Luc. Jeezus, it's good to hear your voice. Where are you?" She suddenly felt happier and less stressed. She stubbed out the cigarette.

"Still down in Luxembourg. We have authority to target Groupe Franco Belge direct. So, research their background. We need to *prove* the link between them and Vandenhove, and prove he's issuing the instructions. But be careful."

"When will you be back?"

"I'll be leaving in an hour, so say three hours. How's Dukakis getting on?"

"Fine. He needs some stuff from the Commission and to show his face if we're to avoid suspicion. And I need some stuff from the guys in Leuven."

"All right, get one of the duty drivers to take him and bring him back."

"Is that really necessary?" asked Joanna.

"Absolutely."

"Okay. See you later." Joanna rang off and went to talk to Sophie, the Director's secretary, to arrange things.

Half an hour later, a black Audi A6 carrying Paul Dukakis rumbled up the ramp from the underground car park and headed towards the European Quarter. Shortly afterwards, Joanna, on her yellow BMW 1100 GS, roared up from the car park and swung left. She crossed the tram tracks and turned right under the railway bridge. As she approached the traffic lights, she swung round a grey Mercedes 300 as it edged its way into the traffic.

Joanna waited patiently for the lights to change. The run to Leuven should take about thirty minutes as traffic was reasonably light and she was in no hurry. It was a pleasure to be out and about rather than inside slaving over a computer.

She eased the bike up a couple of gears as she passed through the Place Louise tunnel and headed for the Porte de Namur. She took the right-hand lane through the Place du Trône tunnel and came to a stop at the lights at the top of Rue Belliard. From here, she would take the tunnel round to the E40 autoroute to Leuven. The lights changed and the traffic edged forward and then started to roll comfortably down Rue Belliard at fifty kilometres per hour.

As the bike dipped under the futuristic footbridge that linked the European Parliament complex with the buildings on the east side of Belliard, she checked her mirror and saw the grey Mercedes one car length back and matching the bike for speed. Joanna signalled and eased over into the left hand lane, accelerating gently as she dropped down into the curving tunnel.

Her speed was a little over sixty kilometres per hour when the Mercedes hit the rear wheel.

Fighting for control as she slid towards the outside of the curve, Joanna had no real understanding of what had happened. Another jolt and her balance was gone.

She fought to steady the bike but there was no way to save it.

No time for panic. No time for anything. Ground rushing towards her. The wall of the tunnel approaching. The squeal of brakes. Pain as her left leg took the weight of the bike and then the bike was gone. A huge sound. A large object rushing towards her from above.

Oblivion.

The sounds of cars braking and tearing metal as they collided were of no consequence to Gärtner in the grey Mercedes 300 as he checked his mirror to watch the result of his efforts. He watched the bike slide across the carriageway, collide with the right-hand wall and crash down on the rider still sliding across the road. Good enough. He accelerated away.

"Call an ambulance and the police," shouted the first driver to reach the scene.

"Don't move her," warned another as a group rushed to aid the fallen rider.

"Help me get the bike off her," ordered a large man who had been driving a delivery van.

Carefully a group lifted the heavy bike off the body of the rider and the pool of blood became evident.

"Don't touch the helmet," shouted a biker.

Behind them engines were dying and voices carried clearly through the cool air. A small crowd had gathered.

"It was a grey Mercedes. It deliberately hit the bike and then drove off." A small, dark-skinned man, possibly Moroccan, was speaking to anyone who would listen.

Drivers from the cars nearest the fallen bike were now moving through the closely packed vehicles in the tunnel entrance, advising and assisting others. The sound of approaching sirens echoed in the tunnel.

But Joanna Donnelly lay in a pool of blood and knew nothing.

Luc was beginning to get annoyed. The drive back into Brussels had been slow and as he approached the bottom of Avenue Louise, everything came to a standstill. The outward-bound traffic was particularly heavy and blocking the junctions. Luc swore quietly.

A gap appeared and Luc took it, joined Avenue Louise, and worked his way past the Peace Monument and the Blue Tower and swung left onto Vleurgat. Twenty minutes later, he entered the underground car park at the office.

Luc walked into his office and sat down. He switched on the computer and a message-waiting icon flashed. He opened the message and recognised the name immediately: Dirk Wauters of JDB Systems in Leuven. He reached for the telephone.

"May I speak to Dirk? This is Luc Hansen."

"*Met* Wauters."

"Hi, Dirk, it's Luc. I have a message to call you."

"Luc, I'm sorry to have to tell you this, but Jo was involved in a major road accident in the Belliard Tunnel a couple of hours ago…" Luc felt himself go cold. "…and she's been taken to UCL St Anne. She's alive but badly hurt…Luc, you still there?"

"Yes, I'm still here. Do you have a contact number for the hospital?" He wrote it down. "Thanks. I'll call you later." He hung up. *Merde*!!! "Think, Luc, think."

He reached for the phone. All the hospital would tell him was that, at that moment, the patient was alive and in surgery. He put down the phone and headed for Radcliffe's office.

A frustrating hour later, Luc walked through the main doors of the hospital. The receptionist directed him to the Accident & Emergency department.

"She's still in surgery, *Monsieur*," said the A&E receptionist firmly but gently. "Are you the next of kin, *Monsieur*?"

"No, she has no next of kin in Belgium. I'm her colleague."

"Ah… anyway, could you sign here…" she indicated the place on a form "… so that we keep the records straight. Is your organisation going to be responsible for the accommodation costs?"

"Yes." He signed and handed the form back. "Is there anyone who can tell me anything about her condition?"

"I'm sorry, *Monsieur*. The doctors are with her now. Please wait and I'll ask someone to talk to you as soon as they are free."

He knew his anger was wrong, but he could not help it. He was annoyed and if he was honest with himself, seriously worried. He wanted to know now how Jo was. He needed a cigarette. He forced himself to be calm.

"I'll step outside for a while." He mimed smoking and the receptionist smiled knowingly.

"I'm sure someone will be out to see you shortly, *Monsieur*." She smiled and Luc put all his effort into smiling back.

Outside the air was cold. Luc found a quiet place to smoke, his thoughts focused on Joanna. He now realised his attachment to her was more than just professional. He tried to push personal thoughts to one side and failed.

He finished his cigarette and went back inside. The receptionist smiled but shook her head. "Nothing yet, *Monsieur*. Why don't you get yourself a coffee and I'll come and get you when the doctor is free."

"Thank you." He was grateful and showed it.

An hour later, the receptionist touched him gently on the shoulder. Luc looked round with a start and realised that he had drunk two coffees and smoked another cigarette.

"*Monsieur*, the doctor can see you now. Please come with me."

The receptionist led him to one of the consultation rooms and ushered him in. The only occupant was a young, dark-skinned female in a white clinician's coat. Her name badge said she was Dr Farah Aziz.

"Please sit down, *Monsieur* Hansen." Her voice was light, her French pronunciation revealing a slight Arabic accent. "You are the friend of *Mademoiselle* Donnelly, yes?" Luc nodded. "Well, she's a lucky young woman. The protective clothing absorbed most of the damage. She's okay and in no danger medically."

Luc felt a rush of relief.

"Can I see her?" he said.

"In a moment. Let me tell you about her injuries because she's rather covered in bandages at the moment. She must have slid across the road for some distance, as there is bruising along her left side from ankle to shoulder and lacerations on her torso and left shoulder consistent with such road contact. Unfortunately, she has a badly strained left knee and, judging from the damage, she must have twisted it as she fell. The cast will have to stay on for about six weeks. There are no head injuries at all — her helmet saved her — and the fact that no one tried to remove it. The motorbike seems to have landed on her and there are some internal injuries and a puncture wound plus a lot of bruising in the abdominal area. She lost a lot of blood, both externally and internally, and we've had to give her several transfusions."

"But she's going to be all right?"

"Oh, yes, *Monsieur*. She's very fit indeed and should heal well. The leg will be fine. She was lucky she was brought here and that I and my team were on duty." She smiled in a way that indicated that she really knew just how good she was. "We've had a lot of experience with this sort of thing. Yes, she'll be fine."

"Can I see her now?"

"Yes, of course. She's still unconscious from the anaesthetic. We did a complete body scan, including the head. There may be some bruising to the brain and she'll need to be under constant observation for a few days. Concussion is a probability and we want to be sure there are no complications if that happens." She stood up. "Come with me and I'll take you to her. She's on the third floor."

Joanna was lying in a bed surrounded by monitoring equipment. A drip entered her left arm and the electronic equipment mounted to her right trailed cables that led to her head and upper body. Her dark hair on the pillow accentuated her pallor, but her breathing was gentle and regular. Her face was, Luc noticed thankfully, completely unmarked. Her left leg was elevated within a framework that might easily have proven useful to the Inquisition, although the doctor would doubtless claim that it was only light traction.

Dr Aziz carefully checked all the equipment and then pulled back the sheet to check the various wounds. Luc turned away, it was not right he should see Joanna exposed like this. After five minutes, Dr Aziz was satisfied.

"We did a good job on her. Stay with her if you want. She'll wake up shortly and would probably want to see a friendly face when she does. Don't use a mobile telephone in here because it'll upset some of this equipment."

"I'll slip out and let the others know the news and then I'll stay with her." He accompanied the doctor out of the private room. They said good-bye and Luc remembered to thank her. He entered the lift, headed for the lobby and then out into the cold.

Two minutes later, he heard Radcliffe's voice.

"Sir, she's going to be all right. A badly strained knee, some internal bleeding and other damage but Dr Aziz says she'll be fine."

"I assume you'll stay with her, Luc. You'll need to check in periodically but at the moment everything is under control."

"Have we anything on what actually happened?"

"The police have confirmed that she was deliberately rammed by a Mercedes, which then stopped to see the result. They're checking the security cameras from the tunnel to see if they can pick up anything that would be useful. Oh, and Luc, I've just heard from London that the Met have finally identified video footage of a man inspecting Morgan's car in the garage. They're sending it over."

Luc considered the information and made a decision. He needed watchers to guard Joanna. He dialled Benoît's number and issued instructions. It was not a perfect setup but it would have to do. With all the teams engaged in operations and Gregor not yet back in Belgium, Benny would have to use a freelancer, predictably yet another ex-Legionnaire and thus 'family': tough, reliable and extremely professional with lots of close-protection experience. Although unarmed, he could do lethal damage without a weapon.

Inside Joanna's brain, images were forming: the bike leaning over, the ground coming up to meet her, the wall rushing towards her, the bike crashing down, blue lights, white coats and pain. More images: a woman in a white coat bending over her, a familiar face in the background. She opened her eyes but could see nothing for a moment and then things started to come into focus. A figure in a chair. She focused on the face and smiled as she recognised it.

Something made Luc turn and he saw her looking at him. He smiled and reached for her hand and gave it a gentle squeeze.

"Hi, kid! Glad to have you back."

She closed her eyes and went back to sleep.

In Luc's office, Paul Dukakis watched the monitor screen intently. It had not been difficult to work out how the photo-enhancer program worked and he was pleased to be doing something useful. Radcliffe was watching from another chair as Dukakis manipulated the image and sharpened the picture that they had received from the British police. The over-enlarged pixels slowly smoothed and sharpened and the image resolved into a reasonably clear picture of a man with pale features, darkish hair and a stubble beard. The next challenge would be the images from the Belliard Tunnel camera.

Dukakis was enjoying himself and the work was interesting. The second picture took only a few minutes to enhance. He printed it and pushed it across to Radcliffe.

"Definitely a match."

"You're a hundred percent sure?"

"Yes, Mr Radcliffe."

"Well, I suppose that counts as proof that the same man tried to kill Jo but it'll never convict in court." He looked at Dukakis for a few minutes and then said, "Mr Dukakis, if we wanted to find out if there was a computer record showing that Groupe Franco Belge knew about the false accounting, how would we do it?"

"Basically, you'd have to hack into their computer and see what you can find."

"Could you do that?"

Dukakis leant back in his chair and considered the question. It was both risky and illegal, but the DER team had dug him out of a hole and he owed them.

"Yes, Mr Radcliffe, I could do that."

"And would the security measures you find reveal who had set them?"

"Possibly. All the major players in the field leave their own sets of mouse-prints, so to speak, including Jo, and if they are on record somewhere, or in one of the hacker's databases, then we'll know who we're dealing with."

"Did you record Jo's, Paul?"

"No, sir. And she isn't on record either or I'd have found it." He looked quizzically at Radcliffe and then continued, "She's too good to be a 'gifted amateur' so she's bound to be on record somewhere, unless someone has removed the record."

"Is that so? Is that so?" murmured Radcliffe.

"Do you want me to have a go at the Franco Belge computer?"

"Oh, I think so, Mr Dukakis. But not just yet."

Joanna woke a number of times during the early evening and each time took comfort from Luc's presence. She did not speak but she did respond by squeezing his hand whenever he spoke to her. Later, he told her he had to go home and would be back the following day. She smiled painfully, but her eyes lit up when he kissed her gently on the forehead.

Joanna felt nauseous from the anaesthetic and she was thirsty. A nurse helped her drink, but her throat was very dry and swallowing was difficult. Sitting up was extremely painful. The doctor authorised a small increase in the anti-nausea drug and painkiller administered through the drip. After a while, Joanna slept. And while she slept, her body started to heal itself.

The following morning Luc arrived at the DER offices early and was surprised to find Paul Dukakis already working at the computer. They exchanged greetings and Paul explained what he was doing.

"Will your continued absence cause problems in your unit?"

"I doubt it. I've taken some long overdue leave and am officially on vacation somewhere in Greece. Your people have even arranged for witnesses and cover if needed, so I am told."

"Actually, that sounds like a good idea to me." Luc grinned and reached for a cigarette but paused with his lighter halfway up. "Have we checked on the output of the bugs recently? Jo was doing it daily, usually in the afternoon."

"What bugs?" Dukakis responded in surprise.

"The bugs in Vandenhove's office," Luc replied as he reached over, opened the computer file and started to read.

"Fuck it!!" He read the transcript again. It was from the morning of the previous day and, among the normal conversations of a busy office, it contained two one-sided conversations, the first between Vandenhove and an unknown caller on his mobile phone, and the second with a man called Gärtner.

09.45: Sound of mobile phone ringing

Vandenhove: "Yes, my dear… They've done what?…
When did this happen? They're getting too damned close.
Who turned Dukakis?…Luc Hansen. Okay. Can we do
anything about him?… Okay, no he's too senior. Who's
Dukakis working with…Joanna Donnelly. Right, I've got
that. Is she DER as well?…I'll make arrangements. Let me
know when they leave. Yes, I miss you as well and I'll come
and see you soon."

Sound of call terminating and a new call made on mobile
phone.

Vandenhove: "Gärtner, the DER have compromised
Dukakis. My contact has just told me that he's working
with the DER and is at their offices right now. She

says he's been there since yesterday morning…Yes, but discreetly. He's working with some computer expert, a female called Donnelly. This could compromise the entire project, so just make them disappear without arousing suspicion."

Call ended at 09.48

Then, around two hours, later a second sequence

11.45: Sound of mobile ringing

Vandenhove: Yes, my dear?…Thank you.

Call ended 11.46 and new call made

Vandenhove: Gärtner, Dukakis is going to the Commission under escort but the girl is going to Leuven on a yellow BMW motorbike. They'll be leaving in a few minutes.

Call ended 11.48

Half an hour later Luc watched as Radcliffe read the transcript. There was one inescapable conclusion. "There's no question about it, sir. Someone, almost certainly female, called Vandenhove on his mobile and told him Dukakis was here. We can assume the same person called again from here when Dukakis and Jo were about the leave. And we know the result."

"And your conclusions, Luc?"

"It's obvious, sir. We now have proof there is a mole inside the DER. We also have the name of the killer — Gärtner — and we have proof that Vandenhove ordered him to kill Jo."

"I agree, but do we know who the mole is?"

Luc nodded. "I've checked to see what Jo did here after I called her. She went to Sophie to arrange transport for Dukakis and Sophie got authorisation from the Duty Officer Claudia Chalon. Sophie then ordered a car from Transport. The Transport Officer logged the request at 11.36 with no passenger name, only a destination and to await the passenger's return. Sophie says she was then in with you from 11.40 until 12.15."

"That's correct. So, you're seriously suggesting that Claudia is leaking information to Vandenhove," said Radcliffe neutrally.

"Yes, sir. Since Sophie was with you when Jo left, Claudia is the only female who knew the full details and could have made the call."

"What about other support staff?"

"No one else knew Dukakis' name or who he was working with."

Radcliffe nodded in agreement. "We'll need proof, of course. Set up full electronic surveillance on Claudia including her house."

"I'm also going to bug Vandenhove's mobile," said Luc. "He's got a pay-and-go number and ProxiStar don't keep a call record. We need to know who he's calling and what is being said."

"Very well. Arrange it. But first take a look at these." Radcliffe slid two photographs across the desk. They showed a well-built man in his late thirties with dark hair and a stubble beard. The cameras had caught him from the left-hand side and the image was reasonably sharp.

"Do you know him, Luc?"

Luc studied the pictures carefully, the face had a strange and disturbing familiarity, a memory stirred, a memory of *la Légion*, but he could not pin it down. He would have to think about it.

"Possibly, sir. Who is he?"

"The driver who attempted to kill Jo. The same man was seen in the garage looking at Morgan's car in London. That's our killer, Luc. So now we know what Gärtner looks like."

Luc's memory stirred again. Damn, he'd have to think about it but in the mean time, he needed to go and see Dirk Wauters.

Friday 14 March, Leuven

Luc's interest in computers, electronic surveillance equipment and other technical gadgets was confined to their utility value and the quality of the output. He simply could not share Joanna's passion for them. As a result, he left that side of their work entirely to her. Despite that, he found it surprising that he had never been to the offices of JDB, the DER's electronics section.

The building turned out to be a three-storey townhouse in an area of Leuven that Luc knew to be predominantly student residences. The building itself was impressive but distinctly in need of some maintenance. There were a number of bell pushes by the front door but none had names. Luc pushed them all.

The door buzzed and he pushed it open and stepped into a dark hall in which was parked one ancient-looking pushbike and one very shiny, new mountain bike. As the front door closed, a light came on and a voice called him to come in. Picking his way carefully past the bikes, Luc entered the room from which the voice had come and was stunned by the array of computers, wires and other gadgets; a techie heaven.

A man in his mid-sixties with long grey hair pulled back in a pony-tail, half-moon glasses on his nose and clad in a loose, red polo shirt and camouflage trousers, rose to meet him, revealing himself to be a bit over two metres in height. He held out an enormous hand, but when he spoke, his voice was surprisingly soft.

"It's good to see you again, Luc."

"And you, Dirk."

"Do you want some coffee? Only the best stuff here, and we've our own espresso machine." Luc followed the older man through to a small kitchen that housed the shiny and immaculately clean coffee maker.

A voice called from somewhere else in the house and Dirk gave an answering roar. Feet pounded on the stairs and a few moments later a young man, mid-twenties, with long black hair, a tie-dyed T-shirt and ragged blue jeans bounded into the kitchen like an over-friendly Labrador dog.

"Hi, Luc." He rummaged in a box and produced some biscuits, which he handed round.

"Morning, Bart." Luc accepted a biscuit. According to Joanna, Bart Jongen was an outstanding and gifted technician.

The young man smiled broadly before saying, "Dirk, I've got the stuff set up."

Dirk Wauters looked up from the delicate task of preparing the best smelling double espresso that Luc had tasted recently. "Good boy. You can show it to Luc in a minute."

The young man nodded, grabbed his coffee and ambled off.

"A nice lad and very good." Wauters led the way back into what was clearly his main work area and they sat down.

"Now, Luc, tell me what happened, what's going on?" The older man sat listening without interruption.

"It seems that you've got yourselves involved with some rather nasty people."

"That's one way of putting it," Luc said as he finished his coffee.

"And will Jo be all right?"

"Yes."

"Then I think now would be a good time to use some of our new kit. Come with me."

They left the main room, climbed the stairs to the second floor and entered a large room in which various computers hummed softly. Bart was reading a cartoon book at a table.

Dirk pointed at the monitor. "That allows us to track GSM mobile telephones and locate them geographically. What's your number?"

Luc told him and Bart quickly entered it. After a few moments, a map of Belgium appeared with a small blinking dot more or less over the town of Leuven. Bart hit a few more keys and the map resolved into a much larger scale map showing the street plan of the town. The dot was clearly visible and Luc checked the name of the street. He was impressed; this was a most useful tool.

He gave Bart a new number. The screen resolved first into a map of the Czech Republic and then into a map of the Little Quarter in Prague. Now that was very interesting indeed, and useful.

Dirk looked quizzically at Luc, "And who might that last one be?"

"Someone we're very interested in." He noted down the street name. "What's the accuracy of the location?"

"Currently about fifty metres in a town and about 200 metres in the countryside. If the phone is a new one, we can get to within a few metres or so 'cos they have a GPS code in the transmission string. Old phones have no such code and the accuracy is limited to which cell the phone is in."

"Can this only be done from here?" Luc indicated the equipment.

"No. It uses our server but we can load the interface on any laptop." Dirk took out a pipe, lit it and watched a cloud of smoke drift towards the ceiling. "Now, what else is on your mind?"

"Two things. We need to do a thorough electronic surveillance inside a house, sound and video if possible."

"No problem. Just get us inside and we'll do the rest. And …?"

"I want to bug a mobile phone."

"If it's a GSM, it's easy really. Young Bart here has already miniaturised the necessary chip and all we have to do is insert it in the phone. It'll then transmit via a separate channel to a monitoring device, even when switched off."

"The easiest way of making it all work," continued Dirk, "is if we can get Bart into the room with the phone so he can substitute a doctored one for the original. I assume you have ways of doing that." He looked at Luc expectantly.

"It can be arranged — how much time would you need?"

The young technician answered. "Maybe ten minutes max. I'd pre-code the receptor number before going in. That takes about two minutes off the operation."

Luc looked out of the grimy window as he considered the options. The bugging of Claudia Chalon's house was straightforward. All it required was to get her away from the place long enough for Dirk and Bart to do their work. But getting them into Vandenhove's office and locating his mobile phone would be riskier and much less certain of success. However, the intelligence they would collect warranted the risks. He reached a decision.

"The target for the telephone bug is a *fonctionnaire* called Vandenhove. Now what we need is an entry route."

CHAPTER SEVEN

Monday 17 March, Brussels

High in the Breydel building, the computer maintenance crew was painstakingly checking the fault that the *Chef de Cabinet* to Commissioner de Foucaud had reported in his computer. They were being very discreet and Karel Vandenhove continued his work while seated at the round table that occupied one corner of his office. The younger of the two men glanced at the *fonctionnaire* and then nodded at his older colleague who positioned himself between Vandenhove and the desk.

Bart reached out and slipped Vandenhove's mobile phone off the desk. It was a common enough model. He quickly copied the settings and directories across to his laptop. Then he removed the covers, took out the SIM card and dropped the phone into his bag. He selected the appropriate model from another compartment, inserted the SIM card, copied the settings and directories to the new phone, and clipped on the covers.

He placed the phone back on the desk and said, "Okay, I think I've found it. Yes."

The older man spoke. "*Monsieur* Vandenhove, it's all fixed."

Vandenhove merely nodded and the two men left the room.

Out in the corridor, Dirk Wauters spoke briefly into his mobile and then turned to his companion. "Right, reception's good, when off and when on."

"Of course," replied Bart with a smirk.

Dieter Gärtner was frustrated and angry. He could not find Dukakis, and Vandenhove had not been able to find out where the DER had hidden him. However, Vandenhove had given Gärtner a piece of disturbing news, the importance of which Vandenhove had no idea about. He had given him the name and address of the man leading the DER enquiry: Luc Hansen.

Gärtner rubbed the scar on his cheek. Hansen had been the name of the bastard who had given him the scar. Was it possible that this Hansen was the same one? If so, then he'd waited ten years to get even.

He settled into his observation position carefully. He was obliquely opposite the building in which Hansen lived but he was sure that he could see the only entrance his target would use. Some ninety minutes later, a car drove up the street and entered the garage.

Gärtner glimpsed the face of the driver and felt his heart rate go up. He was reasonably certain it was the same bastard. He touched the scar again.

Gärtner considered the idea of entering the garage and wiring the car. What a pity he had no *plastique* left and his normal source was not in town. He approached the building carefully before retiring in irritation. The garage door had two video cameras set above it, one looking directly down at the door and the other out towards the street. That suggested a higher than normal level of security.

He walked back past the main entrance and was annoyed to find that the entrance area had a similar setup along with an armed guard. Unusual precautions for a residential block! He watched unobtrusively for a few minutes and then saw the discreet symbol to one side of the entrance that identified this as a diplomatic residence. That would explain the security. Gärtner was reasonably confident of his ability to get in and deal with his target but it wouldn't be easy. It would be safer to get him outside the building.

He went back to his observation post and waited. An hour passed before his target drove away from the building. Gärtner moved discreetly to the waiting motorcycle and followed at a safe distance. The target had turned onto the Boulevard de la Woluwe and was heading out of town. It was obvious that he was watching for a tail so Gärtner accelerated, overtook and settled back into line. Tailing from the front was not easy but there was no other way.

The traffic lights had turned to red and Gärtner had just seconds to adapt to the fact that his target was signalling to turn right towards UCL St Anne hospital. He flicked on his indicator and stopped in front of his target. The light turned green and Gärtner preceded his target up the road to the hospital. The target was parking, so he obviously had business here.

Gärtner parked the bike and walked back to the main entrance just as Luc Hansen entered the lift. Gärtner watched the indicator and saw that the lift went straight to the third floor and then began to descend. A nurse got out and walked past him.

He looked around for the information board, which was uninformative in that there were a number of departments on the third floor, but there was also a surgical recovery ward. Why the hell was Hansen visiting a surgical recovery ward? A chill cut through him. Perhaps the DER girl was still alive.

From the increased movement of staff, it seemed that the evening shift was coming on duty and an idea occurred to Gärtner. Following the general movement, he quickly located the laundry room near the staff rooms. Once inside, he found a reasonably clean set of 'greens' and a mask, pulled them on and headed for the third floor.

The surgical recovery ward occupied a long corridor and Gärtner could see down its entire length. A man in dark blue combat fatigues stood guard outside one side ward, which suggested a particularly important patient. Boldly, he walked up the corridor as though he belonged there and glanced right as he approached the room. Yes, there beside the door was the name of the patient 'J. Donnelly'. So, he had not killed the bitch.

He continued walking, took the next corridor on the left and circled round. He needed time to plan the assault and his escape route. He took the lift.

Inside Joanna's room, Luc sat beside the bed holding her hand. She was awake and had spoken to him for the first time. He had her computer bag on the floor beside him.

"I've brought you some toys for when you feel better."

"I feel better when you're here, Luc." She squeezed his hand.

"Tell me about Dirk Wauters?" He tried to sound businesslike but it was difficult while she held his hand.

Tentatively and then with growing confidence, Joanna explained about her past as a hacker and how she and Wauters had established a friendship via the Internet. Wauters was, she said, one of the best hackers she had ever come across and great fun as well. They had kept in touch over the years, and when the DER had agreed to set up the specialist unit, she had gone to meet the tall, Flemish computer expert. They had remained firm friends ever since. He and Bart had gone straight and JDB Systems had been born. Now they spent their time putting together computer solutions, developing useful pieces of electronic gadgetry and conducting covert electronic surveillance. Dirk and Bart handled the hardware side of the business and Joanna handled the software.

"And he's been hard at work ever since by the look of it. He sent me away with a whole load of stuff for you to play with." He bent down and picked up the computer case. "There's a telephone socket in the wall. We should be able to make it work." He plugged in the cable and, following the instructions given him, started the program.

When the computer connected to the JDB server, he entered the password Dirk had given him. Joanna watched as he entered his mobile number and, sure enough, located it in Brussels and the map then resolved to show the hospital. He typed in her mobile number and that resolved to the Police headquarters. Well, they would have to get that back shortly. Then he typed in Gerald Darbly's number and it resolved to the Little Quarter in Prague. The bugger was still there.

"I did that at Dirk's place and Darbly was located in the same street. That's his apartment."

He sensed she was getting tired and would rather just have him talk so he put all the equipment on the side table. Outside it was getting dark but, in typical hospital style, she had been fed nearly an hour previously.

"Luc, be a love and help me get more comfortable."

"I'll call for a nurse."

"No, just help me, please."

"My extremely elegant outfit has rucked up and the sheet is wrinkly so you're going to have to be careful. I can't lift myself at all, it's too much strain on the stomach muscles, but I can roll so let's get this done."

Luc pulled back the sheet that had provided some privacy and gently smoothed the bottom sheet first one side and then the other and then it came to the more intimate task of what she was wearing.

"It's all right, Luc. In my current condition, modesty is very unimportant." She laughed painfully and Luc carefully re-arranged her clothing while trying hard not to look too long at the shapely buttock and leg that was exposed.

"Thank you. You'd make a great nurse. Now, go and get yourself some coffee while I get a nurse to help me with something more basic." He got up as she pressed the call button. Coffee would be a great idea.

The guard on the door accepted his offer of coffee and Luc went down the corridor to the lift.

The snack bar was busy and it was some fifteen minutes before Luc had drunk his coffee, smoked a cigarette and returned to the third floor with the coffee for the guard.

But the corridor was quiet and empty, the guard nowhere to be seen.

Sensing danger, Luc felt his skin prickle with tension. He walked faster, reaching Joanna's room in a matter of seconds.

The door was ajar, the room itself in semi-darkness. The light had been on when he left, something was very wrong.

He heard Joanna call out.

He kicked open the door, wishing he had a gun.

A man in hospital 'greens' and mask whirled round as the door crashed open and Luc saw the knife.

For a moment, there was complete stillness.

Luc flung the contents of the coffee cup and the man threw up his right hand to protect himself.

Luc moved in fast. He felt a sharp stinging sensation across his chest as he dodged the upward slash of the blade and landed a quick strike to the man's ribs.

The man grunted and shifted position, the knife held left-handed in a classic knife fighter's grip, blade uppermost.

Above the hospital mask, Luc saw the top of a scar and was momentarily distracted by a memory flashback to a scene in Rwanda ten years previously. He knew this man.

His opponent was moving, inadvertently telegraphing his intentions as he shifted his weight onto the right foot.

Luc readied himself and then hit the light switch on the wall.

The pale blue eyes reacted instantly giving Luc the edge. He stepped to his right, reducing his opponent's attack vector, then kicked out connecting with the knife hand. The weapon spun away.

The man launched himself at Luc, delivering a vicious blow that numbed the muscles of Luc's left arm.

Stepping backwards out of range, Luc stumbled against a chair and took a strike to his upper chest.

Then the man was gone.

"Get a doctor here," shouted Luc as he scrambled to his feet and then took off after his opponent.

The stairs next to the lift echoed with running feet. Luc followed, spinning and bouncing his way down the flights of stairs. He heard a crash as a fire door opened and then he was outside. It was too big a lead and Luc ran more in hope than expectation. He heard a motorcycle start up.

He had a partial on the number plate, which he quickly wrote down before telephoning the police. He called Benoît for additional back up and then headed back to the third floor.

There were a lot of people in Joanna's room when he arrived and, in the mêlée, he recognised the calm competence of Dr Aziz. Joanna was in good hands. He slumped against the wall and sank to the floor, his chest wet.

"Doctor, over here!" A quick swish of a coat and then gentle hands checking his pulse. More hands unbuttoning his shirt, the sting of antiseptic.

"He'll live but I'll need to stitch that up. Keep pressure on it while I finish with the girl." The calm and controlled voice of Dr Aziz made it through Luc's rapidly fogging brain. *Damn, the bastard must have caught him with the knife.*

"We've another one over here," a male voice called from the next room. "He's alive but unconscious."

"Get an emergency team up here — we'll deal with them *in situ.*"

Cool hands were at his chest again and the calm face of Dr Aziz bent over him. He felt the sting of the local anaesthetic and the prick of a needle.

"You and the girl are really in the wars, aren't you?"

"Is she all right? The bastard had a knife."

"Well, he didn't have a chance to use it. She's okay but must have been stretching for the alarm because she's caused one of her wounds to open. I've stitched her up again and she's fine. She's more concerned about you. What a pair!" She shook her head.

"What happened to the guard?"

"He's all right. Got hit over the head." She smiled again and was gone. Other hands helped him up and onto a chair.

"Did you get the bastard?" Joanna reached out and took his hand rather limply.

"No…This isn't funny anymore."

They stayed as they were and said nothing. After a while, they dozed and were still half-asleep, hand in hand, when Radcliffe walked in. "Do you two always sleep together?" They laughed the pain away.

"How did he find us, sir?"

"Probably followed you. We know he's good and we know good tails are difficult to spot. It's not important. What is important is that the two of you are all right, if somewhat the worse for your adventures. There are now three armed guards in the corridor and I need Luc to go through the video footage to see what we can find. So, young man, off you go to the security office and leave Jo to me."

Tuesday 18 March, Lasne, Belgium

Dr Aziz hadn't liked it, but with the safety of all the patients in mind had finally agreed that they should move Joanna to a more secure location. She had, however, insisted that she, and she alone, should supervise the treatment of all her patients. Radcliffe had demurred briefly but had been secretly thankful. Although the DER and their Belgian security service 'friends' would provide the very best of staff and facilities down at the Farm, the safe house out beyond Lasne, having Dr Aziz was a useful bonus.

"We'll move Jo tomorrow by helicopter and I think it would be a good thing if you could come too, Doctor."

"I'll arrange it, but it'll have to be in the afternoon. I have three procedures to do in the morning and we'll need to prepare Miss Donnelly for moving."

The transfer went smoothly. Joanna had had a good night and her wounds were dry and clean. The move had taxed her but she had not complained and had lain quietly watching Luc as he sat with Dr Aziz and the medics on the opposite side of the helicopter.

The flight took less than twenty minutes and willing helpers stretchered Joanna into the main building and up to an airy room with an excellent view over the surrounding farmland. Outside, the security guards patrolled with their automatic weapons and dogs. Dr Aziz immediately cast a professional eye over the equipment and nodded with satisfaction; the DER had obeyed her instructions explicitly. She turned to examine her patients.

"You, Mr Hansen, will need that dressing checked daily but you can ask them to remove the bandage and use tape as from tomorrow." She gave a wry smile, "And try not to get into any fights for the next few days."

Luc saluted her.

"As for Miss Donnelly, she just needs rest. I've left instructions here…" she tapped a pad of paper, "and I'll be back tomorrow if your Mr Radcliffe can arrange transport. Helicopters! What is my husband going to say?" She shook her head and walked out of the room to talk with the nursing staff.

Luc went over to the bed, stroked Joanna's face with the tips of his fingers and then kissed her gently before leaving.

Later that evening back in his office in Brussels, Luc gazed at the latest pictures of the killer taken from the hospital CCTV. He allowed his mind to empty and form random connections. The scar on the face triggered memories. He closed his eyes. The memories were forming, memories from ten years previously, from Rwanda and *la Légion*.

The post-dawn heat and humidity were already heavy. He brushed an insect from his face, shouldered his pack, checked his weapons and moved out.

It was his first experience of an African equatorial forest; but nothing in his three years in the Legion had prepared him for what he had experienced in the last week. The mutilations, the rapes, the genocide by Rwandan Hutu militia and army units were unbelievable, and the lives of their Tutsi victims could not be put back together.

Luc had arrived in Rwanda via Djibouti. Officially, he was in the 2nd REP, the Legion's paratroop regiment, but he and two 2nd REP friends, Gregor and Benoît, were mission specialists and their orders were specific: the three of them were to handle any air extractions. They didn't know the rest of the platoon.

They marched through thick jungle for the first three kilometres and emerged on higher, more open ground. The Lieutenant in charge of the mission signalled a halt and sent the sergeant and two others forward to reconnoitre.

Then they were moving again. Luc could smell burnt flesh and hear the screams. The Legionnaires fanned out. The village was below them and they could see three army trucks and a number of Rwandan militiamen. Several huts were on fire.

The Legionnaires took the village by storm. There had been nearly sixty Rwandan militia but most were now dead. The Legion had taken casualties as well: the Lieutenant had a leg wound, and the sergeant and two others were dead.

A group of Hutu militiaman suddenly appeared in front of Luc and his two companions. Crazed with bloodlust and armed with machetes, they attacked fast. Luc got off a short burst taking out two. A third had his machete up for another strike at Gregor who had blood on his face. Luc shot the man by reflex and looked round for others, then secured the area. Benoît applied a field dressing to Gregor's face; the wound was not serious but would leave a scar.

There was more firing further into the village and a woman screamed. Luc and the others moved forward cautiously. Another scream, this time from a hut close by. Luc kicked the door in and saw something he had hoped never to see: a Legionnaire raping a teenage Tutsi. There was blood on the girl. Against a wall, an older woman cowered under the threat of the assault rifle held by a second man.

Luc swung the butt of his rifle down between the shoulders of the rapist and pulled him away. Benoît disarmed the second man and marched him out. Gregor helped the woman and the girl.

The rapist was up on his feet, his knife in his left hand gleaming dully as he launched his attack. Luc sidestepped the lunge, tripped over the girl's legs and fell. The knife arced down. Luc rolled and came up holding his own knife. He watched his attacker approach, judged his time well and slashed the man across the face, opening up a deep gash from his chin to his right eye. The fight was over.

The rapist was a German with blond hair and pale blue eyes. At his court martial, other Legionnaires described him as the Angel of Death but his real name was Dieter Gärtner.

Luc slowly focused on the picture. Yes, it was the same man: older, of course, and the hair colour had been changed, but certainly the same man. It would have been better if he'd killed the bastard in Africa.

CHAPTER EIGHT

The headaches and indigestion of the last few days, and even weeks, had left Karel Vandenhove short-tempered and irritable with his staff, his colleagues and even with his boss. Now, as he sat in his office in the Breydel Building, he reviewed recent events. The Commissioner had insisted that the latest Foreign Policy Strategy paper contain the new Iraq Aid Policy. The President and the other Commissioners had been rather horrified, if horrified could describe the reaction Vandenhove had observed: more a recoil from a plagued rat. But Commissioner de Foucaud had played it well for a Frenchman and the whole document was at least on the agenda. Much good that would do, thought Vandenhove sourly. It just meant that the Commission would shovel it off to the Committee of Permanent Representatives, where they would bury it. Shit, the internal politicking was such a pain. Vandenhove stretched and reached for the phone as it started to ring.

"*Met* Vandenhove."

"Karel…" the voice of his mistress brought some relief to an otherwise bad day and he smiled.

"Yes, my dear."

"Karel, they're getting close and I'm scared."

"Then we'd better meet and have a chat." He liked it when she was scared; it made her more passionate and that could do wonders for his tensions.

"I'm at home now. Why don't you come round?"

Vandenhove looked at his watch and then at the remaining papers on his desk. "I need to finish a couple of things, my dear, and then I'll be right over."

It was nearly an hour later when Vandenhove parked his Mercedes in the quiet tree-lined street. She would, of course, be ready for him. He opened the door of the small townhouse with his own key and stepped inside. He could smell her perfume.

Vandenhove felt himself becoming aroused, as he did whenever he came here. She was sitting in the living room waiting for him. An attractive forty-year-old with a penchant for rough sex, her body language betrayed her own arousal. He smiled in anticipation: this was going to be pleasurable.

"My dear, you and I are going to have to talk but first there are things you must do." He stood in front of her, his arousal evident. She stared in fascination and Vandenhove saw her pupils dilate and sensed the increase in her breathing rate.

Almost as though controlled by forces beyond her, Claudia Chalon shifted position and then knelt in front of him, her face only a few centimetres from the bulge at his crotch. She reached out and gently touched him and then, with more confidence, she grasped his belt and undid it. Her breathing was shallow and fast and he knew exactly what she wanted.

She slipped his trousers down, released the engorged penis and gently started to lave it with her tongue. He knew that her own arousal would be nearly complete. Slowly she took his penis into her mouth and began to suck. His hands were in her hair as he held her head tight against him and he felt a wave of pleasure. His penis was now very firm and her tongue was hard at work; he knew she wanted him to come inside her mouth but he would not. He had other desires, desires she shared.

At an unspoken command, she stopped sucking and allowed him to help her to her feet. Without any instruction, she turned away from him, grasped the table and slowly bent forward. He lifted her skirt, exposing her bottom. His engorged penis was against her skin for a moment and she trembled. He moved slightly and she readied herself. The first smack was always the best and Vandenhove knew exactly how hard to make it. She let out a deep sigh as his hand made contact, her head arched back and she moaned. His hand descended five more times and her buttocks quivered. He knew she was desperate for the next phase but he would not be hurried.

He gripped the top of her panties and she lifted her body a little away from the table to help him. The silk underwear pooled at her feet and his penis was against her flesh again. She spread her legs and he entered her. She sighed, her back arched as he thrust hard, his hands on her shoulders. He could feel that she was nearly climaxing and was fighting to control it. If she came too soon he would be angry, but if she could hold out then it would be better for them both. With each thrust, he could feel himself expanding inside her and then it was too much. She almost screamed as she came and collapsed face down on the table. Vandenhove thrust again, shuddered and came.

As he left her, she turned and sank to her knees, took his now flaccid penis in her mouth and licked it clean. Then she stood up, stepped clear of her underclothes and sat down in the chair she had first occupied and watched as Vandenhove dressed himself. He felt complete, refreshed.

Vandenhove went through to the kitchen and, after a while, returned with a bottle of chilled Chablis and two glasses.

"Claudia, my darling, we have to talk." He sipped his wine and looked at her. She really was good looking and he had needed the release. He would take her again later when she would do things that most men could only dream about.

"Tell me about this man Hansen."

Later, when she had no more to tell, they went upstairs to the bedroom where she demonstrated her skills as a lover. There was no time for talk; the physical desire in each of them was too great, and the lovemaking was all that Vandenhove had hoped for. He felt relaxed, drowsy, all tensions now gone. Beside him on the satin sheets, Claudia lay on her side facing him, her tousled hair half covering her face, a sheet decorously covering her lower body. The scent was now of sex with overtones of her perfume and his aftershave. The strains of his favourite Beethoven symphony wafted up the stairs. He reached out and stroked her shoulder and breast and she moaned slightly. He felt himself getting aroused again and she moved closer, their coupling less frantic now.

Vandenhove woke and realised that it was late. He felt hungry. Claudia was dozing, her auburn hair lustrous against the cream pillow. Vandenhove smiled and sat up quietly.

"Where're you going, Karel?"

"The shower, *ma chérie*, and then I need to eat — you make me hungry."

"Then come back to bed." She made a playful grab at him but he was already moving away.

The bathroom was ultra-modern in design, which reminded Vandenhove rather uncomfortably of a doctor's surgery. However, the water was hot and his favourite soap was always available. There was even some of his deodorant and aftershave beside the basin. He turned on the shower.

Twenty minutes later, Vandenhove entered the sitting room to find a pot of fresh coffee, some white wine in a cooler and some Melba toast with smoked salmon. The music centre was playing Gershwin. He smelt her perfume before he was really aware that she had entered the room. He focused.

"Karel, the DER has got a *carte blanche* from Luxembourg and they've just extended the range. But they don't have proof…yet."

"Then, my darling Claudia, we must make sure they don't get it."

Claudia Chalon reached forward and poured some wine, her silk dressing gown falling open slightly to reveal her breasts. Vandenhove looked away and concentrated on what she had said.

"I assume it's too late to do anything to stop them?'

"Yes. And they've shut me out. I think they suspect me. I'm scared."

Vandenhove sucked in his breath. *Damn and more damn.*

Thursday 20 March, Brussels

The smell of coffee permeated the office as Luc switched off the recording and looked across at Radcliffe.

"There's no doubt about it, sir. I checked the voice prints to be absolutely certain and the video confirms it."

"Damn." Radcliffe sounded disappointed and no one spoke. When the decision had been made to place electronic surveillance in Chalon's home it was with the expectation of catching Vandenhove on tape, not to hear and see Chalon and her lover in the midst of sexual activity and then discussing DER secrets.

"We'll have to bring her in," said Luc.

"Agreed. And the sooner the better. The question is: do you want someone else to handle it?"

"No, sir, I'll deal with it. I need a couple of days to get everything ready. We also need to beef up the personal security of the team."

"Especially on Jo and Dukakis."

"I'm using Benny and his team to guard Jo at the Farm, but we'll need some others for Dukakis and it would be better if you had someone as well."

"Thanks, Luc. Please arrange it even if you have to pull them off other assignments. But no visible weapons on the streets."

"I'll get on it right away."

Radcliffe shifted position and then said thoughtfully, "Luc, all our evidence in this case comes from intercepts and activities that are inadmissible, legally. Unless we can come up with admissible evidence, we'll never get this to court. We might also never get the killer there either for much the same reason."

"Is that what we're trying to do, sir?" Luc asked, quizzically.

"What you do mean?"

"Sir, this is an authorised but deniable operation: there is no way that Mr Ashley wants this in court. As he said the other day, if this gets into the public domain, it could seriously damage international relations with America as well as within the Union."

Radcliffe said nothing.

Luc stood up and picked a picture from the board. "Mr Radcliffe, this man is Dieter Gärtner. He's an ex-*Légionnaire*. I had a run-in with him in Africa ten years ago and gave him that scar. The psychologist at the court martial described him as a psychopathic killer. We need to find this man quickly and take him out and I don't mean arrest him. And then we need to take down Vandenhove."

CHAPTER NINE

Luc grasped Claudia Chalon's arm as she was reaching for her front door keys. She tensed, tried to pull free and turned.

Luc spoke softly. "Please come with me, Claudia."

She looked past him and saw Benoît waiting just inside the gate.

"What the fuck do you want, Luc?"

"We'd like you to come with us and not make a fuss, Claudia."

"And if I don't?"

"Then I'll break your arm. Now, come with me." He spoke calmly, making the threat stronger.

Chalon looked at him and then at Benoît who, like Luc, was dressed in dark blue combat fatigues with a holstered sidearm.

Luc watched her as she worked through her options. When she saw Michel, the third team member and dressed the same as the others, leaning against the 4x4 twenty paces away, her resistance evaporated.

"Exactly, Claudia. I simply don't think you're that good."
Luc waited knowing she would not fight him but wanting her
to acknowledge it. When she sighed in resignation, he took her
to the vehicle and told her curtly to get in.

She entered the back seat and Luc climbed in beside her.

"Where are you taking me?"

He did not bother to reply.

"This isn't the way to the office!"

"Shut up."

"Where are you taking me?" She leant forward and hit
Michel on the shoulder. "I demand an answer."

Well, you won't get one, thought Luc. He had issued orders
that no one was to speak to the prisoner.

"This is kidnapping. I demand you let me go." Fear caused
her voice to rise to a hysterical pitch.

Luc sighed, and with practised ease attached handcuffs to
her wrists and slipped a black hood over her head.

In the enveloping darkness, Chalon screamed.

Luc administered a sedative and she sank into oblivion. He
checked her pulse. "All right, guys, that'll hold her for about
forty minutes."

They crossed the Ring at the Groenendaal junction and headed
for La Hulpe. Twenty minutes later, just beyond the village of Lasne,
they entered a densely wooded area and immediately turned onto
a narrow, cobbled road that led down to a walled farm
complex.

Benoît spoke quietly into the radio and the huge farm gates
opened. Michel eased the 4x4 into the courtyard and stopped
by the waiting medical team.

Chalon groaned but made no movement as she was half
lifted, half pulled from the vehicle, placed reasonably gently
into a wheelchair and taken to what was the old barn. Luc and
his two companions headed for the main building.

"You two wait here." Luc indicated chairs and then left the room.

"Hey, Benny, what is this place?" Michel looked round at the elegant furniture and imposing paintings.

"Belongs to Belgian Military Intelligence and is used for secret meetings. We use it as a training base and we've got Jo stashed here as well."

Luc came back ten minutes later.

"Right, our immediate objective is to find out how much Chalon has leaked and how compromised the investigation actually is. Our secondary objective is to find out everything she can tell us about the opposition."

"And you want us to do what, Luc?" Benoît asked.

"Our 'friends' are currently working on her in preparation for questioning. That'll take about twenty-four hours. Benny, you take over here again and make sure this place is one hundred percent secure. Michel, you come with me — we need to search her house."

Sunday 23 March, Lasne

Claudia Chalon was feeling nauseous. She was also cold and she could not see anything. She turned her head slowly and realised that she was lying down. Somehow, her body did not seem to be feeling anything. She tried moving her hands but discovered she could not. There was someone else in the area, she was sure, but she could not hear anything. Someone was moving close behind her and she felt hands on her face. She screamed, only no sound came from her parched throat. Suddenly she was very afraid.

Someone gently removed the hood and Claudia blinked. At first, she saw nothing but an eerie red luminescence, but slowly a dark figure came into focus, a slim woman bending over her. Cool hands held her face and a sharp bright light shone into each eye in turn. The hands returned and laid a cool damp cloth across her eyes. She could smell eucalyptus. Her head was clearing.

She felt a straw press against her lips and when she opened them, a welcome trickle of water came out and she swallowed compulsively. The trickle continued and she swallowed again but in a more controlled manner. Her throat felt less dry and the nausea was fading.

The cloth across her eyes was removed. She moved her head a fraction and could see the tubes of a drip in her arm.

She sensed that, out of her sight, a door had opened and a third person had entered the room but she could hear nothing. The air seemed cooler now and things were coming into focus. The red glow appeared to be from a small light beside her and she sensed she was on a bed. Mental activity was returning and she could vaguely remember some people and a car journey. Perhaps there had been an accident and she was in hospital. She closed her eyes and the oblivion returned.

When she woke again, she was immediately aware that the red light was still on but that a pool of white light was also visible. She tried to speak but could not hear her voice. A figure got up from behind the light and came over to her and a tube was pressed against her lips. A distorted female voice seemed to speak directly into her brain.

"Suck on the straw and you'll get some water."

She sucked greedily and was rewarded by a thin stream of cool water. The woman was, she assumed, some sort of nurse and seemed to be doing nurse-type things. She felt the nurse moving her and making her more comfortable. But still there was silence.

The distorted voice spoke again. "There, that's better. You'll feel a bit disorientated for a while. Now here's someone to talk to you."

"Good morning, Claudia." Again, the voice seemed to enter her brain directly but she recognised it as that of Luc Hansen. "You can't see me, Claudia, but I'm behind you. In case you're wondering, you're in a medical facility and sedated. I'm going to ask a few questions."

She tried to tell him that he was a bastard, that she'd kill him, but she could not hear her own voice.

"Now that you've got that off your chest, shall we begin?"

How the hell did he know what she had said when she'd made no sound? And why did his voice sound right inside her brain?

"Claudia, you're here to answer some questions. If you cooperate, then the conditions will improve. If not, then they'll go the other way. So, let's start. Is your name Claudia Chalon?"

She told him to fuck off and immediately a sharp pain hit her brain.

"That was not wise. Now, answer the question. Is your name Claudia Chalon?"

She again told him to fuck off and again the pain lanced through her brain.

"Understand that lack of cooperation automatically results in the pain. Now: is your name Claudia Chalon?"

She thought for a moment, capitulated and answered in the affirmative. Immediately, she felt a sense of indistinct pleasure, but no less real pleasure.

"Good," said the voice of Luc Hansen deep in her brain. "Do you work for the DER?"

Again she paused, and then she answered in the affirmative. Again, she felt pleasure.

"How long have you worked for the DER?" The voice in her brain held no emotion.

She told him the date she joined. She still could not hear her voice but the response brought more pleasure.

"Thank you, Claudia. Now let's move on. Who was the man you had sex with three days ago?"

Her brain answered that it was none of his business and immediately the pain returned. Sweat beaded and dripped from her forehead as the pain subsided.

"Who was the man you had sex with three days ago?"

Fuck off.

Pain.

She squeezed her eyes shut, feeling sick.

"Who was the man you had sex with three days ago?"

She couldn't take the pain. *Karel Vandenhove.* She felt no rewarding sense of pleasure, but at least she felt no pain.

"Who is Karel Vandenhove?"

Oh fuck off, you bastard.

This time the pain went on until she passed out.

She regained consciousness and sucked greedily on the straw.

Hansen's voice returned. "Claudia, cooperation is better than non-cooperation. Now, who is Karel Vandenhove?"

This time she told him and received a small jolt of pleasure as her reward.

"Good. How long have you been having sex with Karel Vandenhove?"

She hesitated and the pain reappeared. She had to stop it quickly before it took hold, she had to make it go away, she couldn't take any more. She answered and the pain retreated.

"What is the relationship between Vandenhove and Groupe Franco-Belge?"

I don't know.

Pain.

She screamed. Bright spots of light made her squeeze her eyes shut. She felt sick.

I don't know.

Pain.

She could hardly breathe. Her head felt like it was about to explode.

"Why are you lying, Claudia?"

I'm not. I don't know.

Pain.

Her whole body was on fire. A terrifying void was opening up before her.

"I don't believe you, Claudia."

Please no more. I'm not lying. I don't know.

Pain.

She lost control of her bladder and she could feel the warmth of her own urine. She knew she was finished and nothing could save her now. She would tell him anything and everything he wanted to know just to avoid the pain.

"All right, Claudia. I'll believe you. Now, we know what you told Vandenhove three days ago — listen." The sounds of her and Vandenhove talking, the sounds of them having sex, filled her head. "So tell me, Claudia, what else have you told him about the investigation?"

Slowly, Claudia completed the deconstruction of her professional life and told him everything. About her recruitment by Vandenhove and the money he paid her. About secretly reviewing case files and warning Vandenhove about each move that the DER made. About Gerald Darbly and his work as Vandenhove's fixer. About Gorsky and the purchase of arms. About Gorsky's sister being Darbly's mistress. She told Hansen everything and held back nothing. And when she had finished, feeling a great drowsiness, she sank into oblivion.

As Chalon slept, Luc left the interrogation complex and walked slowly back to the main building, revelling in the March sunshine. It would take the transcription people a few minutes to complete their work and then he would be able to make some decisions. He had been surprised at how quickly she had caved in. They usually held out much longer but he did not like the work. *C'est la vie,* he thought.

Radcliffe was waiting for him in the main sitting room.

"Let's take a turn in the garden and you can smoke," Radcliffe suggested as though sensing his need.

The sound of birdsong was balm to Luc's brain. Daffodils swayed gently under the trees. The grass was still damp from recent rain.

"So what's the damage?" Radcliffe's voice brought Luc from his reverie.

"The bottom line is that the investigation is completely compromised. She's told Vandenhove just about everything we know and she knows we have no admissible proof. We must assume that they know that as well and that's why they feel able to act the way they do. We now have confirmation that Gärtner works directly for Vandenhove."

The two men walked onto the grass as Luc added, "Vandenhove dreamed up the whole project, apparently, and some high officials in the Belgian Government are aware of it."

"Are they, by God? Now that puts a different slant on the matter."

"Darbly is the fixer. And this is interesting, sir. His mistress, Svetlana Nikolaevna, is the sister of the arms dealer called Gorsky who we identified in Hungary. Claudia was responsible for introducing Darbly to Svetlana and, when I searched Claudia's house yesterday, I found a picture of Darbly and Svetlana, along with another man who may be Gorsky. I'm sure I recognised him."

"Do we know anything about this Gorsky?"

"Only that he's the arms dealer and almost certainly ex-*Légion*. I need to check him out."

"And what is their next move, in your book, Luc?"

"She simply doesn't know. She just spies for them and gets some rough sex as a reward."

"Very well. We target Vandenhove and Darbly. We also need to get the word onto the streets to find Gärtner before he kills anyone else." Radcliffe paused for a moment and then said, "Good work, Luc. Now, I've another task for you. We've just heard from Gregor in Hungary. The arms shipment is on the move."

CHAPTER TEN

The monotonous thuds of the rotor blades, the vibration of the airframe and the pitching of the helicopter made it difficult for Luc to concentrate on the mission. The Turks had been quick to offer the DER assistance and it was one of their military helicopters that was carrying him on the last leg of his journey to the town of Nusaybin close to the Syrian border.

The pilot's voice crackled in Luc's headphones, the helicopter banked sharply and began to descend. The landing zone was a little-used military facility. The helicopter flared and the deceleration caused Luc's rucksack to slide across the small cabin. The crewman opposite pushed it back with his foot and Luc acknowledged his help with a salute.

He felt the helicopter touch down and was out the door the instant it was pulled open. He raised a hand in thanks, turned and ran towards a blinking flashlight. Behind him, the helicopter was already airborne.

The flashlight continued to blink and, as his night vision steadied, Luc could make out the shape of a Land Rover and two men. He flicked his flashlight in the prearranged signal and jogged towards the vehicle.

Luc gave the password — *kamal* — and pulled himself up on the roll bar and swung onto the seat — the vehicle was already moving. The night-time insertion of an operative into a hostile environment called for speed and silence. Also, the less the Turks knew the more deniable the operation.

One of the Turks switched on a red night-vision light and played it over a bundle on the floor. Luc quickly unwrapped it and checked the contents: one M16A2 NATO-issue rifle with a night scope and flash suppresser, four fully loaded spare magazines, a fine pair of night glasses, a 9 mm Glock 17 automatic with silencer plus a dozen clips and a generous supply of field rations. The weapons were exactly as requested. Luc chambered a round in each and stowed the spare magazines in his battle vest. The rations went into his rucksack, he hung the night-vision binoculars around his neck and clipped the attached halyard to his belt.

The Major had told him the road journey would take about twenty minutes, so Luc reckoned that about five remained. He checked his watch, confirmed the estimate and extinguished the red light, plunging the Land Rover into total darkness; even the dashboard lights were off to protect their night-vision adaptations.

The vehicle stopped and a hand touched his shoulder. He grabbed the rucksack and followed the dim shape of the Turkish soldier already disappearing down a gully. The vehicle immediately moved off and Luc dropped down next to the Turk who had hand-signalled him with the usual flat palm indicating the ground. The soldier used his night glasses to scan the area and, after five minutes, he pointed out over the berm they had hidden behind. Luc could make out a small building. It was nothing more than a shack but it was on the other side of a fence.

Keeping low, the two men made their way down to the fence and directly into a ditch. A hundred metres more and the Turk dropped to the ground. Luc followed suit and noticed a gap under the fence. He scanned the other side of the fence with his night glasses, then turned his head to see what was next, but the Turk had gone. Luc silently acknowledged the professionalism of the disappearance in the low grass and sandy ground. Apparently this was as far as the assistance went.

Half an hour later, and sure there weren't any guards coming by on some sort of rota, Luc edged forward. He pushed the rucksack ahead of him and easily cleared the gap without touching the fence. He crawled slowly forward towards the cover of some rocks he had seen to the left. He was now in Syria. He gave two quick farewell flashes of his torch towards the darkness of Turkey.

The airfield at al-Qamisli was ten kilometres to the south and he needed to be in position before dawn.

He made good time and the first hint of dawn revealed the airfield across the fields in front of him so he knew the road to the Iraqi checkpoint eighty kilometres away was immediately behind him. He slung a camouflage net over his hiding place among some low bushes and settled down to wait.

He switched on the small battlefield computer and rigged the satellite link. The pressure switch in the GPS tracking devices would only activate once the plane was near ground level but he could at least double check. There was nothing. He opened the secure communications program and reviewed the latest information from Brussels. An icon flashed and he read the message.

> *To: Luc*
> *From: Gregor via Director DER*
> *Subject: Shipment*
>
> *Text: Two 35-tonne containers, numbers UN23895 and UN24860, safely loaded Batumi and marked 'EU Kurdish Aid Programme – Agricultural Equipment'. Arms stowed in boxes marked tractor parts. Both containers have genuine equipment as well. Trackers working well at take-off. Take care.*

Luc sent an acknowledgement, did some stretches, then relaxed.

The huge Antonov AN-124 Condor came in from the north, circled to the west and made its approach. Luc switched the computer to GPS tracking mode and received two clear signals. He watched the cargo plane land and taxi to the hangars. It was time to move.

Three hours later, Syrian–Iraq border

An antiquated truck came to a halt at the back of the queue at the border post three hundred metres away. Luc studied the old truck carefully and decided it would serve his purpose: a canvas-covered load and a single driver. Now all he had to do was get across the border and onto the truck before it built up speed. Not as simple as it sounded but, south of his position, the actual border seemed to be nothing more than a line of poles. But it was very open terrain and he was aware that there could be land mines.

Luc could hear shouted commands. The Arabic was easy enough to follow and it was clear that each truck was going to be searched before being given clearance to proceed. He studied the line of poles that marked the border and then he saw what he needed: a dry wadi two hundred metres to the south. He checked the progress of the truck at the border post and began to crawl.

It took nearly two hours to get across and back to the border post from the Iraqi side — only to see the truck pulling away. He cursed quietly. But then fate intervened and the truck pulled into the car park at a teashop. *Yes. Now, if he was quick.* Minutes later he was safely hidden under the canvas cover.

He heard the Syrian driver shout something to a man inside the building and readied himself, easing the Glock clear of its holster. It all depended on whether the driver wanted to check the load.

The Syrian driver, an old man, was muttering to himself but made no movement towards the load. The truck tilted slightly as he entered the cab and then they were moving. Luc shifted position and pulled the battlefield computer free of its case. His plan depended on him reaching the junction at Kasik ahead of the trucks carrying the arms shipment; the GPS showed that they were still a long way behind but moving steadily.

According to Turkish intelligence, there was a military base near the junction between the road from Tall'Afar and the main road to the south. Luc located the junction and calculated it was less than forty kilometres from Mosul, which was close enough. Any closer would be seriously dangerous. If the arms passed through this junction, then it was reasonable to assume their destination was the Sunni Militia in Mosul or beyond.

The GPS showed that he was still some sixty kilometres away. He closed his eyes and slept.

An hour later Luc awoke with a start as the truck lurched heavily and canted to the right. He pushed away a box that had slid against him. From what little he could see out of the crack in the wooden side, the truck appeared to have slipped off the main road and into a ditch. He heard the driver curse. The engine revved hard and the truck lurched forward, stopped, then slowly ground its way back onto the road. The driver was cursing again. Other trucks rumbled past and then there was silence.

The truck started moving again but Luc could hear the sound of metal on stone and from the motion of the truck, it was clear that a tyre had burst. He eased the boxes away from his cramped hiding place and checked his equipment. The computer showed that they were less than five kilometres from Kasik and that the arms shipment was still some way behind. Time to bail out.

The driver was cursing all Iraqis as sons of camels whose mothers were goats and the colourful image made Luc smile as he crawled to the front of the flatbed and then pulled himself into a standing position. The canvas flap that had allowed him entry was still loose and he eased it aside. Immediately the bright sunlight caused him to screw up his eyes.

They appeared to be in a desolate, arid area and a careful reconnaissance suggested that there was little more than scrub cover on either side of the road. Luc could hear the driver muttering to himself again about sons of camels as he laboured at the rear of the truck, clearly struggling with a jack and the spare wheel. Then there was silence. Luc risked a look to where he supposed the driver to be and saw him some distance away spreading a prayer mat in preparation for afternoon prayers.

Luc pulled himself and his equipment clear of the load and then waited. The driver was now facing away from the truck, his hands in the position of supplication. Luc lowered himself down to the road, looked to see if it was clear, ran quickly across and scrambled down into a wadi.

About a hundred metres to the northeast, away from the road, he could see some inviting rocks interlaced with gnarled, stunted trees — but to walk there was madness. *Merde! Give me the jungle anytime.* He would have to crawl or be in full sight of any passing truck. Behind him, the driver had finished his prayers and was again cursing the Iraqis and commenting on the parentage of those who had made the jack he was trying to use.

There was nothing for it. Taking care not to dislodge rocks, Luc started the laborious business of crawling through the low scrub. He was confident of his own ability to make the trees without being seen but it had to be taken slowly so that his outline would appear to be a rock or piece of scrub. This was a well-practised exercise in the Legion — one he had been good at and one of the reasons he had come to be trained as a sniper — that, and his ability to shoot straight. Luc smiled to himself at the thought.

Twenty minutes later, concealed in the rocks, he watched a military convoy rumble past the still motionless truck. There was little time: the arms shipment was less than forty kilometres behind and he still had five kilometres to cover. Once over the ridge, he could move freely out of sight of the road. He started to climb, reaching it within ten minutes.

Keeping parallel with the road, Luc made good time and within an hour could see the military compound ahead just to the southeast of the small town and close to the Tall'Afar road junction. He scanned the area. The main road dropped down sharply into the town and the main northbound road was clearly visible just beyond the military base. Luc checked the location of the arms shipment. He had only just arrived and they were converging with his position. He looked down at the road below him and saw them, their EU Aid markings in large white letters across the sides of the containers.

The trucks descended the turn that would take them down to Kasik, their engines complaining under the stress. A herd of goats crossed the road and ambled off to chew the spiky thorn grass to one side. The trucks slowed and, to Luc's surprise, the first one took a small northbound road towards the bridge that would carry it across the Tigris river. The second headed into Kasik and a few moments later drove into the military compound.

A stone rattled behind him and he started to turn. An immense pain exploded in his head and he felt himself falling.

Wednesday 26 March, Kasik, Iraq

Pain and darkness. Sound but no light. Cold and numbness. Returning consciousness sending flashes of light and pain through his brain.

The shock of returning light and full awareness, eyes and senses struggling to cope.

A forceful dousing of water brought Luc around. His head hurt. He could not move but he could see people, a figure behind a desk, lights…all blurred.

Concentrate above all. They had stripped him to the waist and tied him to a chair. He was a prisoner.

"Is he conscious?" asked a voice in Arabic.

A hand on his face. A face in close up, distorted, a bushy moustache, the smell of cigarettes. A light probing his eyes.

"Yes."

The first voice again, this time in English, "You are an American spy."

Make no response. Analyse, consider.

"American Pig…answer when you're spoken to."

Pain thundered as the blow caught him across the side of the head. Feign unconsciousness. Play for time.

"Chuck him in a cell. And, doctor, give him something to put him out. But I want him ready for interrogation in two hours."

A prick in the arm…darkness returning.

He was thirsty and he smelled of urine and blood. He pressed the wound on his head and it oozed. He smelled and then tasted the dampness on his fingers. The blood was clean. His trousers were wet with urine and water but he was alive.

He cautiously stood up and moved each joint slowly to check for structural damage. Nothing apparent. He stretched, putting each muscle set in tension and then relaxing completely. Except for the head wound, he seemed to be undamaged.

There was no light.

A careful exploration of the cell by touch revealed that the walls were smooth and the ceiling out of reach. The cement floor was dry except where he had been lying. A drain in one corner gave off the acrid smell of excrement. The door was metal and beside it was a bucket containing liquid. He smelled the contents, put his hand in cautiously and lifted a little of the liquid to his lips. It was water, not very clean or fresh, but water all the same. He drank slowly.

Luc sat down against a wall and concentrated on the 'no mind' technique he had been taught. The Legion's instructors had been adamant: when facing interrogation, empty the mind, concentrate not on what was about to happen but on staying alive and finding a way out. He followed the training and relaxed his body.

The door crashed open and light flooded the cell. Two men entered, one carrying a gun. Luc did not move. The man with the gun motioned for him to stand and the second quickly tied his hands behind his back. They pulled a hood of a dense black material over his head and hustled him from the cell.

The guards forced him onto a stool and removed the hood. The room appeared to be a larger version of his cell. A large man seated at a table was watching him.

"What is your name?" The man asked in English, his voice surprisingly soft.

He said nothing.

"I suggest you answer, it would be better for all of us," the large man continued. "We know you speak English, we know you are an American spy. Cooperate and things will be easier for you."

He said nothing.

The blow caught him across the back of his shoulders. They must have used a hosepipe, judging from the sound and pain. A second blow knocked him off the stool, face down on the floor. Hands grabbed him from behind, forced him into a kneeling position and pulled the hood over his head.

He knew that whatever he said or did would make no difference to what would happen next. In the Legion, they had called this part of the interrogation process the 'shell phase', referring to the idea that it was necessary to crack the protective shell around the prisoner. The correct response was to remain passive as this robbed the interrogators of the responses they needed to feed their violence. He waited patiently for the next blow.

There were two of them working on him. One used a hosepipe, the other a cane and they did not care where the blows struck him. He knew he was bleeding but they were methodical and he willed himself to stay still. One blow caught him above the kidneys and he nearly gave into a scream.

They were using their boots as well now but he concentrated hard, and when he felt himself falling again, he managed to land with his face and genitals protected. The beating continued. Eventually they lost interest. The blows stopped and a bucket of water was sloshed on his back. He did not move. Rough hands hauled him to his feet and dragged him back to his cell.

He lay where they had dumped him. His body was on fire and he could feel the warmth of fresh blood on his back. He mentally checked his body. No bones broken but massive bruising on the back and arms. He breathed deeply and winced — perhaps a cracked rib on the right-hand side. He attempted the 'no mind' technique again but could not focus because of the pain. He mentally moved to the 'focused pain' technique, seeing the pain as a red colour covering his body and then mentally changing the colour to bright gold, triggering the natural painkilling endorphins.

Slowly the pain subsided.

Later they came for him again and half-walked, half-carried him back to the interrogation room.

"Why are you in Iraq?" asked the same voice he had heard before. He knew it belonged to the chief interrogator and not one of the guards.

He said nothing. It was important, his instructors had said, not to respond. Silence, according to them, was the best weapon.

A guard removed the hood and he blinked at the light. On the table in front of the interrogator were his papers and the battlefield computer.

"Interesting toy. Not American. Perhaps it's British. Are you British?" The interrogator tapped the computer.

"I said: are you British?" But he had already looked down at the papers. "No, I think not. These seem to suggest you're

Belgian. What's a Belgian doing in Iraq with a battlefield computer and American weapons?"

Luc remained impassive.

"If you're not going to be cooperative then we'll have to see if we can encourage you to assist us." The interrogator sighed when he said nothing.

"Very well." He turned to the guards. "Don't kill him. I want to talk to him later."

The guards started with a beating then moved to suspending him from the ceiling by his wrists and alternately hitting him and applying electric cattle prods. They worked methodically until his body was a mass of pain and lacerated nerves. Blood dripped from various wounds and he let loose a primal scream of pain on a couple of occasions, but still he refused to speak. Eventually they took him back to his cell, untied him, removed the hood, threw a bucket of water over him and walked away.

Later, back in the interrogation cell, they chained him to a metal frame against the wall.

Feeling was returning and the pain was red-hot fire. He forced himself to think. His brain was numbed but he managed to focus on the pain and exert a modicum of control. He tried to breathe deeply: there was definitely a cracked rib. He tensed and relaxed the muscles: badly bruised, yes, seriously damaged, no. These guys were experts at inflicting maximum pain with minimum damage and for that he had to be thankful. It was also his biggest weapon.

From the look of things, they were going to use sleep deprivation next. The lights were too bright and the entire room was silent. This forced the prisoner to bear his own weight in such a way that if he tried to ease the strain then the pain would return. It was impossible to sleep vertically and it was sleep he needed.

He went into the 'no mind' sequence again, this time successfully. He allowed himself to go down deep, to still the pounding of his heart, to slow his breathing to the minimum and to encourage his body to start repairing itself.

He had no idea how long he remained that way in the interrogation room, but when the guards returned, he was aware that the recovery techniques had worked. Through half closed eyes he studied their faces as they untied him: typical northern Iraqi Arabs, with bushy moustaches and abundant black hair. Their uniforms carried the lapel flashes of the Mukhabarat, the old Iraqi Security Police. He would have no compunction in killing them when the time came.

They took him along the corridor and up some stairs. He could see daylight. He had a sudden and almost overwhelming desire to break free and reach the light. But before his thought turned into action, the guards pushed him into a cell and slammed the door.

He hauled himself to his feet and looked round. The cell had a window with bars across it and this admitted the only light there was. He could see two filthy mattresses, on one of which was a body. He moved closer and saw the blood and the half-closed eyes of someone who had taken a severe beating. He sat down on the other mattress and studied the cell carefully. He knew it was standard procedure to put a prisoner in a cell with another man without completing the interrogation. The idea was that the prisoner would talk to a supposedly sympathetic fellow human while the guards monitored what they said. And that meant there had to be microphones somewhere in the cell. He started an inch-by-inch search with his eyes.

It took him less time than he had expected to locate the two microphones and the small camera lens. *Never underestimate the enemy and use all observations to your own advantage*: he could hear the voices of his instructors in his head. He had not enjoyed the interrogation course in the Legion but he was grateful for having undergone it; it had kept him alive a couple of times in Africa and it would keep him alive again.

The muscles in his back were aflame and the pain from the cracked rib made breathing difficult but the rest of him seemed intact. He would be able to suppress the pain and to function providing he remained focused but his mouth was parched with a bitter acid taste in his throat. He needed a drink and that was the first challenge. He struggled across to the water bucket and drank a little, and then a little more.

His captors would expect him to check on the other man so that would be a good idea. He pulled the bucket across the room and knelt beside the body. The blood was fresh and clean and the welts on the upper body were new. A half-closed eye flickered slightly and the man groaned. Luc dribbled some water onto the broken and bloody lips, they parted and the man licked tentatively. More water yielded a stronger response. The man groaned again and tried to move. Luc helped him sit up.

The man spoke in a language Luc did not recognise. He shook his head and then pointed to the camera and the microphones. The man frowned, tried to focus and then dipped his hands in the water and washed the blood from his eyes and tried again. He looked back at Luc and nodded.

The man started to tap the bucket rhythmically and spoke very quietly in Arabic.

"Who are you?"

"A prisoner like you," Luc replied in the same language.

"You're not an Iraqi — your accent is wrong."

"Nor are you," Luc replied.

"Kurd," said the man tapping his chest and then, whispered, "My name's Birkim."

"I'm Luc. Where are we?"

"Kasik, the old Mukhabarat barracks — the bastards work for the Sunni militia now."

"How badly hurt are you?"

"About as bad as you look but I can still fight." Birkim patted his own leg.

An idea was forming in Luc's mind. He needed more information but without the guards hearing. He looked round the cell and then he saw it in a corner: a small pile of excrement left by a previous occupant. He quickly outlined what he intended and Birkim nodded his understanding. Luc dragged the bucket back to the door and looked closely at the microphone inset in the wall close to the ceiling. It was doable if they worked together. The other microphone was next to the camera in the ceiling and that would be trickier especially if the bastards left a light on at night. He looked round. There was no light fitting visible.

Keys rattled in the door, a flap at floor level opened and a small amount of bread appeared. The flap closed.

Luc retrieved the food and sat beside Birkim, more ideas forming in his mind as they ate. Later, when it was dark, he stood up and went to the pile of excrement. It was hard. He got some water and softened it, making a paste. Birkim stood directly under the wall-mounted microphone.

"Tread carefully, my friend," he whispered.

Luc put his foot in the cupped hands and reached up. Birkim lifted, Luc steadied himself with a hand against the wall and pushed some of the paste into the microphone's aperture.

The two men moved under the camera and the second microphone in the centre of the room. Birkim grabbed Luc tightly round the legs and lifted. Luc located the twin apertures and covered them in paste.

"You're not a light man, Luc. Now, tell me how we're going to get out of this hell hole."

CHAPTER ELEVEN

The guards came for them later that same night as Luc had expected they would.

There was no light, but he knew Birkim was in the corner near the door. As the keys rattled in the lock, Luc lay down on one of the mattresses.

The door opened and, through half-closed eyes, Luc watched a guard enter the cell. A second stayed in the corridor, his AK47 assault rifle slung over his shoulder.

The guard bent down and grasped Luc by the left shoulder, then let out a small grunt and collapsed as the heel of Luc's right hand drove the cartilage of his nose back into his brain. The second guard stepped quickly into the cell, his AK47 coming to the ready. Birkim moved and the guard went down silently as a double-handed blow broke his neck.

Silently, Luc and Birkim stripped the guards and put on their uniforms before arranging the bodies to look as though they were prisoners. They checked the assault rifles and Luc looked carefully into the corridor. It was empty. He stepped clear of the door followed by Birkim who shut and locked it.

There were two options: out into the courtyard or back through the building. The first could trap them in an enclosed space; the second allowed them the opportunity to inflict considerable damage if they were stopped. Neither was a safe option but surprise was on their side. They headed away from the courtyard. The light on the stairs leading down to the interrogation room was on. Luc led the way.

The interrogator was alone and did not look up from what he was reading. He died without a murmur. Luc wiped the blade of the knife on the man's uniform. The battlefield computer was on the table along with Luc's papers, his Glock and his watch. Silently he checked that the weapon and the computer were working. He looked round and saw the rest of his equipment in a corner, including the M16A2. It was still loaded and the spare magazines were with it.

From the doorway, Birkim gave a small warning sound and stepped back out of sight. A guard entered, saw the body of the interrogator, reacted too slowly and slid to the floor with Birkim's knife embedded in his throat.

Silence.

Luc put the computer, the spare magazines, his papers and other items into his rucksack and settled it on his back. He pushed the Glock into his belt.

"Let's go," he signalled, picking up the M16A2.

"What about the other prisoners?" asked Birkim.

"No time," replied Luc and Birkim shrugged.

The two men climbed the stairs and reached the main corridor. They could hear voices coming from a room about halfway down.

"Guard room," whispered Birkim.

"Leave it."

Luc stepped past the open door and then motioned Birkim to wait. Both men focused on the guardroom door but there was no challenge.

Luc then motioned Birkim forward and as the latter stepped close, Luc could see the Kurd's body tension and the intense concentration on his face. Luc looked him straight in the eyes trying to gauge the Kurd's resolve, found strength there and the man stepped past him to take up his station on one side of the main door.

The main entrance gave onto a badly lit parking area, across which Luc could see the outline of an army truck. There was no sign of the container with the arms. He checked his watch: an hour until dawn and sixty hours since he was captured. He'd lost a lot of time and he needed to know where the second container of arms had gone.

A sentry moved across a pool of light, stopped, lit a cigarette and stood smoking. *Merde*! Luc tapped Birkim on the shoulder, indicated the sentry and made a circling movement with his hand.

Birkim nodded, shouldered the AK47, sauntered over to the sentry and engaged him in quiet conversation. Luc watched warily because it was still possible that Birkim was a plant working for the Iraqis. That's where it could all go wrong. He withdrew the Glock, fitted the silencer and waited. Birkim stepped in front of the sentry and there was the brief flare of a match. The sentry began smoking and was now looking away from the truck.

Luc recognised the coolness of the tactic. Birkim was a real professional. Luc moved quickly and silently through the shadows until he was next to the truck, the pain in his ribs and back forgotten with the pleasure of positive action.

The truck was empty.

He circled round to the fuel tank and slowly opened the cap. The tank was full. *Good.*

He crouched down and looked under the vehicle. Birkim and the sentry were four paces away enjoying their smoke. He whistled a single note. The two men turned. The sentry brought his weapon to the ready and stepped towards the vehicle. Luc shot him from a distance of two metres.

Birkim placed the dead man in the back of the truck, climbed into the cab and hot-wired the ignition as Luc clambered into the passenger seat, Glock in hand.

"According to the sentry, there are three men on duty at the gate." Birkim drove slowly towards it.

"Be ready to ram the barrier," Luc suggested and Birkim nodded.

As the truck approached the barrier, a single guard came out and signalled them to stop.

"We've got to go to the bridge to bring back some more Kurdish pigs," said Birkim casually and offered the man a cigarette.

The guard lifted a hand in acknowledgement and raised the barrier.

Saturday 29 March, northern Iraq

The two men took it in turns to sleep during the day. Birkim had found a disused building in which he hid the truck and had taken the first watch. They buried the dead man and Luc located a first aid box. The rather basic contents, combined with his own, were sufficient to patch them up. Even the pain from his cracked ribs was easing and he was able to lie down without excessive discomfort.

About three hours before sunset, Luc broke out some emergency rations and Birkim produced cigarettes.

· "We need to talk, my friend," he said as they lit up.

Luc said, "How did you end up in Kasik?" This was critical. If Birkim was a Sunni spy, he would have to die.

"I lead a PKK People's Defence Force unit this side of the border. We took delivery of a large shipment of weapons near Dahuk, about sixty kilometres north of here. My unit acted as the rear guard."

"And what happened?"

"We were about five kilometres south of the transfer point. About fifty Mukhabarat came at us. I lost six men."

"How come they took you alive?"

"Martyrdom in the name of Allah is one thing but being killed by Iraqi pigs is another. There were five of us left at the end. They knew who I was but they killed the others."

"Is Kasik the nearest Mukhabarat base?"

"No, but it's the biggest and there are no Americans around here. They wanted information and they know how to get it in Kasik."

"How long were you there?"

"They beat me up and threw me in the cell. You arrived a couple of hours later." Birkim drew deeply on his cigarette. "They were talking about an American spy they had caught a couple of days previously. I guess that was you."

"Probably."

"So how did you survive two days in that place? Most men are dead in less than twenty-four hours."

Luc replied, "I've been well trained."

"Where?"

"The French Foreign Legion."

"Well, that explains a lot. What now?"

"We go north to your people."

Birkim looked straight at him. "Are you going to help us?"

"Why not?" Luc shrugged. He had most of the answers he

needed, except for where the Kurds were getting their weapons. Logic suggested the second truckload of arms had gone to the PKK but he needed to confirm it and find out who arranged it.

"Then we'd better get moving. There's a checkpoint about twenty kilometres north of here so…"

"We'll just have to be careful, eh?"

They reached the Iraqi checkpoint at sunset. Luc dropped from the back of the truck about four hundred metres from the barrier and headed into the scrub and boulders on the slight rise behind the buildings. The truck drove slowly up to the barrier.

Luc did not want to start a firefight and if Birkim could bluff his way through there would be no need. The Kurd was very cool and Luc admired that. He watched the guard approach the vehicle and raised the M16A2. He had a clear line of sight of the man and held him in the cross hairs but, after a minute or two of conversation, the guard raised the barrier and waved the truck through. Luc relaxed but continued to watch the checkpoint. He saw no sign of activity and the truck was already two hundred metres away gathering speed. Luc scrambled across the ridge to rejoin it.

"That was pretty cool, Birkim."

"Or pretty routine if I'm a Mukhabarat agent. A bit harder if I'm not." Birkim threw him a casual toss of his head.

"Yes." Was he kidding? Or did Luc have a problem?

"Well, I'm not. So rest easy, my friend." Birkim lit a cigarette and passed the packet across. "The checkpoint guards were the remains of an army unit and knew nothing about Kasik. They're part of the unit based at the Ain Zalah oilfield."

He drove in silence for a few kilometres and then said, "Luc, up here the Mukhabarat and militia are hated by the Kurds and the Iraqis equally, and the Iraqi Army is no longer in the Zagros. We used to live peacefully enough with the Iraqis but since the US arrived, there are only Mukhabarat in the mountains."

"That could make this truck a target for your own people. Have you any way of contacting them? I didn't break us out of Kasik to get blown away by your lot!"

"There's little danger of that until we're well north of Dahuk," replied the Kurd. "Is there a map anywhere in this she-camel?"

Luc got out the battlefield computer, switched it on and opened the relevant map. The GPS locator was working and the icon flashed over their current location.

"We're here. There's Dahuk and here's Sirsenk airfield."

"And that's where we have to go." Birkim's stubby finger pointed to a river north of the airfield. He paused for thought. "We should be okay until here." He pointed to a junction. "After that, *In'sh Allah*."

"Can we contact your people?"

"This is not the 21st century up here." Birkim sighed. "If we can get past the airfield it might be best to abandon the truck and walk."

"So be it." Luc closed the computer.

Once through Dahuk, they found a secluded, dried-up river valley and slept. They started moving again at dawn and saw no one except for some distant herdsmen. The route through the mountains and down into the next river valley was slow going. Birkim insisted on driving and Luc used the time to sleep some more.

"Wake up, Luc."

"What?"

Birkim pointed. "That's the airfield. It's not been used by the Iraqis since 1994 and it's not used by the Americans either, but it's a large Mukhabarat and militia base."

Luc studied the compound through binoculars. "I wonder… Birkim, what was in the weapons delivery?"

"I don't know for certain but likely small arms and ammunition."

"Have you got rocket launchers?"

"Yes. My unit has four and about twenty rockets. Why?"

"We could take out that base."

"How?"

"Let me lay it out for you."

Sunday 30 March, Zagros Mountains, northern Iraq

Birkim looked around at the assembled PKK fighters. "And so, my brothers, if we're in agreement, I think we should go with Luc's plan."

The leader of a group from the east asked, "Who is this man anyway?"

"I'd say he's probably an American spy!" ventured another.

The discussion had been going on for over an hour already. Luc looked on in concealed amusement. He thought that getting this lot moving in the same direction was like trying to herd cats.

They were speaking in Kamanji, the local Kurdish language and Luc understood very little. He stretched. The bruising was already subsiding but he needed to keep moving. He checked his head wound and found it dry and clean. He could deal with the bruises from the beating but the likely cracked rib was troubling him. He missed the discipline of the Legion that was a given and could always be relied upon…

Birkim held out his hand and pulled Luc to his feet. "Luc, we are agreed. Please explain the details."

"Does everyone speak Arabic?"

"If they don't, I'll translate."

Luc walked into the firelight and surveyed the men. They were seasoned fighters, all of them. Luc reckoned that if they followed orders then the raid he was proposing would be a big setback for the Iraqi militia.

Thirty minutes later they were nodding in agreement.

The PKK commander for the region, an immense man nearing seventy, signalled for silence and spat into the fire. "This is a good plan, my young friend, and we can do it, but why are *you* doing this?"

Luc noted narrowing eyes of the men around the fire. He had expected this question and was prepared for it. He explained about the arms shipments and how he had been tracking them, then related the key fact that one truckload had headed north while the other went directly into the Mukhabarat compound at Kasik. The men were particularly enraptured by the story of how he had been captured, his description of how he exercised the protective self-discipline he had been taught in the Legion and how they had escaped. In this setting, he thought later, he had been inspired to speak with the eloquence of an old-fashioned storyteller.

"*In'sh Allah*, we will destroy the Mukhabarat out there with your help." The PKK commander looked across at Luc. The men in the firelight nodded in agreement. Women entered the circle and served mint tea. A man started to sing a folk song.

"Where did you learn your Arabic?" The PKK commander spoke as he sat down beside Luc.

"From my mother. She was Moroccan."

"So you are half Arab. Are you of the faith? Are you one of Allah's children?"

Luc shook his head. "No. I was brought up a Christian. My father was a Belgian Catholic and he had strong views."

"Ah, but that still makes you of the Book, Luc, and that is good." He offered a cigarette and lit up for both of them. "We know how to use the weapons and the rocket launchers, and we've even got some light field artillery if we need it. But we still need you to train the men in the precise movements and timing in what you want us to do."

"This is a hit and run operation so no field guns, but you are right, Commander, we need to accurately coordinate the attacks."

"We have good radios. They work at two kilometres, even in these mountains."

Luc held his hands in the Muslim position of supplication and spoke with deference. "Please understand...I have to ask this. Who has been supplying your weapons?"

"Ah, yes, I understand. You must talk to Kosaran." He indicated a young man and spoke rapidly in Kamanji.

"I'm Kosaran. I'll tell you what you want to know."

To: DER Director
From: Luc
Subject: Iraq

Shipment tracked to Kasik 40 km north of Mosul. Half went direct to Mukhabarat/Sunni militia, the other half to PKK People's Defence Force north of Sirsenk Airfield. PKK confirm supply arranged by Gerald Darbly identified from picture and by name. Delivery arranged by Gorsky identified from picture. PKK not happy about split delivery providing arms to the Iraqis. Total of eight (8) deliveries to PKK in four years.

Ten minutes after transmitting the message the computer beeped and an incoming message blinked on screen. Luc smiled. Brussels was still at work.

To: Luc
From: DER Director
Subject: Well Done

Information acknowledged. Well done. Where the hell have you been?

Luc responded:

To: DER Director
From: Luc
Subject: Hell right word.

Spot of local difficulty. Got caught watching delivery. Unpleasant few days not answering Mukhabarat questions. Escaped north to PKK.

Luc smiled to himself, he knew that the Director would probably appreciate the description. A few minutes later, a new message arrived.

To: Luc
From: DER Director
Subject: Physical Condition

How 'unpleasant?????' What's your status?

I bet Jo is in the office with him, thought Luc. The Director wouldn't have asked.

To: DER Director
From: Luc
Subject: Re: Status

Damaged but functional. Perps killed. Two days on run. Now in secure position with PKK. Will try border crossing in about a week.

He'll want to know why the delay. Best to tell the truth…
not that there is anything the DER can do about it, thought
Luc. As he touched the keyboard a message came through:

To: Luc
From: DER Director
Subject: Crossing

You can walk faster than that!!! Rumour of Kurdish
offensive to coincide with US offensive against Mosul militia
next week. You are NOT authorised to join in…officially.
Don't get yourself killed. There's work for you back here.
Turks are standing by to extract by helicopter. Jo says hi.

Well, I'll be buggered…

Tuesday 8 April, Zagros Mountains

Luc had drilled the PKK fighters hard all week and now it was
time to see what they were made off. The Iraqi guard post was an
easy target, front-lit by the setting sun. The young PKK soldier
set the sights of the shoulder-launched rocket, armed the firing
mechanism, waited until the red light went off and the green light
was steady, then slowly squeezed the trigger. The rocket streaked
away and the other men in the group watched with satisfaction
as it hit the entrance spot-on target, followed by a huge explosion
that hurled a storm of smashed masonry high in the sky.

Luc slapped Birkim on the back as they watched the
command post vanish. "An effective weapon, eh, my friend?"

"I wish we'd had one or two of these earlier," he replied,
shaking his head in wonderment.

"Let's go," Luc ordered.

Luc expected stiff resistance from the estimated hundred men housed in the main Mukhabarat barracks and his attack plan called for a two-pronged assault. Birkim was to set up an enfilade at the back of the barracks, while Luc and his team would take the front. He heard the sound of small arms and then the heavier thumping of the light machine gun. He signalled his men forward.

The first bursts of small arms fire coming at them did little damage, but then came the flat crack of a high-powered rifle. A man to Luc's right fell with half his head missing and their group hit the sand. He used the shoulder of the man next to him as a rest, took aim with the M16A2 and had the satisfaction of seeing the sniper crumple.

Small arms fire was now coming from the barracks. Luc crawled over to the young man with the rocket launcher.

"Have you got a clear sight of the door on the left?" The man nodded. "Good. Take your time and put a rocket through it."

The rocket struck the door squarely. "Good shot, now follow me." Luc crawled back to his first position.

"I guess the main support for the building will be just to the right of that door. I want you to angle the shot…" A bullet hit the tree a metre to their right. "…*Merde*! Wait a moment." He took up his binoculars. "I see the bastard." A bullet smacked into the gnarled tree just above their heads; the tree was not large enough to provide full cover. Luc quickly knelt, used his own arm crooked in support of the rifle and squeezed the trigger. The sniper vanished, knocked backwards by the impact.

Luc turned back to the man with the rocket launcher. "Aim to hit just a forearm's length to the right of the door." He extended his forearm to illustrate.

The man eased himself into a prone; he had obviously been well trained. The rocket streaked away, hit precisely on target, giving a modest puff of white, then a few billows of darker smoke came out of the windows. For a long moment there was almost silence. Then the building slowly collapsed. The Iraqi fire immediately ceased.

A structure about four metres square remained standing to the right of the collapsed barracks. Luc keyed his radio. "Birkim, where are you?"

"We're in a fire-fight well clear to your left."

"Now put one into the wall, midway, on the right." The man complied, and again, there was only a puff of white smoke. When it cleared, they could see that the wall had been damaged but not breached. If their intelligence was correct, that was the armoury, so it was understandable that the walls would be much thicker. They had only one rocket remaining.

"Now, lad. You need to put the last one in the same spot as the first." Luc thought there might be some question about that and the precision required, but the young man calmly loaded up, took his time and fired. Once again there was a modest puff of white smoke, a delay, but then a most satisfying, truly magnificent explosion followed. The men were cheering as volleys of for-real fireworks streaked into the sky, framing a huge mushroom cloud of red fire slowly turning black as it rose and capped off. Luc had seen, and himself engineered, a few before this, perhaps one or two even larger, but none more satisfying.

Luc launched a green flare into the sky and it was met with Kurdish voices filling the air as they stormed the collapsed building. As planned, they first used grenades, reverberating and deadly in the enclosed spaces under the collapsed roof. Then it was the dirty business of fierce hand-to-hand fighting at which the Kurds excelled.

He turned and put a hand on the shoulder of the man beside him, now closing the rocket launcher. "Good. I've never seen better." The young man smiled broadly.

Sporadic single shots now issued from the building, with only one possible meaning.

Luc shrugged: "*In'sh Allah.*"

CHAPTER TWELVE

For Joanna, the passing days represented one physical challenge after another. At first, too weak to do anything for herself, she had been totally dependent on the medical staff who, having no other patients to look after, gave her their undivided attention. Dr Aziz had visited daily for the first week, then declared herself satisfied with the progress of her patient and the care. She only came every few days after that.

Joanna had found the inactivity of early recovery irksome. Now she could look forward to the physiotherapist, and welcomed the pain and exhaustion that was beyond anything she had ever before experienced. The cast on her left leg was a drag, but she eventually got used to it and even began to appreciate its added weight for the lifts and other exercises designed to strengthen it.

But her real problem was simple, gnawing worry. The news from Iraq was good. The Kurds had reached Mosul that morning, ahead of the fast moving Americans, but Luc had been out of touch for five full days when heavy fighting had trapped them around the town and in the Zagros Mountains. Radcliffe had not seemed overly concerned but she still noted that the first thing he asked on arriving each morning was for news of Luc. When none was forthcoming, he did sit down to work, but she felt he wasn't settled into it. But he said nothing more about his missing agent.

Joanna had asked why the operation was now being run from the Farm and was told it was a security issue. She left it at that.

They had not allowed her to do much except monitor the electronic surveillance, but she had insisted on standing a shift in the communications room each day as they waited for Luc to make contact. That contact had finally come the previous morning: a brief encoded transmission requesting extraction.

The sound of a car woke her. She looked at her watch: 05.30, far too early for it to be the DER Director. She heard voices, got out of bed and started towards the window, misjudged her mobility without her elbow crutches and fell heavily. Tears of frustration welled in her eyes and spilled down her cheeks as she struggled to get up again.

Then Luc was beside her.

"Hey, what's up, kid?"

He gently lifted her into a sitting position and she hugged him hard, her relief at his return unrestrained. "What were you trying to do?"

"I wanted to look out of the window," she said, not wanting to admit how much she had missed him and how worried she had been. Luc smiled and put his arms around her again.

"I guess it's time we gave you something to do. Let me get you back to bed and have one of the nurses check you over…"

"There's nothing wrong with me."

Luc did not respond and stood up, lifting Joanna as he did so to place her in the bed.

"Show off."

"Now, the nurse…"

"I don't *want* the nurse. If you think the wounds need checking then you do it." She still had hold of his hand and was casting him a mischievous smile. She kept her eyes locked on his, challenging him. Her voice was suddenly husky: "Check my wounds."

Sensing that they were both about to cross a line, she opened her pyjama top revealing her nakedness. There was no longer any danger of blood or discharges, and as he started to close her jacket, she took his hands and pressed them to her breasts.

"You are supposed to check me over." She spoke in a low voice looking him straight in the eyes. He bent forward and kissed her. For a moment she savoured the kiss and then put her arms around his neck.

"I want you to check me over properly, Luc Hansen." She kissed him hard. He sat back and looked at her. Then he put his hands back and she sighed as he gently stroked her there, and then all over. They both knew what they wanted.

He chided, "You've got too many clothes on."

"Then help me do something about it." She raised her hips as his hands reached for her pyjama bottoms. Gently he eased them away from her waist and pulled the soft cotton down, his eyes fixed on the dark mound between her legs. He reached out and gently touched her there. She moaned quietly.

"Be very gentle with me Luc." She knew her arousal was genuine, that this was the right time and that her feelings for Luc were real and mutual. She shifted slightly and reached for his belt.

The sun had come around to the window and was flooding the room as they lay savouring the moment. Luc had not hesitated to stand before her naked and she had taken him in hand without a word, and he her equally, reaching between her legs. Then gently moving them apart, he lay beside her. It had not been the most actively passionate or easiest coupling for either of them but there was genuine affection, and attraction, and they had found a way. Joanna had wanted him on top but that was not practical and he took her carefully from behind, then to remain curled together fully relaxed.

"Luc…?"

"Ummm…."

"Thank you."

He looked startled. "For what?"

"For being gentle."

"My pleasure…I've wanted you for long time."

"And now you can have me whenever you want." She kissed him and he started to become aroused again. He put his hand on her bottom and stroked it, running his finger into the top of the cleft between her buttocks. In this way, they came together: it was easier and longer. Then they dozed.

When they awoke, Joanna insisted on touching every part of him as if to reassure herself that the damage to his body was healing. He winced once or twice but said nothing. She kissed the raw wheals on his back and then gently rubbed some of the physiotherapist's oil into them. She gently touched the wound on his chest where Gärtner had caught him with the knife four weeks previously. Finally, she bathed the wound on his head.

Sunday 13 April, Lasne

Luc opened the picture file of the man the Kurds had identified as Gorsky. The quality was excellent: sharply focused with good contrast and little shadow.

Joanna swung into the room on her crutches and sat down next to him.

"What you got there?"

"I need to know who this guy Gorsky really is, but the database comes up blank."

"Try taking off the glasses." She reached past him and called up a photo manipulation program. A few keystrokes later, the face reappeared without glasses. "If that doesn't work, I'd suggest changing the hair colour, then longer or shorter hair, and do it twice each time, with and without glasses."

"How's Dukakis working out?" Luc felt a minor twinge of jealousy and tried to keep his voice neutral.

"Okay. He's very good and I'm learning a lot. The DER should recruit him."

"Has he found anything we can use?"

"He's searching the Commission's system for anything and everything connected with the ZX programme but it's a long, slow process."

Luc nodded absently, then said in frustration, "Damn. I know that face!"

Joanna lit cigarettes for them both and put one in his mouth.

"Thanks, but when did you start smoking again?"

"Coffee?"

"Answer my question."

"Bully. When you were away. I was worried."

"Well I'm back so you can stop again. Now, what about that coffee?" He laughed as Joanna, scowling, stubbed out the cigarette.

"I'll make us some. I know where the guards keep their supply." She was suddenly the mischievous urchin.

Luc's eyes followed her departure and then returned to the screen. He saved the image Joanna had concocted and ran through the other possibilities.

Joanna returned with mugs of freshly brewed coffee on a tray that she carried with difficulty. She carefully set them down on the desk and peered at an image on the screen. "That face looks Slavic to me, definitely not western European. Try the racial stereotype utility."

Luc did as he was told and selected Russian. The image faded and then reappeared, the hair colouring and style now changed to match the stereotype selected.

Luc exclaimed with conviction, "That's him! I'm certain now but I'll be damned if I know who he is."

"Your immediate past, or distant past?"

"Distant, I think." He moved aside as Joanna leaned over the keyboard. A whiff of perfume made him look up.

"Distant past as in, the Legion?"

"Possibly."

Joanna worked the program for a moment and the image re-appeared looking about ten years younger.

"Well, I'll be damned. That's him. Can you hack the *Légion*'s archives?"

"At this time of night? No bloody chance. The Director would murder us if he found out."

"Chicken."

"No, but the last time I did it to check up on a certain Luc Hansen it took a couple of hours."

"All right, hotshot, how about we call this quits and I'll get you a beer?" Luc headed for the door.

"I'd rather you took me to bed."

"You hussy." His lips pressed against the back of her neck, his hand found her breast and she moaned as the nipple hardened.

"But I'm *your* hussy," she responded breathlessly.

His tongue flickered on her neck.

"In that case…" He pulled her round and his lips found hers. She reached up and clung to him.

"Help me to bed, you bastard, and I'll show you who's a hussy."

Luc grinned and pulled her upright. The next moment she was in his arms, her face buried in his neck, as he carried her up the stairs.

Monday 14 April, Brussels

Rain shrouded the École Militaire, a neo-classical building facing the Parc du Cinquantenaire. Luc parked his car and dashed across the road. A guard stopped him just inside the entrance and, when Luc had explained his mission, made a telephone call while indicating that the DER man should wait.

A young uniformed cadet, a member of the duty guardroom, appeared and invited Luc to follow. After a labyrinthine walk involving several sets of stairs, they arrived at the Archivists' Office. A middle-aged sergeant dismissed the cadet and then disappeared through a doorway, only to reappear within seconds.

"This way, sir." The sergeant opened the door and ushered Luc inside. The room was as comfortable as any army office can be and there was the pleasant smell of fresh brewed coffee. A large man with a heavily scarred face got up.

"Luc Hansen, you bastard. Good to see you." The timbre of his voice was unchanged from his days as a drill sergeant.

"René…" but before he could say more Luc found himself in a bear hug that left him gasping as the pain from the cracked rib flared up.

"Damn, but you look well. What are you now? A policeman or something I seem to remember?"

"I work for the DER."

"And who the hell are they?" René Lachapelle thrust a coffee across the desk and slid a packet of Gauloise alongside it.

Luc lit up before replying. "Well, a sort of security and intelligence unit within the EU."

"And what brings you here?"

"I need your memory, René, and your help." He slid the modified photograph of Gorsky across the desk.

Lachapelle put on a pair of reading glasses and studied the picture. "Seems familiar. From the old days, yes?"

"I think so."

"What's he done wrong?"

"I'm not sure he's done anything wrong but we think he's an arms dealer. He looks older of course…" Luc showed the original to Lachapelle.

"Africa!" Lachapelle studied the pictures, nodding thoughtfully. "Definitely Africa. Must be nearly twenty years ago. Before your time, huh."

Luc waited, patiently smoking his cigarette and occasionally sipping the coffee. Lachapelle turned to his computer.

"Ah, yes. Gorsky, Valentin — Sergeant. They gave him a Russian *nom de la Légion* 'cos he's a Russian émigré. Real name: Alexis Nikolaevnich. Got shot up in some stupid West African affair and was shipped back to Castelnaudary. I guess you might have come across him there. I think he taught explosives and urban warfare. According to this, he was discharged ten years ago. Take a look."

The face on the screen was a certain match to the one on the desk, younger and rather more stylish but definitely the same.

"Any idea where he's based now?"

"There's nothing on this record. Let me ask around. This is going to cost you lunch, you idle bastard." Lachapelle bellowed, "Sergeant!" The desk sergeant stuck his head into the office.

"Louis, my young friend here wants to know how to contact an old acquaintance. Details on the screen. Dig around and get me some answers. We're off for lunch."

The sergeant grunted.

Luc smiled an apology and allowed Lachapelle to march him from the office.

Wednesday 16 April, Lasne

The first floor conference room at the Farm was pleasantly warm, the windows were open onto the garden, and Joanna could see the ever-vigilant guards patrolling the perimeter beyond the helicopter that had brought James Ashley from Luxembourg.

She heard voices on the stairs. Luc was the first to enter and he came round to kiss her. James Ashley and Radcliffe sat down round the table as Joanna struggled to her feet.

"Sit down, young lady, sit down." She subsided gratefully. "Now, tell me, how are you?"

"I'm fine, thank you sir."

"And now how about telling an old man the truth?" He sat down beside her to listen.

Luc poured coffee and then sat facing them.

"We're all up to speed," said Radcliffe from the head of the table. "So this meeting is to decide where we go from here. I assume you've all seen the newspaper reports and TV coverage of the renewed fighting around Mosul, spearheaded by the Kurds. The Sunni militia are taking a pounding." He looked round and everyone agreed.

Ashley added, "I understand that de Foucaud was very eloquent on the subject in the Commission meeting yesterday, and there are murmurings about changing the EU policy towards the Kurds. The German and French are at the forefront of those supporting the move, including, it goes without saying, the Belgians."

Joanna handed out transcripts of the intercepts. "Vandenhove was busy on the telephone yesterday and again this morning. He was lobbying for a change in policy amongst the other *chefs de cabinet* and even spoke to some of the more influential Commissioners. He's very persuasive."

"Exactly," replied Radcliffe. "So, it appears that his plan has worked, up to a point, but that need not concern us. What does, is that this has to remain deniable — no arrests and no courts. We have to keep them out of the public gaze." He drank some coffee and looked round for reactions.

"You mean kill them." The pencil Luc was playing with suddenly snapped in two.

"Or give them to the Americans," offered Radcliffe quietly.

"One way forward might be to make the conspiracy implode."

"And how do you propose we do that?"

"By closing down the funding and the arms route and then telling them what we've done. But at the same time we continue to focus on Vandenhove and Groupe Franco Belge covertly."

"What about the others?" asked Joanna.

"Gorsky isn't an issue — he's a legitimate arms dealer. And there is no evidence that he was involved with either the fraud or the acquisition of false End User Certificates. I'll find him and warn him off."

"And Darbly?"

"Darbly…Well, if we close down the arms route and let everyone know it, he becomes a serious liability. I think we can leave it to Gärtner or the Kurds to deal with him."

"They'll kill him," Radcliffe asserted.

"Probably, sir. But does that matter?"

"We're not in the business of setting up murders."

"Aren't we? Isn't that what you just asked me to do?" Luc angrily replied.

Joanna was uncomfortable with the tension between the two men. She agreed with Luc but understood where Radcliffe was coming from. She looked across at Ashley but he was lost in thought. "Surely we should focus on locating and eliminating Gärtner."

"Are you suggesting we sanction him?" Radcliffe came directly to the point.

"No, Mr Radcliffe. But from what we now know about the man, it seems unlikely he'll be taken alive." Joanna wondered if she had pushed it too far but then received support from an unexpected quarter.

Ashley steepled his fingers and leant forward. "It's an exceptionally risky strategy but I'm inclined to agree with it."

Joanna saw both Luc and Radcliffe relax and she breathed a sigh of relief.

Ashley continued, "I have, of course, already discussed this with my colleagues in Luxembourg, and we're of the opinion that all the major players need to be disposed of quietly and away from public view. Luc's basic approach is in line with our thinking. It's politically incorrect, I know, but I think we have little real choice in the matter."

Joanna watched as the others took this in. It would have to be a deniable operation so if it went wrong, Luc would be the fall guy and that bothered her. But Luc had openly accepted the risks. Who was she to argue?

Ashley turned to Luc. "Where will you start?"

"Prague."

CHAPTER THIRTEEN

Friday 18 April, Prague, Czech Republic

Luc watched Svetlana Nikolaevna enter a café and order coffee. He and the team had been following her, hoping that she would lead them to Gorsky. It was a long shot and a strain on resources, but ever since he had discovered that Gorsky was the arms dealer involved, Luc had been trying to find a way to make face-to-face contact with him. Joanna's tracking system showed the Russian's mobile phone was in the Czech capital, but locating the man in the crowded, medieval streets was proving difficult.

A man approached Nikolaevna's table and sat down. Luc compared the face to the one on the photograph from Chalon's house. It was a probable match and when the man turned Luc was certain. He let out a sigh of relief.

The couple spent about twenty minutes together and then Nikolaevna stood up, kissed her brother and walked off. Gorsky ordered a beer and started to read a newspaper.

Luc took the recently vacated seat and Gorsky looked up in annoyance.

Luc spoke softly, "Hello, Valentin, long time no see, *mon Sergent.*"

"Who the hell are you?"

"One of the men you taught explosives to in Castelnaudary. Now, let's have a Pils and I'll tell you all about it."

"Tell me about what?"

"How the funds have dried up and how you've made your last shipment to the Kurds." Gorsky tensed. "No, don't even think of it, Valentin, there's a silenced automatic pointing directly at you right now."

Gorsky looked at Luc coldly and shrugged.

"What do you want?"

"To give you some advice. So come on, Valentin, another Pils, or would you prefer Marc like the old days?"

"Who are you?" Gorsky asked again.

"A friend from *la Légion*. But I work for the DER now. Do you know who they are?"

Gorsky nodded.

"Good, that saves a lot of explaining." Luc waved away the hovering waitress.

"We've been investigating your illegal supply of arms to the Iraqis and the Kurds and we've closed down your operation."

"I have no idea what you're talking about." Gorsky started to rise.

"Sit down," Luc snapped, and the Russian subsided into his seat.

"You are shipping arms to Iraq; we know that. You're using false Czech EUCs to purchase them in Hungary; we've closed that down. The money comes from a EuropeAid contract via Gerald Darbly and we've closed that down too."

"Why are you telling me all this?" Gorsky had regained some composure.

"In the hope you might make a wise decision."

"And what might that be?"

"That you go back to Russia and forget all about Iraq."

"And if I don't?" Gorsky asked casually.

"Then we'll tell the Americans or the Kurds exactly where to find you. They already know you were supplying to both sides and they don't like people who do that."

"And what about the others?"

"I'd advise your sister to get away from Gerald Darbly."

"Thank you. We won't meet again." Gorsky stood up, put some money on the table and walked away.

As the Russian merged into the crowd, two of Luc's team moved to follow.

An hour later Luc approached a bar on the *Kampa* opposite Darbly's apartment. His mobile phone buzzed.

"Hi, Luc." Joanna's cheerful greeting rang in his ear.

"Hello, you gorgeous thing."

"I suppose you're having a good time without me, huh?"

"Actually I'm outside Darbly's flat, wondering if the BIS security people have finished installing the electronic surveillance."

She laughed. "I believe you, but thousands wouldn't. Luc, I've got the latest from the Vandenhove bugs. Darbly phoned him a short time ago and went ballistic when Vandenhove told him that the Hungarians have closed down the arms route."

"Good."

"Oh, and Gorsky hasn't disappeared, he's still in Prague."

"I know, I spoke to him just over an hour ago and he's been a busy boy since then. He went to the Czech Ministry of Defence and came out looking very unhappy. According to Gregor he just missed seeing Darbly."

"What are you going to do now?"

"I think it's time to spy on Svetlana Nikolaevna."

"Well, keep your hands off any pretty women or I'll have something to say."

"Yes, dear." Smiling, he turned and approached an unmarked beige Renault van that he knew belonged to the BIS, the Czech Security Service.

Luc tapped lightly on the rear door and was immediately admitted. Inside were two Czech security personnel. A young female agent with blond hair in a ponytail silently acknowledged him, while a technician wearing headphones monitored the wide-angle view of an empty office with his hand on a joystick.

The technician started the playback, and Luc watched as Gerald Darbly and a second man appeared on the video monitor.

The woman narrated: "The man with Darbly is Albert Cerný, in Procurement at the Czech Defence Ministry. We set up surveillance on him when you identified the target."

Luc replied, "Anything of interest since then?"

"Enough to convict Cerný of embezzlement and put him away for years…but nothing on your case until today."

"When was this recorded?" Luc pointed at the screen

"About an hour ago."

Luc picked up a set of headphones and heard Darbly ask about the End User Certificate for the final shipment.

"I'm afraid I can't help you there, Mr Darbly," replied Cerný.

"But it is just an extension of the previous certificate!" Darbly exclaimed.

"As I said, Mr Darbly, I can't help you." Luc watched Cerný turn away, clearly showing the interview was over.

"Why not?" Darbly demanded.

"Because, Mr Darbly, I can't." Cerný took a piece of paper and wrote on it. He slid it across the desk to the Englishman.

The technician quickly zoomed in and Luc was able to read what the ministry official had written:

> *The police are investigating. I'm under suspicion and I'm under surveillance. If you come here again they'll probably arrest you.*

"How true," murmured the female agent.

"I'm sorry that your journey has been wasted, Mr Darbly. I'm sure we won't be seeing each other again." Cerný pressed a bell push. Another man entered the office and escorted Darbly out.

Luc turned to the female agent. "Are you going to arrest Cerný now?"

"Yes, unless you have a reason for us to wait." Luc shook his head.

"Who did Gorsky visit while he was there?" Luc showed her a picture of the Russian arms dealer.

She flipped open her phone and called headquarters. After a long and, to Luc, unintelligible conversation, she looked up from her notes.

"Well, two things of interest. Gorsky did not visit Cerný but he did visit the section that actually processes the applications for EUCs. We don't know what was discussed but we do know who he spoke to and will investigate. The second thing is that Cerný has now been arrested. Thanks for that, Mr Hansen."

The technician said something and the agent spoke to Luc again. "According to Josef here, the surveillance equipment was successfully installed in the apartment as you requested and he now confirms that the female target has just entered."

Luc's mobile buzzed.

"Yes, Gregor."

"We're just descending the steps from the Charles Bridge."

"Right, the surveillance vehicle is a beige Renault beside the police station."

The security agent pressed a switch and a monitor showed Darbly, tailed by Gregor, approaching across the square. As Darbly unlocked the front door of his apartment building, Gregor crossed the square and sat down outside the bar.

The technician spoke, "Mr Hansen, the woman has just taken a call from a male called Alexis."

Luc picked up the headphones. His Russian was serviceable and it appeared that Valentin Gorsky was warning his sister. *So far, so good.* The telephone conversation ended and he could hear Darbly enter the sitting room.

Luc looked up at the video monitor. The quality of the picture was excellent and he could see Svetlana Nikolaevna beside the window with a stormy look on her face.

He watched as Darbly went to a sideboard and splashed some whisky into a glass.

"Typical. I suppose a drink cures everything." The sarcasm in Svetlana's voice was cutting.

"Where the hell have you been?" Darbly's normally cultured tones sounded harsh in the headphones.

"Do I have to tell you everything I do? If you'd told me when you were coming back, I might have been here."

"I said, where have you been?" Darbly's frustration was turning to anger.

Svetlana ignored the question and stalked off-camera and into what Luc knew was the bedroom.

"I'm leaving you," he heard her say.

Darbly put his glass down with a snap and it shattered spilling whisky over the carpet.

"What the hell are you talking about?" Darbly's off-camera voice was clear.

"I've just spoken to my brother. It's over, Gerald."

"Damn it, Svetlana, what are you talking about?"

"Oh I think you know, Gerald." She sounded contemptuous.

"Know what?" Darbly sounded barely under control.

"He's losing it," observed the security agent and Luc nodded.

"My brother's been warned off. The money has gone. And the ministry won't help you." Her voice had risen to a shout.

She came back into view.

She spoke over her shoulder. *"I suppose you're going to claim it's all lies, huh? You see yourself as a hero to the Kurds, don't you, just because you sent them arms."*

Darbly entered into view.

Svetlana continued, *"You idiot…did you really think they would give construction contracts to you and your friends for a few rifles? You're fucked good and proper now. The DER is after you and the Kurds know you've been selling to both sides. You're a dead man, Gerald Darbly."*

Darbly grabbed at her. Her arm came up and her nails ripped into his face. *"Don't you touch me, you bastard!"*

The technician altered the focus. "A right little tiger…she really got him."

Luc could see the blood on Darbly's cheek. He hit her hard and she stumbled.

"Typical. Can't take the truth so you have to hit out. No wonder your wife threw you out. No wonder your daughter hated you. She was going to report you, you know. That's why Vandenhove had her killed."

Darbly froze, his fist raised. *"You're lying."*

In the surveillance van, Luc held his breath as Darbly's face revealed profound shock. So, Luc thought, the bastard didn't know.

In the apartment, he heard Svetlana say sadly, *"No, I'm not. Emma was investigating your little project and Gärtner killed her."*

Darbly's clenched fist caught her on the side of her face,

sending her stumbling backwards. A stool caught her behind the legs, she lost her balance and fell heavily onto the glass coffee table. It splintered, she screamed and Luc saw blood appear.

Luc tore off the headphones. "*Merde*! He's fucking killed her!"

The BIS agent was already on the telephone as Luc leaped out of the van.

Luc ran to Gregor. "Follow him and stay in close contact.

Darbly exited the building, blood clearly visible on his face. Gregor nodded at the bill on the table and made off to follow. Luc dropped a banknote on the table as the BIS agent joined him. They walked quickly across the street.

They took the steps two at a time. The front door of the apartment was open. Luc pulled on a pair of surgical gloves, stepped into the short hallway. On the floor in front of him was a bloody footprint. He stepped carefully to one side and looked again. There was another, a right hand shoe each time. He moved down the hall and gently pushed a door open.

The woman was lying in a large pool of blood, all tangled up with the wreckage of a glass coffee table. He moved round the side of the room until he was by her head and then reached over and checked for a pulse. There was none, which did not surprise him when he saw the large shard of glass deeply embedded in her neck.

He stepped aside, surveyed the room and took a photograph of the dead woman with his mobile phone's camera.

The Czech security agent looked down at the dead woman. She's said, "Dead I suppose."

"Very. Can I leave this with you to sort out?"

She flashed him an ironic smile, "My pleasure. You going after Darbly."

"Yes."

"I'll sort it out with the police, but Mr Hansen, this time leave it tidier, yes? And keep us fully informed." She held eye contact with Luc.

Two minutes later he was back in the street and heading towards the Charles Bridge. He called Gregor.

"Where is he?"

"In the Blue Monkey and getting drunk."

"Stay with him, but don't intervene no matter what happens."

Luc dialled Gorsky's number and when the Russian answered, he sent him the picture of the dead woman and told him where to find Darbly.

CHAPTER FOURTEEN

Karel Vandenhove was worried. The collapse of the Sunni militia and the fall of Mosul after just three weeks of fighting were astounding, and nothing short of disastrous for Groupe Franco Belge and the projects Vandenhove had spent so much time and effort establishing. It was all coming apart and, with the DER closing in, he needed reliable information. He also needed Claudia Chalon but she was missing.

It was not unusual for her to be out of touch for a couple of weeks but four weeks was very unusual. He had reached her answer phone each time he tried calling but he had not left a message. Now he was seriously worried. He needed to know what was happening with the DER enquiry.

Dieter Gärtner entered the sitting room silently and sat down in the armchair opposite his employer.

Vandenhove looked at him. "I need you to find someone or, at least, find where they are."

"Okay."

"Her name is Claudia Chalon, the details are in here." Vandenhove handed over a slim file.

Gärtner flicked open the file, quickly read the notes and then looked carefully at the picture.

"Who is she?" he asked dispassionately.

"She's our contact inside the DER. She's the reason we've been able to stay ahead of the bastards," Vandenhove replied.

"When I find her, do you want me to get rid of her?"

"No, just find out what has happened to her. She's been out of touch too long." Vandenhove held out a small bunch of keys. "These are the keys to her house. There is an alarm system and the control pad is just inside the front door. The code is in the file."

Gärtner let himself into the house and carefully closed the door. He turned the alarm system off and listened. Silence.

He started to search.

The sitting room revealed Vandenhove's real interest in the owner of the house. A good photograph in a silver frame showed Karel Vandenhove and Claudia Chalon in a pose that suggested great intimacy between them. Gärtner considered it for a moment: the fat man keeps her as his mistress. "*Mein Gott*! And he managed it without anyone knowing." Gärtner moved on, methodically checking each room, but found no sign of anyone having been in the house for some time.

The first floor study contained a desk; the contents were interesting but not particularly helpful. The bedroom revealed nothing further. No sign of a hurried departure, no sign of anything. The house was as normal as though its owner was about to return.

Gärtner returned to the study. He could not see a computer but from the cabling and equipment, it appeared she used a laptop. On the desk was an answer phone and the message-waiting light was flashing. Gärtner pushed the playback button and listened: nothing unusual.

Gärtner opened his rucksack, took out a monitoring device and switched it on. Almost immediately, the digital readout indicated the presence of a source of radio signals with a frequency that he did not recognise. He swept the monitor around the room and identified three 'hotspots'. He left the room and swept the rest of the house. Hot spots turned up in most rooms.

He returned to the study and searched for the source near the telephone. There was nothing visible. Gärtner took out a set of screwdrivers, disassembled the telephone itself and found the bug in the handset. Gärtner replaced it and reassembled the telephone. He repeated the operation with three other hotspots.

The house was under very sophisticated electronic surveillance and that suggested the DER.

Monday 21 April, Brussels

Radcliffe pushed the newspaper across the desk towards Luc.

> *MEP found drowned.*
> *The Czech State Police recovered the body of English*
> *MEP Gerald Darbly from the Vltava River in*
> *central Prague late on Sunday evening, according to*
> *a spokesman. Initial medical reports indicated that*
> *Darbly had drowned and had been in the river for*

*about 24 hours. There was no sign of foul play. The
Czech State Police had been wanting to interview
Darbly in connection with the death of a young woman
in the city on Friday.*

"Well, he was alive when he ran off," said Luc as he put the
newspaper down.

"Is he likely to have committed suicide?" asked the DER
Director.

"I doubt it, sir."

"So who would want him dead?"

"The Kurds, Vandenhove possibly, especially as his usefulness
was over."

"I think we can rule out Vandenhove. Or at least his tame
killer. The surveillance team on Claudia's house still have a video
link running and obtained some excellent shots of Gärtner poking
around on Sunday. He found quite a number of the bugs."

"The Kurds wanted Darbly dead. They didn't like the fact he
was selling guns to the Iraqi regime."

"What about Gorsky? You said the dead woman was Gorsky's
sister."

"Possible, sir," replied Luc neutrally.

At that moment, the Director's secretary entered the room
and smiled apologetically. She placed a note in front of Radcliffe
and waited. He looked up, "Where are they?"

"In the main conference room, Mr Radcliffe."

"Very well, we'll be along in a moment."

Luc waited patiently and then Radcliffe said, "Very well, I
don't think we'll bother with the late Mr Darbly. The Czechs
can have the case. We've got another problem now. Come
with me."

There were three people in the conference room when
Radcliffe and Luc entered. All three stood up. Luc recognised

Christian Declerq, the DER's chief legal officer.

"Good afternoon, I'm Alan Radcliffe, and you are...?" Radcliffe spoke to a tall young woman with long hair.

"Dominique Sombreville of the Public Prosecutor's Office." She did not introduce the man with her.

"Please sit down. Now, what can I do for you?" Radcliffe sat down and waited.

"According to information placed before us, we have reason to believe that the DER is holding a Belgian national by the name of Claudia Chalon. And she has not yet been brought before a court." Dominique Sombreville consulted her notes.

Radcliffe remarked offhandedly, "Well, I hardly think that is a correct statement of the situation."

"Mr Radcliffe, I must inform you that an application has been made to our office for the release of Miss Chalon pending further investigation."

"Oh."

"I beg your pardon, Mr Radcliffe."

"I said, Oh."

"Well, are you holding her or not?"

"Miss Sombreville, let me see if I can shed a bit of light on this for you. Miss Chalon is a DER officer and is involved in a very sensitive case with major international ramifications in the political and security field." Radcliffe smiled tightly.

"That is as may be, Mr Radcliffe, but our information suggests you have arrested her and I have an order here for Miss Chalon to attend the court so that a judge may decide the facts of the matter." She held up the document and the DER lawyer took it, quickly scanning the legalese. He nodded at Radcliffe.

"Exactly, Mr Radcliffe. As your colleague can confirm, Miss Chalon is to appear before the judge tomorrow morning." A hint of triumph entered Sombreville's voice as Declerq nodded again.

"Very well, Miss Sombreville. I'll let her know. I will, of

course, have to remove her from the case she's on. Now, since this is a highly sensitive international security case, I assume you have arranged for an 'in camera' hearing."

"Please don't fence with me, Mr Radcliffe."

"Oh, but my dear Miss Sombreville, I'm not fencing with you. Under European Union law and the directives signed by the Belgian state when the DER was set up, no DER officer can be questioned about anything in open court. But, there again, I'm sure you knew that." Radcliffe smiled at the prosecutor who looked nonplussed. "Tell me, Miss Sombreville, where did your information come from?"

"I'm not at liberty to say."

"Well, I'm sure you understand, as I'm sure your director does, that you are asking me to imperil a major international investigation on the basis of information that comes from a source you refuse to reveal, who could possibly be the *subject* of our investigation. Had you thought of that? And if you can't be a bit more cooperative we'll seek an injunction requiring you to tell us."

The prosecutor paused to consider her options.

Luc broke the extended silence. "Perhaps Miss Sombreville would like the opportunity to take instructions."

"Excellent idea. Miss Sombreville, please feel free to use a mobile phone. This room is not subject to surveillance." Radcliffe stood up and, with Luc and Declerq, left the room.

"Right, Luc, what's on your mind?" Radcliffe asked as soon as they reached his office.

"They're trying to force our hand, sir. This has got to have come from Vandenhove. That's why they can't or won't say where the information comes from. Let's give them Chalon. We can still use her but they'll think we've no more leads."

"Do we have other leads, Luc?"

"Only that the evidence is inside the Franco Belge computer.

We can step up surveillance on Vandenhove. And I think we have a way of tagging Chalon who should then lead us to either Vandenhove or Gärtner."

"Why would she do that?"

"Because they know her house is bugged and she's nowhere to go. I think she'll make contact with Vandenhove so he can pull her out."

"There's some merit in that, Luc. Risky…but let's do it."

Tuesday 22 April, Lasne

Claudia Chalon had lost track of the number of days that she had been in her prison. With no real idea of time, she split her waking hours between reading the ample supply of books brought in by her guards, eating the not unpleasant meals that arrived regularly and dreaming about getting out. Deep down she knew that the DER would not, could not, let her go, but she pushed the thought to the back of her mind. Occasionally she raged inwardly and sometimes audibly at her captivity.

Her cell door opened and Luc Hansen entered. Behind him, a guard placed a box on the floor and stood by the open door. The guards never spoke so it was a shock to realise that Hansen was talking to her.

"…Claudia, you've not been listening. Please pay attention."

She refocused trying to concentrate.

"You are to shower and dress and when you're ready, you'll be taken to see Mr Radcliffe. Please don't delay. He's expecting you in forty minutes."

She watched him walk out, followed by the guard. She heard the door lock. Her brain refused to work coherently. If it was just more interrogation, then why should she shower and dress?

Why didn't Hansen just come in and do his worst? After a few minutes of pointless speculation, she crossed to the box and opened it. Inside were her clothes, all neatly laundered and folded, along with most of her own cosmetics and make-up. It didn't make sense. Then the urge to wear her own clothes became unbearable: she quickly showered and dressed.

What were they going to do this time? Her mind started playing tricks again: surely they were not going to let her go. The door opened and Luc Hansen entered.

"Come along, Claudia, the Director is waiting."

She stood up and held her wrists forward for the inevitable handcuffs but none were forthcoming. She was confused. She felt herself taken gently by the arm and escorted to the door. She was unaccountably afraid of crossing the threshold but her escort was insistent. She stepped hesitantly into the corridor expecting to see armed guards, but there was no one other than Hansen and another man. To her surprise, the latter entered the cell and returned with all her other things in the box.

She walked unsteadily and was secretly glad of the support of having her arm held. The stairs were an effort but she could see sunlight and it pulled her upwards. The room at the top of the stairs was clearly the guardroom and she recognised some of the guards.

Nobody looked at her. Nobody spoke. It was as though she was in a dream and this wasn't really happening. Going down another long corridor she started to shake. They were merely moving her to another cell. She struggled.

Hansen held her firmly but gently. The corridor gave way to an entrance hall and then they were outside in the sunlight.

Unable to see, she stopped.

Hansen handed her a pair of sunglasses.

She gratefully put them on and her eyes adjusted to the

glare. She felt the luxurious warmth of sun on her skin.

She looked around. They were in a cobbled courtyard. It appeared to be an old farm complex. She thought she recognised it. Her disorientation was terrifying and she stopped, but Hansen gently moved her forward.

They entered the main house through a side door that opened into a large kitchen. Three men and two women, all in dark blue fatigues, were at a long table drinking coffee, but no one looked at her and no one spoke. In the corner, she could see a flight of ascending stairs. Hansen guided her towards them. Climbing tired her, but with each step, she felt renewed hope and returning strength.

They passed along another corridor with a long room to the right, computer screens flickering, the sound of people talking.

They entered a large conference room. Sunlight flooded in. Claudia suddenly felt weak, reached for a chair and sat down at the long table, beyond which several tall windows overlooked a garden.

"Would you like some coffee?" Hansen asked.

She nodded dumbly. What was going on? Why were they being so nice?

The coffee smelt and tasted wonderful: the deep blackness of the best espresso with just the right amount of sugar. She savoured the taste and determined that whether this was her last or not, she would try to relax and enjoy it — the first — for how many days?

She watched Radcliffe take a seat with his back to the windows, a bright halo of light surrounding him. She almost laughed out loud as it reminded her of a picture of the haloed Christ in her childhood home.

"Claudia." She sat up and tried to concentrate. "Claudia, we've completed our investigation into your actions and we're not going to keep you here any longer."

Claudia regarded him closely as the words sunk in. So, they

were going to ship her off to some crummy Belgian jail. Shit!

Radcliffe's next words came as a complete shock. "I'm going to have to suspend you from duty, of course, and you'll have to surrender your passport but, providing you report daily to the local police, you're free to go."

"Aren't you going to put me on trial?"

"Not yet. The Investigating Magistrate has not finalised her report and it could be a couple of months before you'll know. You'll have to go to court tomorrow morning but that's a formality. However, please remember if you discuss your work, or reveal any information that could jeopardise the DER's investigations, you'll be arrested immediately and sent to prison. Is that clear?"

"So what happens to me now?" She hated sounding so weak and hesitant but she had not spoken to anyone for so long that even thinking was difficult.

"You can go back to your house. As I said, you'll have to surrender your passport and report to the local police daily but otherwise you're free to do as you want." Radcliffe placed her handbag on the tabletop and pushed it across to her. "Please give me your DER warrant card and your office security card."

Falteringly, still not believing what she had heard, she found the card and her official DER papers and slid them over to the Director. She took out her purse and found all her personal documents intact, credit cards, cash and her mobile phone.

Radcliffe picked up the items on the table. "Wait here. Luc will drive you back into Brussels." He left the room.

The sounds of people talking, computers humming and the occasional noise of a fax filtered through from nearby rooms. She could hear Luc Hansen talking to someone on the telephone. She stood up, walked to the window and looked out at the sunlit garden. The house was set in well-maintained grounds with some substantial trees. To one side of the large lawn, she could see the 'H' of a helicopter landing-pad and further out, towards the boundary, she could see armed guards with dogs. A vague memory was forming but she still could not work out where they were.

"Come on, Claudia." Luc Hansen spoke from the doorway and she followed him down a sweeping staircase and out into the bright sunlight.

She got into the car and was relieved to see no one around. Hansen got in beside her and started the engine. He handed her a blindfold.

"Put this on, please. It's for your own protection."

She meekly obeyed. Thirty-five minutes later, they stopped outside her house. During the entire trip they had not spoken. She removed the blindfold.

"Here's a set of instructions concerning tomorrow. Just remember you have to report to the local police everyday. They're expecting you between 09.00 and 16.00 daily. Take your passport in on the first visit and don't try to leave the country in the meantime. You're under surveillance until you start reporting to the police."

She got out and shut the door with a snap. Would he follow her? She walked unsteadily up to her front door and rummaged for her keys. Clumsily, she opened the door and stepped into the house. She heard the car start and drive away. She was alone again.

Two hours later, Lasne

"The bugs are working fine," said Joanna as she climbed the stairs beside Luc. "She sat in the sitting room for an hour saying nothing, then made herself some tea. She's just rung Vandenhove who is sending someone to collect her. The GPS locator in her watch is also spot on. We can track her easily enough now."

"Well done."

As they entered the conference room, they saw Radcliffe by the window talking on the telephone. He finished speaking and turned.

"Very well, Mr Ashley has authorised the next stage. Luc, please explain exactly what you are proposing."

"We need to get into the Groupe Franco Belge computer. We need to find out who else is involved with Vandenhove and his schemes."

"So, you want me to hack into their mainframe?" said Joanna.

"Yes."

"And Mr Ashley has approved that?" she looked directly at the DER Director.

"He has, Jo. I've just spoken to him. We're all unhappy that it has come to this but we need to clean up this whole mess discreetly."

"And what happens if the evidence is not there or I can't find it?"

Radcliffe spoke frankly. "If that's the case, Jo, then Vandenhove will walk. Either way, you mustn't leave any tracks…this has to be clean, start to finish."

"Jo, the conspiracy is dead. The arms route is closed. We'll get Gärtner. But we don't want Vandenhove to walk." Luc sounded angry.

"Don't worry, Luc. I'll do it."

She looked thoughtfully at the two men. It was not that hacking the computer bothered her, she'd done lots of that in the past, but taking down Vandenhove seemed to have taken on a personal dimension for Luc. She had seen this happen in the past and it worried her. It had not so far impaired his operational efficiency, but she felt he would take greater risks and ignore the rules too freely.

CHAPTER FIFTEEN

In the six weeks since the motorbike accident, Joanna had become proficient in getting around with elbow crutches but today things were different. The orthopaedic surgeon and Dr Aziz had removed the cast and announced themselves satisfied. Joanna had gingerly swung her legs to the ground and had taken her first steps unaided. The effort and concentration needed was immense and she tired quickly.

Luc had brought her back to the Farm. The physiotherapy would continue there and she would be able to work. Luc had watched with concern as she climbed the stairs for the first time unaided and looked rselieved when she gave him a 'thumbs up' from the top.

Joanna had spent the last two days planning her assault on the Franco Belge computer. She had discussed possible approaches with Dirk Wauters and Paul Dukakis and together they had formulated a plan. It was not going to be easy but it should work. She had tried explaining it to Luc but lacking the specialised computer knowledge that she and her team had he could do no more than understand the basics.

She was both scared and excited by the challenge. The responsibility for the success of the operation now lay with her and she worried about not letting the team down.

Luc had the Groupe Franco Belge offices under surveillance and had noted that everything closed down at six o'clock each day. Joanna calculated that any computer maintenance would take place immediately after the offices closed and that by ten o'clock they should have finished. She had selected 10.30 p.m. as the time to launch the attack.

She and Dirk had carefully created a 'clean' computer with its own high-speed Internet link and a back up. This was essential to protect the DER system.

She checked her watch. "Ready, Dirk?"

"Go for it, Jo." He checked the stability of the system and its link to the back up. Every step would be logged. As Dirk had laughingly said, it was like defusing a bomb: one person did the dirty work and the other monitored, ready to profit from the information gathered if the bomb exploded. Joanna had not appreciated the analogy.

"Starting the probe, now." She keyed in her access code, located the Franco Belge server and bypassed the firewall.

A list of directories appeared.

"You want to download everything?"

Joanna shook her head. "No, I don't think so. There's at least four hundred gigabytes and we don't have the capacity, and anyway, bulk downloads will attract attention."

Dirk spoke calmly: "Jo, they have an access tracer running."

"Shit."

"According to the parameters, you've got ten minutes before it triggers."

"What does it do?" Joanna continued the search.

"It will start tracing the connection."

"Can you disable it?"

"Yes."

"Wait. I've found the ZX programme files."

"It's a two-gigabyte file, Jo you'll have to hurry."

She started the download.

"One minute to go," warned Dirk.

The computer pinged and she quickly shut down the link.

"How do we stand, Dirk?"

"The registry is updating. No alerts." The relief in Dirk's voice was palpable.

Joanna fumbled in her purse. "Jeezus, I need a cigarette."

"Have some chocolate, it's better for you." Dirk quipped as he lit his pipe.

It was midnight and Luc was standing on the terrace gazing at the stars. His favourite constellations were Cassiopeia and Ursa Major. They had led him to safety many times with their unfailing identification of Polaris, the North Star. Out here at the Farm, without the city's light pollution, the stars were bright and reassuring.

Joanna stepped onto the terrace to stand beside him. He absently put his arm around her.

After a while, he looked down at her. "How has it gone?"

"We've found proof that GFB knew all along about the arms and the split account in Prague. And that they knew where the arms were going. We've also found that Darbly was on their payroll as a consultant."

"Well done."

"However, we've found nothing that links GFB with any politician and we haven't found anything that proves

Vandenhove is issuing the instructions to GFB directly," said Joanna in disappointment.

"Oh."

"Luc, we have discovered one other thing though…" she spoke hesitantly.

"Which is?"

"Gärtner is on the GFB payroll as Head of Security. He's salaried, pays his taxes and social security."

"So the tax man gets everyone including the bad guys."

"Yes, but that's not the point, Luc. If Gärtner is their Head of Security and Vandenhove is issuing instructions direct to Gärtner, which we know he does from the telephone intercepts, then that links Vandenhove and GFB, doesn't it?"

"Not really — it only shows a link between Vandenhove and Gärtner."

"Shit!" Joanna looked at the stars for a while. "But the telephone intercepts show that a crime is in progress — therefore we can officially get the hard drive from his office computer."

"If we do that, he might just do a runner. At the moment he knows we're looking and he also knows we haven't enough to arrest him, but if we show our hand then…"

"Okay. So we snatch the hard drive."

"Why do we need it?"

"Because that's the one he uses for his communications to GFB. We can't get at their email file without getting caught, so we need his original hard drive to do a forensic examination and recover the erased data."

"Can't you just make a copy of the disk?" Luc frowned.

"No. That would just give us the current files; we need all the files that have been deleted from it and for that we need the original disk.

"Surely it will have been overwritten by now."

"He has a standard forty-gigabyte hard disk so it's unlikely. But in any case, unless he has security software to shred the files by multiple overwriting with random data, we can look back through the last three or four erasures even if overwritten."

"You can do that?"

"Yes, and there are specialists we use sometimes who can help. And I think he'll have an email program on his machine linking through to a personal address somewhere and we need that as well."

Luc considered the situation. It was risky but no more so than anything else in this operation. It would take twenty-four to thirty-six hours to set up and would have to be carried out by Joanna with Bart Jongen to assist.

"He'll catch on if we keep the disk."

"Luc, we copy the disk *in situ* if we have time, then put the duplicate back in his machine. He'll never know the difference."

Monday 28 April, Brussels

Just before leaving the lift, Joanna made a final check on the audio bugs and decided Vandenhove's office was empty. She and Bart were dressed as maintenance personnel, confident that their baseball caps should be sufficient to avoid recognition by the security camera in the corridor itself. According to the security register, the *Chef de Cabinet* had left the building at six o'clock and his staff shortly after that. It was now eight o'clock and the building was quiet.

They entered the office. Bart immediately took a hard drive from his bag and quickly connected it to the desktop computer on Vandenhove's desk.

"Remember there's a Trojan running." Joanna said quietly and Bart nodded.

The link stabilised and Joanna watched as Bart entered the necessary commands. The plan was to copy the entire contents of the computer to a new hard disk then strip out the original and replace it with the new one. The operation would probably take forty minutes or more to make the copy and a further twenty for the swap so they might need an hour and a bit. There was no way they could be up there for that long without a security check but Joanna had already thought of that and had forced Vandenhove's machine to log a malfunction requiring a maintenance team to be in the office.

As Bart worked on the computer, Joanna hacked the Commission's email system from the secretary's machine in the outer office. If Vandenhove had used his Commission email address for any private communications, she wanted to know. But a forty-minute search through the files revealed nothing. Vandenhove simply had not used the Commission system for his private affairs and probably knew that all emails would be kept.

She went back through to Vandenhove's office just as Bart disconnected the two machines and started to exchange the disks. Her mobile vibrated.

"Vandenhove is on the move," said Dirk from the Farm. "And he's heading your way."

"Anything else?"

"According to the bug, he wants some report from his office safe."

"Shit! Where is he now?"

"About ten minutes away," came Dirk's reply.

"Let me know when he gets here. Where's Luc?"

"In the car as planned. I've already told him the situation."

Bart had the computer cover off and the hard disk was safely in the bag. He slid the duplicate hard disk into place and made the connections. Joanna was getting impatient it was going to be very close. The computer started up without a hitch.

Joanna's mobile vibrated again.

"Vandenhove has just entered the building."

They were out of time. Bart had everything back in place and was ready to leave. Joanna went through to the outer office and looked out into the corridor. It was clear but she could hear the lift at the far end. She turned to Bart and thrust the bag into his arms.

"Do you know a way out without going through the security zone?" she whispered.

"Yes. The fire stairs across the corridor go to the basement."

"Okay. You first and whatever happens, keep going. We have to get that hard disk to Dirk." Bart looked as though he was about say something. "Don't argue, just do it."

She looked out of the door again. The lift doors were opening.

"Go." She hissed. Bart stepped across to the fire stairs. Joanna followed but, as the door closed behind her, she heard running feet and shouted commands. She was halfway down the first flight when her damaged knee gave way and she fell.

"What happened? Where's Jo?" Luc demanded as Bart scrambled into the car.

"I'm sorry Luc, there was nothing I could do. She ordered me out."

"What happened, Bart?"

"We were just leaving when Vandenhove and a security guard arrived. We couldn't use the corridor so we went for the fire stairs. Luc, there was nothing I could do."

Luc forced himself to calm down. The young man was a technician not an operative. "Tell me what happened."

"Jo fell. I was three flights down when the guard got to her. I stayed where I was in case they heard me but Jo got him talking. It went quiet so I went back up the stairs and saw Jo entering the lift with the guard and Vandenhove. Then I went down to the basement."

"It's all right, Bart. Then what?"

"I saw Jo and Vandenhove being driven away in a silver Mercedes 300 with tinted windows."

"Yes, I saw it. You did well in the circumstances."

Luc thumbed his radio "Dirk, Jo's in a car with Vandenhove. Where are they now?"

"Heading north towards the airport."

"*Merde*!" What the fuck was going on? Why the hell did she get into that car?

"Has she called in?" It was an off chance.

"No."

"Perhaps she doesn't want them to know she has a mobile with her," Bart said.

Luc nodded. It was as good an explanation as any. He needed more information. Unless she had been recognised or given herself away, it seemed unlikely that Jo had been snatched, but what other logical explanation was there?

The radio crackled and Dirk said, "The car has just joined the Antwerp motorway. They don't seem in any hurry."

"Did it stop anywhere?"

"No. Vandenhove has made a call to Groupe Franco Belge, but we couldn't hear what was said."

Bert went on, "If that Merc is Vandenhove's usual car then he's got something in there that makes radio signals break up — we've had issues with that before. We can follow the GPS signal which is what Dirk will be doing with Jo but we can't listen to the bug."

Luc thumbed the radio.

"Dirk, tell Benoît to meet me at the service area south of Antwerp and to bring some kit. And tell him to hurry."

Luc was leaning against the car smoking when Benoît powered up to the service area in a Land Cruiser 4x4.

Benoit jumped out and spoke cheerfully, "Hi, Luc, ready for action then?"

Luc said nothing but looked grim.

"Oh, come on, *mon ami*, if we know where she is then we can get her back and the sooner we start the better. So let's get our collective arses in gear. Okay?"

Luc said, "I think they're heading for the GFB offices near the docks."

"Well, Luc my friend, I've not been idle." He opened the rear door of the 4x4 revealing two piles of assault equipment.

Luc nodded approvingly. "Good man." He slipped on a shoulder holster, selected a Glock 17, chambered a round and settled the pistol comfortably under his jacket.

Benoit added, "I've sent Gregor off to watch Vandenhove's house. He's got all his favourite toys and is itching to use them but he'll need assistance. And I've rousted the others out of bed and told them to be ready at fifteen minutes notice." He clapped Luc on the shoulder. "We'll get her back in one piece."

Luc smiled his thanks. He turned to Bart as the younger man approached, "What tracking devices have you got on Jo?"

"The phone's got a GPS locator in it, she's got another in her watch, a tiny one with a range of about half a kilometre in her earring and we can tell them apart."

"And we track them with this?" Luc tapped on his battlefield computer.

"Already set up and running. I modified the battlefield radios you guys use so you can track them as well. It's not a hundred percent reliable because of the different technologies involved but the only one we might lose is Vandenhove."

"You've done well, thank you."

"She's our friend too, Luc," said the young man quietly.

"I know, Bart. I'm sorry." He pointed at the car. "You get that hard disk to Dirk. It may contain something useful for us on this as well."

"Will do."

"All right, let's go."

At the Groupe Franco Belge headquarters, two guards escorted Joanna to the security office and left her there, locking the door behind them. She tried the door, but only out of curiosity. The room was under surveillance from a rather obvious closed-circuit television camera.

They would expect her to protest, so she tried the door again, banged on it a few times and shouted. Then she sat down hunched over the table feigning despair. There was no need to text Luc — he would be tracking her and it would be better to hide the fact she had the mobile. She discreetly checked to see if it was safely in the special inside pocket of her trousers. It would be safe there unless they did a strip search.

She thought back to the moment the security guard had shouted at her to stop. She had done so but only because her knee had given way. She replayed the scenes in her mind. Something had gone wrong and she needed to know what it was.

"Who are you and what are you doing on this floor." The guard asked as he came down the stairs.

"Christine Dickinson of JDB Systems. I was sent over to fix a computer in the office over there." She pointed to Vandenhove's office.

"Your security pass, please." The guard's attitude was perfectly normal. She handed over the pass and the 'order for work' docket.

The guard studied the documents and handed them back.

Just as Joanna thought she had got away with it, Vandenhove came out of his office and demanded to know who she was and why she was there. Joanna repeated her story and showed her pass and docket.

Vandenhove studied the documents and then said, "Take her to the main security office, this needs to be verified."

"Why?" demanded Joanna.

"Because I didn't report any malfunction."

"It was automatic. You don't have to report it; the system does it for you." At least this much was true.

"Then it'll be on the maintenance register in the security office, won't it? If it is then everything will be okay." Vandenhove turned to the guard. "Take her downstairs please."

The security guard shrugged and looked at Joanna apologetically. She limped down the corridor towards the lift with the guard and Vandenhove behind her.

They entered the main security office in the basement.

The duty security chief, a thin-faced man with dandruff on his collar and a small piece of tissue on a shaving nick, looked up from his newspaper. "What's the problem?"

"We'd like to check the computer maintenance register please," said Vandenhove. He placed the security pass and work docket on the desk. "I'd like to know if and when this work was requested."

The security chief accessed the computer file and swivelled the monitor round so that Vandenhove could see it. There, exactly as Joanna had planned, was the entry requesting the work.

Vandenhove turned to Joanna and said, "Why was it assigned to JDB Systems? According to this they're not on-call today."

She shrugged. "I guess the on-call team were busy. We get called when they're busy." At least, thought Joanna, that's what the records would show.

At a signal from the security chief, the guard left the office. Joanna watched him walk away. Her skin prickled and she recognised that something had subtly changed in the dynamics of the situation.

A silver-coloured Mercedes drew up and a uniformed driver got out.

"Please come with us, Miss Dickinson." Vandenhove was indicating the car.

"Why should I…everything's in order?"

"Get in the car."

"No fucking way. I was only doing the job assigned to me." She felt her heart rate go up and a tightness in her chest.

She turned to the security chief. "What's going on, man?"

The security chief merely smiled and said nothing.

Joanna knew she was trapped but made for the door anyway despite the pain in her knee.

The driver grabbed her, forced her into the back of the car, slammed the door and then got in behind the steering wheel. Vandenhove sat in the front and the car immediately pulled away.

Joanna hammered on the tinted glass of the window and tried the door handle but the door was locked.

"Let me out of here," she demanded.

The two men in the front ignored her.

As the car reached the ramp, she had a brief glimpse of Bart Jongen as he headed for the emergency exit.

They drove to Antwerp in silence.

As she considered the situation, Joanna returned again to the scene in the security office and reached two unpleasant conclusions: firstly, the duty security chief had obviously been bought and paid for, and secondly, Vandenhove must have known that JDB Systems was a DER cover operation. And the only way he could have known that was if Claudia Chalon had told him.

Shit happens, she thought.

Luc and Benoît entered Antwerp from the south. Luc had the battlefield computer open, monitoring Joanna's location, while Benoît drove.

During the short journey, Luc had considered the situation carefully and knew that if there had been more time, he could have used a Belgian Gendarmerie SWAT team to rescue Joanna. It was not an option now and he would have to rely on his own resources. And those resources were now stretched with the number of targets being watched in this operation. Of the six operational members of his team, two were on standby at the Farm, Gregor was watching Vandenhove, Jo had been snatched, and that left Benny and himself. It was a small group for what had to be done.

"Who do we know who could work with Gregor?" Luc asked.

"We could try Geert Verhaegen — he knew Gregor from Djibouti," replied Benoît.

"I thought he'd gone mercenary."

"Out of necessity. I've used him on some freelance protection work recently. This isn't the sort of thing he'd normally do but he might be willing."

"Where do we find him?"

"There's a café near the old docks."

The centre of Antwerp was quiet as they swung west and entered the old harbour district. Benoît parked the Land Cruiser and entered a brightly painted café. After a few moments, he motioned Luc to join him.

"They say that Geert's in a bar just round the corner."

They approached the bar openly. This area of Antwerp was being renovated and although the buildings were old, the area had a vibrant feeling to it. The bar itself was 'old Antwerp', dark, quiet, with men in small groups around tables minding their own business. Luc had been in many such bars, both as a Legionnaire and DER officer. They could be dangerous places for the unwary, especially in the late evening.

Benoît moved purposefully towards a lone man leaning against the bar. Luc could see that he was both very tall and built like a weightlifter.

He watched Benoît make contact while the others present looked on suspiciously.

After a short exchange Benoit swivelled his head, inviting Luc to join them.

The big man greeted him in a neutral tone of voice. "Benny tells me you want help."

"One of our people was snatched and we want her back."

"And?"

"This took place just two hours ago in Brussels."

"So why are you in Antwerp?"

"Because we know she was brought here to the offices of a company near the docks." The big man downed the second half of a large beer in one draught. Luc rotated his hand to the barman to request another.

"Either you move fast or you have some serious toys."

"Mainly useful toys."

"You were Legion, yes?" The three men drank in silence and the rest of the bar lost interest.

Luc finished his drink and put the glass down. "Do you know if there has been any recruiting going on recently?" It obviously wouldn't do to rush this man and he was deep in thought. He pushed his personal thoughts aside and focused on Verhaegen.

"I heard that some bastard was recruiting down by the docks a month or so ago. He didn't get any takers from the real pros but some of the others might have. Didn't hear what the job was. All I know was that it was not real work." Luc understood that this meant fighting a war.

"Any idea where I might look?"

Verhaegen scrawled an address on a beer mat and slid it across to Luc. "This is where they train, if you can call it that… out towards St Niklaas in the middle of fucking nowhere."

Luc pocketed the mat and ordered more beer.

"Do you need some help? Benny tells me this isn't a *private* enterprise."

"Not private but very deniable."

"Who for?"

"The DER."

"Who the fuck is that?" The big man looked at Luc hard in the eye.

"The people Benny and I work for." Luc explained quietly.

The big man looked back and forth between the two DER men. "Have you got something for me?"

"Yes. I have another old friend, Gregor Szabo, and he needs a partner for this op."

The big man reached across quickly and seized Luc by the right wrist. Luc stiffened but did not resist. The man pushed up Luc's sleeve, saw the tattoo and released him.

"2nd REP. Thought I recognised you. Rwanda 1994. You're Luc Hansen, the one that put away that fucking German rapist…what was his name?"

"Gärtner"

"That's the bastard…they called him the Angel of Death. He's the one who was recruiting among the mercs."

Luc nodded and said nothing.

"Has he got your man?"

"Probably," said Luc. And if he has, we're in deep shit, he thought.

"If Benny and Gregor are still with you then you must be all right. I'm in." Verhaegen finished his drink and stood up.

The clock on the wall showed midnight when Joanna heard voices and the door opened to admit two men in combat fatigues.

"Stand up." The order was given quietly by the first man to enter.

Joanna obeyed. Her knee was stiff but the pain had gone and it took her weight.

"Hands against the wall."

"What for?"

"Just do it."

"Who the hell are you?" She put her hands on her hips and stared at the two men.

"Lady, just do as you're fucking told, will you. It'll be a lot easier for you."

Joanna turned and faced the wall. She placed her hands against it as directed and waited for the search to begin.

It was not a particularly good search, more a pat down. They did not find the telephone in the waistband of her trousers. Fucking amateurs, she thought.

The men went through her bum bag, apparently finding nothing of interest and then checked her jacket, which she had left on the table.

"Come on."

"Where to?"

"Just shut up and come with us."

Joanna followed the men out of the office and down a corridor. A door was thrust open and Joanna saw a large white

Renault van standing in the middle of a garage with its engine running, ringed by four men in combat fatigues.

One of her escorts pulled her arms behind her and she struggled but he was too strong. She felt plastic handcuffs around her wrists.

A hood was placed over her head. She fought down panic and maintained concentration.

"Shove her in the van and let's get moving." It was the first man from the office and despite changing from French to Flemish, Joanna understood.

Hands assisted her and she was made to sit.

The second voice asked, "What are we supposed to do with her?"

"Gärtner wants her down at the training centre."

Joanna's throat tightened. "Maintain concentration," she thought to herself, but it wasn't easy to keep terror at bay.

The doors slammed shut and the van moved off.

At a signal from Verhaegen, Benoît stopped the Land Cruiser. Luc could just make out the farm in the weak moonlight. "Is that it?"

Verhaegen nodded.

Luc checked the battlefield computer but there was no sign of any of Joanna's GPS signals within forty kilometres. *Merde!* As they left Antwerp, the computer had shown that Joanna was on the move and he had made a critical decision: to let Dirk track Joanna while he checked out the mercenary base.

He called Dirk.

"Where is Jo now?"

"Heading south towards Brussels. We have a good clear signal."

"And Vandenhove?"

"He's at his house with Chalon. Gregor reported a positive visual of them both about thirty minutes ago."

Luc looked across at the farm. There were no lights and no sign of activity.

Verhaegen spoke, "Got any weapons in the car?"

"Of course," Luc replied calmly.

"What?"

"M16A2s and Glock 17s with silencers."

The big man whistled, "Serious stuff."

Benoît put the car in motion and slowly drove up the approach road to the farm. They could see tracks in the road suggesting that at least two vehicles had been there recently. They visually scanned the outbuildings — all appeared empty.

They got out and Luc approached the main house to carry out a quick recognisance. Benoît and Verhaegen circled around the back. Luc hit the glass of the window sharply with his flashlight and then picked out the broken shards. He opened the window and climbed in.

The rooms at the back were empty except for discarded beer bottles. The front room contained ammunition boxes casually thrown in a corner and a gun magazine on the table along with a recent, partially eaten sandwich.

"Looking at what's here, and what I've just found outside, I'd say they were testing weapons." Verhaegen dumped cartridge cases on the table. "7.62 x 39 mm and 9 mm shorts, probably AK-47s and 9 mm pistols. The usual favourites for this lot."

"And quite recently," Luc poked the sandwich.

Luc checked his watch. "Right, let's get on the road. I think we're about an hour behind them."

CHAPTER SIXTEEN

Tuesday 29 April, Wallonia, south of Brussels

In the back of the van, Joanna was sitting on what felt like an ammunition box and the men had given her a couple of blankets for padding. But with her hands bound behind her it was impossible to get comfortable.

After a while, her hood was removed and she saw that a canvas shielded the driver and another covered the rear windows. Sharing the back of the van with her were two of the four extra men and she could hear two others in front. She supposed that the rest were in a second vehicle.

She sensed that they were not travelling fast and the men didn't talk much. The oldest of the men silently offered Joanna a bottle of mineral water and some chocolate.

She nodded at the water. He unscrewed the top and held it for her to drink.

It was cold in the van but the pre-dawn light was filtering into the back when Joanna felt the vehicle slow and turn.

The road was still smooth enough but there were more corners and she began to feel slightly car-sick. She asked for more water.

The van rocked violently and she realised that they were on some sort of farm road. Perhaps they were at the end of the journey. She hoped so, as she desperately needed to pee. The van stopped and the rear doors opened. The older man got out indicating she should follow.

She climbed stiffly out of the van and was walked to an ivy-covered farmhouse. She looked around in the half-light and realised they were in an enclosed yard with a second van parked in front of the house. The man hurried her inside.

They climbed a wide staircase and then, on the first landing, the man opened a door and switched on a light. It was a bathroom. He indicated she should enter.

"Undo my hands, please," she said turning her back.

The handcuffs were cut free with a switchblade knife.

"Thank you." She smiled, trying to establish contact with the man.

She used the facilities gratefully and felt better. She tapped on the door and her jailer led her next door to a bedroom. In the corner was a bed with blankets folded neatly on the pillow. There was nothing else. Even the light did not work. She tried the window. It did not open. She looked out on the courtyard where the men were unloading the vans.

The door opened and her jailer returned, inserted a light bulb and tried the switch. It worked. He had also brought some food: a baguette, cheese, some ham, an apple and a new bottle of water. It was not much but she welcomed it.

As she ate she remembered Luc saying that food was a weapon, just as sleep was a weapon. Both helped to calm the nerves and prepare the body for action. She knew she was scared — that was to be expected. But it could also be used as a survival tool as it kept you alert.

She listened to the sounds in the building. Everyone seemed to be downstairs. There was a lot of talking but the distance and the construction of the building made it difficult for her to make out the words. She sat down with her back to the door and studied the room looking for microphones or video cameras.

Satisfied that she was not under surveillance, she took out her phone. She could not risk making a call in case they heard but she might be able to send a text message if she was quick. She looked at the screen and saw the 'message waiting' icon blinking. She listened at the door. No one. She pressed 'read'.

IMPORTANT DON'T CALL OR SMS UNLESS
V IMPORTANT. I'M TRACKING YOU. LUC EN
ROUTE WITH TEAM, ETA NIGHTFALL. DIRK.

She pressed reply:

UNDERSTOOD – NO SIGN OF G, V, OR C – YET!

She signed it with her hacker code name and clicked on send. At least they would know that it really was her and that she was okay.

She put the phone back in her waistband pocket and moved away from the door. She lay down on the bed, wrapped herself in the blankets and fell asleep.

She woke less than three hours later when the man who seemed to be her principal jailer opened the door and asked if she wanted to use the bathroom. Suddenly conscious of her need, she got off the bed and picked up her bum bag.

"Why do you need that?" the man asked suspiciously.

"Girl things." She opened the bag and pulled out a tampon. She felt pleased with herself when the man nodded in embarrassment and let her out. He waited while she used the toilet and washed herself as best she could and then he locked her back in the bedroom.

She finished the rest of the food and drank some water. The fatigue-driven, bitter taste in her mouth and throat eased. She stretched and crossed to the door. An eerie silence greeted her. She went back to the window. It was secured with a basic security lock. She found a safety pin in her bag and tried to pick the lock but it would not yield. It was the same with the door. Shit!

Her jailer brought her a ham baguette and some more water for lunch and allowed her to use the bathroom again, but no one else came near her. The view from the window was not very exciting but at least it eased the boredom and the feeling of claustrophobia. By early afternoon, the sun was just entering the window and she dozed in the warmth.

The sound of a car instantly woke her and she peered into the courtyard. The figure of Gärtner brought a rush of fear and she felt light headed. She sat down quickly, took a few deep breaths and refocused.

Sounds on the stairs.

The door opened and her jailer walked in. "Come with me."

She was shown into a large, sparsely furnished room and found herself alone with the man who had twice tried to kill her.

But Gärtner looked at her without recognition and without emotion.

"Who are you and why are you holding me?"

Gärtner said nothing, merely looking at her from across the room.

Finding herself unable to meet his eyes, Joanna looked round. At one end there was an open-plan kitchenette, while at the other was a conference table and four chairs. The rest of the room was empty except for a group of armchairs near the window.

"Why were you in Mr Vandenhove's office at the Commission?"

"Because his computer registered a fault. I work with the IT maintenance team and was sent to fix it." She spoke confidently trying to sense if he had identified her.

"Mr Vandenhove says he had not reported any fault."

"He doesn't have to. A system check is run every night to identify which machines need attention."

"And why you?"

"Because I'm a software engineer."

"Why didn't they call the duty software technician? You were not listed as being on duty."

"How should I know? Maybe he was engaged elsewhere."

Gärtner continued to look at her steadily. "And what is JDB Systems?"

So he had checked, thought Joanna. Stick to the cover story because it is the truth.

"A systems engineering consultancy in Leuven."

"And what is your connection with the DER?"

"Who?" Joanna's voice cracked. She couldn't prevent it.

"The DER is one of the Commission's security organisations."

"Never heard of them." She regained her confidence. "Why am I being held and who are you?"

Gärtner ignored the question.

"We know JDB Systems is an undercover operation for the DER, so don't lie to me."

"I don't know what you're talking about. I'm just the technician who…"

"Don't waste my fucking time," snarled Gärtner. "You work for the DER. Now, what were you doing in Vandenhove's office?"

"I told you, fixing a computer fault."

"Where is Luc Hansen?"

"Who?" She stared back at Gärtner, willing him to believe she did not know.

Gärtner turned on his heel and walked from the room.

Joanna heard the key turn in the lock and let out a deep breath. Jeezus, but that was close. He did not appear to know her real name and had not recognised her, which was not entirely surprising since the only time he had seen her face to face it had been almost dark. As long as he did not know who she was there was a chance of survival.

She tried the door and checked the windows but there was no escape that way.

Then she shivered. What if they bring in Claudia Chalon? One glance and she would surely tell Gärtner everything and that would be it. She fought to remain calm. Luc always said that keeping a steady grip on oneself and dealing with events as they happened was the key. She needed to get a message to Luc. She looked round the room and quickly located a discreet CCTV camera. Damn! That buggers that!

The sun had dropped to the tree line beyond the river when Joanna heard another vehicle arrive and she quickly identified the occupants as Chalon and Vandenhove. There were angry voices on the stairs and then the door opened.

"Hello, Jo." Chalon stepped into the room followed by Gärtner. "She works for the DER. You've kidnapped Joanna Donnelly and that means all hell is about…" Gärtner brushed her aside, stared at Joanna and walked out. Chalon looked pityingly at Joanna.

"You're in trouble now, Jo," she said casually over her shoulder as she left.

Joanna felt sick and rushed to the kitchenette at the end of the conference room where she threw up in the sink. She was failing to control her fear, adding to the danger. With a powerful effort of will, she forced the fear back through the cracks. Where the hell was Luc?

With no chance of using the GSM to find out what was happening, she was on her own but Luc clearly had a plan, so what was it? She considered the possibilities. Since he would know exactly where she was, but not the location of Gärtner, the most obvious strategy for him was to track Chalon and Vandenhove and hope they led him to the German. The outstanding question was whether she was now live bait or about to become collateral damage.

It was close to midnight when Gärtner returned to the room with Vandenhove and Chalon. Another man came in behind them. Joanna focused on Gärtner — that's where the danger lay.

He attached handcuffs to her wrists, pulled her to her feet and dragged her to the upright chair next to the table.

"Where's Hansen?"

"I don't know."

"You're lying," Gärtner shouted, hitting Joanna across the side of her face with the flat of his hand. She fell to the floor and was pulled roughly to her feet and slammed into the chair.

"Where is he?" Gärtner demanded but Joanna said nothing.

He hit her again.

"Answer my question."

He hit her again.

With each blow, Joanna felt her resolve harden. She would hold out. She would survive.

Gärtner turned to the man who had acted as Joanna's jailer.

"Has the bitch been searched?"

"We did a quick search in Antwerp?"

"Then we'd better do a proper one. Now get out."

Gärtner reached down, grabbed Joanna's top and ripped it open revealing the injuries from the road accident. He took out a large knife, sliced away her bra and proceeded to search both garments. Joanna's brain was still working despite the fear and knowing what was to happen next.

Vandenhove started to protest but a glare from the irate German silenced him. Chalon merely shrugged and moved to the window.

The knife sliced through her belt and she felt her trousers being tugged down. Gärtner found the phone and threw it on the table.

Still he was not satisfied. He ripped off her panties, conducted a quick but through body search and removed her watch. He sliced open the strap to reveal the GPS tracker. He pushed her back onto the chair.

"Give me your watch," he said, turning to Chalon.

"What the fuck for," she replied.

"What the hell is wrong with you, Gärtner," demanded Vandenhove.

"Because those bastards will have planted bugs to track you when they let you go. Now give me your watch or I'll…"

Chalon handed him the watch and moments later the GPS tracker lay in the palm of his hand.

Chalon looked down at Joanna in cold hatred but Gärtner simply looked thoughtful. Then he placed the tip of his knife against Joanna's throat.

"And what have you done to track Mr Vandenhove?"

Joanna knew lying was no longer an option, so she told him about the modifications to Vandenhove's mobile telephone. The fat Belgian listened with a growing look of horror. He pulled out his mobile, handed it without a word to Gärtner who dropped it on the ground and smashed it with his heel.

Gärtner jerked Joanna to her feet. "I think you'd better tell us what your friend Hansen is planning."

"I don't know."

The blow caught her across the mouth and she tasted fresh blood. Tears welled up in her eyes and she felt the tip of the knife against her left breast.

"Leave her alone, Gärtner," said Chalon unexpectedly. "I'll tell you what Luc will do." She smiled scornfully at the German. "He's not like you: a typical ex-soldier boy, all action and no brains. He'll be on his way here with a bunch of ex-Legionnaires and they're seriously good. He's not coming to arrest us — he's coming to kill us. We should get out of here."

"Let him come," snarled the German.

"Oh, for god's sake, man, don't be a complete fool. This isn't about you, it's about all of us. He knows that we're all here and, thanks to you and your stupidity, we're in a trap. We need the girl as insurance — she's our only way out."

"Nobody's leaving. Understand? Now, fuck off, I have something to finish here."

"If you kill her, Gärtner, I will personally blow your fucking brains out. *Verstehen Sie?*" Chalon locked eyes with the German and left. Vandenhove started to follow her when Gärtner spoke.

"You'd better stay, Mr Vandenhove. With your interests, you'll want to be part of this."

Gärtner lifted Joanna off her feet. She squirmed and then felt the knife between her legs. She froze in terror. Vandenhove came up to her, his eyes shining in anticipation. He seemed to know what was expected. He grabbed her wrists, pulled her round and across the table. She struggled but it was useless. She looked helplessly into his face as she felt hands on her bottom and then between her legs. She screamed.

CHAPTER SEVENTEEN

Wednesday 30 April, Wallonia

At 5.45 a.m., the first grey light of dawn touched the sky behind the hill, picking out the brooding shape of the farm with its thinning shroud of mist. The brown brick wall of the barn was unrelieved by any windows or doors and the grey tile roof glistened darkly as the sun's rays picked up the droplets of moisture left by the retreating mist. A man appeared by the front gate.

High on the hill, Luc Hansen shifted his position slightly, focused the binoculars and studied the new arrival. The man had a powerful build and carried a Kalashnikov AK-47 assault rifle. Jackpot!

"Not your average farmer, hey, Luc?" murmured Benoît from beside him.

Their camouflage fatigues and carefully positioned netting hid both men from prying eyes. Luc sub-vocalised through his throat microphone.

"Blue Leader to Red Leader, what have you got?"

"One by the river with a '47," reported Gregor.

"Red Two?"

"One with a '47 at main entrance, one of the Antwerp crowd." The contempt in Verhaegen's voice was evident.

"Green Leader, what have you got?"

"Lights on the ground floor main room facing the river, two men visible."

"Green Two?"

"There's a rear entrance close to the house, it's open, nothing visible."

"There has to be at least one guard on this side." Benoît whispered.

"Agreed. So far we know of four men for certain but the evidence suggests there must be at least eight down there and there could be more."

"You want that I take a look?" asked Benoît.

Luc nodded. "Be very careful. I don't want them to know we're here."

Benoît crawled away and Luc returned to his observation of the buildings below him.

He and Benoît had arrived at the farm at just before 7 p.m. the previous evening having followed Chalon and Vandenhove from Brussels, but there was no way they could launch an assault on the farm with just the two of them, especially as they had no idea about the strength of the opposition. A major accident on the autoroute had delayed the arrival of his men and it was nearly midnight before Gregor, Verhaegen and the other two members of the team had arrived.

Luc had immediately split the group into three sections and briefed them as best he could. His computer told him that Joanna was in the house on the first floor and that Vandenhove and Chalon were also there. He had to assume that Gärtner was at the house as well but they needed proof before they went in.

Just after midnight, he lost all the main GPS signals. Dirk had confirmed that the transmitters in Joanna's phone and wristwatch were inoperative, and that those on Chalon and Vandenhove had also died. Luc had then searched for and found the weak signal from the tiny transmitter in Joanna's ear-stud. With an accuracy of within six metres horizontally and one metre in altitude, the GPS data suggested that the ear-stud was on the first floor to the rear of the main house.

"Green Leader to Blue Leader. The bastard is here."

"Green Leader, say again."

"Gärtner is here, positive visual ID, lawn leading down to the river. He's armed with a 9 mm automatic."

"Roger that, Green Leader," replied Luc

Now the trap could be sprung.

Joanna woke from a troubled sleep as the strengthening dawn light touched her face. She hurt but the pain was bearable…just. She felt between her legs, there was no blood. God she hurt! She cradled herself and rocked back and forth for a while, willing the pain to subside. The rape by Gärtner and then by that fat bastard had been brutal and humiliating. They had hurt her.

Anger welled up. I'll kill the bastards.

She located her trousers. With her wrists handcuffed together, it was not easy but she laboriously dressed as best she could. She looked round for her bag. There were tissues in there and she needed them.

She saw the bag in a corner and started towards it when the door opened and Chalon came in.

"Going somewhere, Jo?"

"Fuck off."

"Now that's not very polite especially as I've brought you some breakfast. After all that sexual excitement you're probably hungry." Chalon put the tray down on the table, undid Joanna's handcuffs and started to leave.

"Why did you do it, Claudia?" asked Joanna.

"Do what?" asked Chalon turning.

"Cross the line and change sides."

"Oh that. That was years ago. Money, mainly," she shrugged.

"And getting fucked by Vandenhove. You suck, lady."

"At least I don't get raped," replied Chalon, turning away.

"Why is that psychopath still holding me?"

"Oh, it's not you he wants, you're just bait. It's Luc he wants. It's payoff time."

"You won't get away with it, Claudia. Luc will track you down."

"If he survives, possibly, but Gärtner's going to kill him." Chalon smiled and walked out, carefully locking the door behind her.

Joanna looked at her watch; it was just a little after six o'clock. She was desperate for a pee. She headed for the kitchenette. She did just manage to get her trousers down and hitch herself up onto the sink. She sat there for some time and then carefully washed. She felt dirty.

Five hundred metres away, Luc watched a blue Audi drive away from the farm. A few minutes earlier, Gregor had seen the car leave through the main gate. He had taken some quick pictures of the driver and registration and had sent them direct to Brussels. If Vandenhove was running they could pick him up later.

Benoît slid silently under the netting.

"The transmitter on Jo is still active and moving so it looks like she's still alive," said Luc.

"Well then that makes getting wet and dirty worthwhile." Benoît grinned. "I've found two of the bastards. One is two-fifty metres to the left and about a hundred below us, covering the approach to the far end of the complex. Green Two could take him out easily — the idiot isn't even under cover. The other one is about a hundred metres to our right and one-fifty down the hill. He's about seventy-five metres from the farm and very well hidden, but he smokes."

"Well done. We don't want to alert the others so you'll have to take the one to the left. I'll take the other. We'll need a distraction across the river 'cos we've about thirty metres of open ground to cover to reach the wall."

"Red Two to Blue Leader."

"Go ahead Red Two," Luc responded.

"We have one man on the road and one by the main gate and Red Leader reports one in the barn our end."

"Roger that, Red Two." Luc considered the possibilities for a moment and made a decision.

In the end, it was the scent of a cigarette on the light morning air that gave the man away. Luc dropped to a crouch and studied the woods in front of him. Yes, there he was fifty metres down and to the right, very well camouflaged. It was going to be a long crawl. Luc started to circle round and down.

His target suspected nothing until a fraction of a second before sinking into oblivion. Luc extracted a length of steel wire, a clip lock, some handcuffs and a roll of duct tape from his rucksack. Luc positioned the man with his back to a tree, hands cuffed behind him and the wire around the tree. The duct tape made an effective gag.

He sub-vocalized. "One down but I've still about seventy-five metres to go."

"I can see the other guy but it's still some way. I'll need another ten minutes."

The woods stopped about thirty metres from the wall of the farm leaving a clear line of fire if anyone was there. He carefully considered the layout. The farm wall was all brick and had no windows or vent holes. The roof was tiled but the wall was too high to climb. He was going to have to find another way in.

The sound of a shot shattered the silence, and rooks and pigeons clattered from their roosts to take flight. Luc dropped to the ground instinctively then cautiously examined his surroundings. The sound had been wrong for the weapons Gärtner's men had. It had been, quite definitely, a shotgun. A second shot rang out. It was away from the building and closer to the river. Again it was a shotgun, and again birds took off in a startled and noisy mass. Luc crawled towards the source of the sound and saw a farm labourer, armed with a shotgun and carrying two rabbits. A curly-coated spaniel scampered in front of him hunting up more quarry. The man moved off and Luc relaxed. His radio earpiece clicked.

"Hill secure. Who got shot?" Benoît asked calmly.

"Two rabbits."

"Green Leader to Blue Leader. We're across the river and heading towards Blue Two's position. We can make the side door without being seen."

"Roger that, Green Leader. Blue team will go in via the main gate when Red team have taken out the guards."

"Red Leader to Blue Leader, what do you mean 'when'?"

It was nice to work with professionals.

The shot brought Joanna to the window but she could see nothing in the courtyard. Wait. Yes, someone was coming out of the house. She watched as the man checked his weapon and headed towards the gatehouse.

Benoît joined Luc and the two ran quickly across the open space and then worked their way along the wall. The farm was still very quiet despite the gunshot. Luc peered around the corner of the building.

A man with a Kalashnikov AK-47 slung across his shoulders stepped through the gateway and stood watching the road. Luc observed the target and hoped that Red team were close. A Long-Legged Buzzard called sharply. It was a bird not found in Belgium but common enough in North Africa. Red team were in position.

Luc sub-vocalised the signal to move, stepped round the corner and came up behind the unsuspecting guard. He clubbed the man hard behind the ear and caught him as he slid to the ground. He stepped over the prostrate body, entered the courtyard with Benoît and dropped behind a parked car.

From the cover of the vehicle he examined the main building and caught a glimpse of a face surrounded by short black hair peering from an upstairs window. Good, Jo was still all right. He looked again and realised that she could see him and was making signs…yes, but what? He watched, then realised she was indicating that the door was to the right of the gate. She was holding up ten fingers and making walking signs. Good girl.

He turned his attention to the downstairs: there was no one visible. The ten paces indicated by Joanna were only about six metres and he was inside the building. There was nobody on the ground floor. He located the stairs to the upper level and started to inch his way upwards. The lookout was standing by the open window of a training room, smoking a cigarette and watching the road.

Luc was still three steps from the top when the man turned and saw him. At first, he did not move and then he reached for his gun. Luc shot him in the thigh.

Luc flung himself up the stairs. The man was reaching for his gun again when he saw the silenced Glock 17 levelled at his head. Slowly, he lowered the gun to the floor and raised his hands. Luc bound and gagged him and attached the handcuffs to the radiator. He quickly bandaged the man's leg. It was time to move.

The sharp sound of a Kalashnikov shattered the silence. From his position just inside the kitchen of the main house, Luc heard Gärtner curse loudly. He readied himself for the shot.

"Get the girl," Gärtner shouted from somewhere at the back of the house.

Claudia Chalon, carrying a 9 mm automatic, entered the hall through a door opposite to where Luc was concealed.

He watched her dispassionately, assessing her tactics. She was a good shot, but from what he knew of her combat skills, something all DER operatives had to practise, usually under Luc's command, she had a tendency to be too tense and likely to shoot without properly identifying her target. That gave him an advantage. He would take her out first. A firefight erupted in the courtyard as Gärtner's men targeted the DER men.

Luc ignored the distraction. Chalon would eventually have to climb the stairs and that's when he'd take her.

He watched her cross the hall. She had not checked for intruders — a tactical error that would cost her. She approached the stairs cautiously. He could take her out easily but they wanted her alive if possible. *C'est la vie.*

Chalon was on the stairs, the gun held two-handed as she had been taught and pointing towards the ceiling. Her back was now towards him. She would have to turn full to her right and down to see him, and that gave him the edge.

"Drop the gun, Claudia."

She turned too quickly and nearly lost her balance but the gun came round and the shot took splinters off the doorframe to his right. She was shooting at shadows. Luc was now directly behind her to the left of the stairs, his rubber-soled boots having made no noise in crossing the hall.

"Drop it, Claudia."

She did not move but she did not drop the gun either. Luc, watching her intently, was ready for the only play she could make, knowing she would try it. She was turning slowly but still facing up the stairs. He stepped back two paces, making no sound as he did so. She had completed her move and she brought the gun round quickly. It was a good move if only her target had been where she had thought him to be. She fired, realised her mistake and in desperation continued the turn. Luc shot her twice in the chest.

He was moving before she hit the stairs. He checked for a pulse. There was one, so at least the bitch was alive. He picked up her gun.

Benoît was already past and covering the landing.

"*Merde!*" he exclaimed.

"What?" Luc joined him.

"Gärtner has just gone into the room where we think Jo is."

The two men crossed to the partially open door. Luc crashed the door open and rolled to the left. Benoît followed, going right.

Gärtner had his right arm across Joanna's throat. His gun was against her face. There was total silence in the room.

"Put it down, Gärtner," Luc taking careful aim.

"Fuck off, Hansen."

"Let her go or I'll kill you." Luc spoke without emotion, his gun steady.

"If you try then the girl will die."

Stalemate.

Benoît had moved further round and was now less than a couple of paces from Gärtner. But Gärtner was ready for him and the gun pressed harder against Joanna's face.

Luc had only a partial target, as Gärtner was sideways on and mostly behind Joanna whose head came above his shoulder. It was a very risky shot. Gärtner had clearly made the same assumption and now carefully eased his way backward.

A burst of automatic fire from the courtyard sent shards of glass, wood and masonry into the room. Luc ducked involuntarily and Gärtner took his opportunity. He flung Joanna at Luc, fired once at Benoît and was gone before Luc could get off a shot.

Luc looked down at Benoît on the floor. There was blood on his chest. His breathing was shallow and blood frothed at his lips.

"Stay with him, Jo," Luc ordered, and scrambled after the fleeing German.

A pistol shot made him duck but not before he saw his quarry clear the bottom of the stairs. Luc raced after him.

Another shot splinted a picture frame to his right as he headed for the main downstairs room. A Kalashnikov came into view and Luc fired as he moved and the gunman slumped to the floor leaving blood and brains on the wall behind him. Luc kicked open the door.

A bullet hit him in the side sending him stumbling forward. He started to turn but a second bullet clipped the pistol, sending it spinning away and numbing his hand. A mental body check told him the damage was not serious, the Kevlar body armour had done its job.

"On your feet, you bastard." Gärtner spoke harshly.

Luc got to his feet swaying.

Gärtner grinned and thrust his pistol into its holster. He took out a large knife.

"Now you're mine, arsehole."

Luc sidestepped the lunge and launched a chest strike but could not get the power to do serious damage. He had the satisfaction of hearing Gärtner grunt. The German came at him again, and again Luc sidestepped the lethal blade.

"Remember Rwanda," Gärtner said.

"I should have killed you then, you murderous psycho." Luc dodged the blade again.

"It would be better for you if you had." Gärtner was moving slower, more purposefully. "I'm going to kill you, Hansen, and then I'm going to go back and fuck your whore again. She likes it in the arse."

The German launched another attack. Luc knew Gärtner expected him to retreat so he used a counterintuitive strike, stepping forward to meet the assault and delivered a numbing blow to the man's right leg. Gärtner went down as the leg gave way and Luc completed the move with a kick to the side of the head. He felt the wetness of blood and knew the knife had caught him on the arm.

Gärtner was up and moving again, the knife still in his hand. Luc stepped away, gathering his breath. The bastard was good. The German moved to Luc's left and feinted a thrust. Luc backed away.

"Come on, arsehole, or are you fucking scared?"

The knife was arching in again. Luc leant back and produced a powerful kick to the German's knee, missed his target and felt it connect with soft tissue. The knife sliced into his leg, drawing blood.

Gärtner was no longer able to move quickly but still he came on. Luc gambled and closed in hard, relying on the body armour to protect him. The knife sliced into the Kevlar, caught on the material and snagged. Luc delivered a double-handed strike to Gärtner's chest, cracking a few ribs. The German stumbled backwards, releasing the knife. Luc pulled it free and went after him.

Gärtner reached for his gun and Luc slashed upwards. He drew blood and the other dropped the gun, cursing. Luc kicked the weapon away as Gärtner closed in again throwing punches and strikes with lethal efficiency. Luc parried and lost his grip on the knife, which skidded away. He struck out against Gärtner's head and made partial contact, shaking the other badly. Then a blow caught him on the hip and he stumbled. Gärtner struck again but Luc got an arm up in defence.

Both men stepped back and drew breath, each calculating attack angles and vectors to the fallen weapons.

"Give it up, Gärtner…there's no way out."

Luc moved, blocking Gärtner's route to the knife and gun.

The German closed in again and almost landed a chest strike that would have broken ribs if it had connected. But it left him open.

Luc delivered two quick strikes below the ribs and when Gärtner reeled away, he went after him and landed two more strikes, one to the arm and the other to the chest.

"You can't win, Gärtner."

"Fuck off, Hansen."

Gärtner was moving slower now, but Luc was unable to exploit his advantage; the wound to his leg was leaching the strength from the muscle. He tried a kick, connected well but landed badly and fell. He rolled reaching for the gun but Gärtner, seeing Luc's move, was already turning away.

Then he was gone.

Luc's leg was bleeding badly. He pulled a field dressing from his waistcoat pouch, bound it tightly, then struggled to his feet. He picked up his pistol, inserted a fresh magazine and cautiously peered into the hallway. Sounds of small arms fire still came from the courtyard, but the house was eerily quiet.

Joanna gently laid Benoît's head down and closed the now dead eyes. The bullet had caught him high in the chest and the Kevlar had not saved him. He had not died easily.

She picked up his Glock and checked the balance — she could use this. She slipped the safety catch off and made sure there was a round in the chamber.

Slowly, she stood up and made her way to the door. She could hear gunshots and the sound of a fight downstairs.

She eased her way over to the banister and saw Gärtner heading across the hall towards the bottom of the stairs. She stepped back and concealed herself in an alcove.

Gärtner climbed the stairs with difficulty. Hansen was very good. There was no obvious way through his defences. Bastard. Well, he'd sort him good now. He'd kill the girl. He stepped over the prostrate body of Claudia Chalon and continued his ascent.

A bullet hit the wall. He turned, fired and took the next flight more quickly. The landing was clear. He could hear voices from the ground floor, shouted commands from outside and then suddenly all was quiet.

He stepped into the room, sweeping it from the right as he did so. He sensed someone and heard the click of an automatic behind him. Then he remembered the man who had been with Hansen. Even for him, there was no point in continuing the swing. He was sure he could take whoever it was but he needed to see them.

"Put the gun down, Gärtner."

Gärtner guessed she was by the door, but where was the man. He lowered the gun waiting for some indication of what was to happen next, but there was complete silence. He started to turn.

"Put it down, Gärtner," she repeated.

Now he knew where she was and could take the bitch.

He had barely started his swing when the bullet hit him in the side of the chest and he stumbled. *Scheiße.* By instinct, he fired in the direction of the shot before collapsing to the floor, dropping the gun, which slid away to the right.

He could not feel his left side, but adrenaline pumped into his bloodstream and he forced his body to function. He struggled to a kneeling position and reached for the knife that he always carried strapped to his right ankle.

"I wouldn't if I were you." It was the girl again. She was very close now.

He ignored her and a second bullet caught him in the abdomen. *Scheiße.*

He knew he was dying. He knew he had lost. He felt cold but his anger burnt and he was damned if the bitch was going to take him out. He willed his body to function. He knew she had not moved so there was still a chance, and if he was going to die, then he would take her with him. He was on his knees now, the knife in his hand. He struggled to turn.

The bullet took him between the eyes, ending his life in a blinding light and splattering blood, brains and pieces of skull over the beige carpet.

Moments later, Luc stepped into the room and quickly surveyed the carnage. Gärtner was obviously dead with half his head blown away. He stepped over the body and saw Benoît. He quickly checked for a pulse but there was none. Fuck it! He spoke into the radio.

"Blue Leader to Red and Green Leaders. First floor secure. Black Boy terminated. Blue Two is down."

He looked across at the body of his friend and felt a tightening in his chest. Salty tears welled up in his eyes.

He turned to Joanna, gently took Benoît's gun from her rigid grasp and pulled her to him. He enveloped her in a strong embrace and said nothing. Slowly the tension eased and she started to cry in long, heaving sobs. She clung to him, gasping convulsively. He kept his arms firmly about her until some semblance of control returned.

There was the sound of running feet and shouted commands. Gregor entered the room, followed by Verhaegen.

Gregor looked down at Benoît and then turned to Luc. "Get her away from here. We'll do the rest."

CHAPTER EIGHTEEN

Monday 5 May, Brussels

"Are you telling me that there was no possibility of taking him alive?" Radcliffe looked steadily at Luc standing to attention in front of him.

Luc nodded. "Yes, sir. The most important consideration was getting Jo out alive. Arresting Gärtner was secondary to that."

"Was any attempt made to get him to surrender?"

"I believe so, sir. But we were in the middle of a gun battle. Asking him politely to surrender was not something that occurred to us." Luc looked fixedly at a point just above his Director's head.

"And who actually shot him?" demanded Radcliffe ignoring the sarcasm.

"Almost certainly Benoît, sir," answered Luc.

"The medical examiner's report says he was shot with a Glock. Was that Benoît's gun?"

"Yes, sir."

"And Ballistics will confirm that?"

"Yes, sir."

"Very well, relax Luc. Please wait outside."

Luc saluted and marched from the room closing the door quietly behind him. Radcliffe sighed and then turned to James Ashley.

"Ballistics confirmed that Gärtner was killed by Benoît's gun."

"So, what's the problem? What's the issue, Alan?" Ashley lit his cigar and watched Radcliffe through a cloud of smoke.

"Well…according to Forensics, Gärtner was hit by three bullets from Benoît's gun. All came from outside the room at a range of about two metres."

"And Benoît was inside and already dead?"

"Yes."

"So we assume that Joanna got hold of Benoît's gun after he was killed, that she shot Gärtner instead of arresting him and Luc is covering for her." Ashley looked steadily at Radcliffe who nodded. "Well…frankly, Alan, I don't see the problem. I assume none of the others will say anything different."

"I doubt it."

"Then," continued Ashley, "I think we accept Luc's version and close the case. Much more to the point is what are we going to do about Vandenhove? I assume you have some plans on that front."

"Luc wants to go after him."

"Then I think we should encourage him to do so."

Tuesday 6 May, Brussels

Karel Vandenhove looked at the package. For anything addressed to him personally to come to the Commission offices was unusual, but what was more unusual was that this one had arrived by internal messenger. He flexed it but it seemed only to contain papers.

He carefully opened it and shook the contents, a plain brown envelope, onto his desk. He turned it over but there was nothing written on it to indicate either origin or recipient. He checked the package again but there was nothing else.

Vandenhove slit the flap and pulled out two colour photographs. He felt his gorge rise. One picture showed the scarred face of Dieter Gärtner in close up, with a dark wound in the centre of his forehead. The other was a full-length shot of Gärtner lying in a pool of blood. Vandenhove retched.

He reached instinctively for the envelope — there simply had to be a note of some sort. He slid the single sheet of paper out of the envelope and read:

> *Herr Dieter Gärtner regrets that he will no longer be able to fulfil the role of Head of Security at Groupe Franco Belge.*

Was this some sort of sick joke?

As calmly as he could, he carried the package through to his PA.

"When did this arrive?"

"It came by mailroom messenger while you were out for lunch."

"Find out who sent it." He tuned back into his office and shut the door.

Picking up the photographs, he fed them into his security shredder along with the letter. His internal telephone warbled.

"Yes."

"Mr Vandenhove, the mailroom says the package was handed in at the front desk by a motorcycle courier."

He put the telephone down and stared out of the window. The telephone warbled again.

"Yes," he snapped.

"Mr Vandenhove, don't forget your 2.30 meeting."

"Thank you." Damn and fuck it. He picked up his files and walked down to the conference room.

Another package was waiting for him when he returned an hour later. He picked it up. No sender's details and the same typed address. He went through to his PA and showed her the package.

She looked up and said, "Came in about ten minutes ago. I asked the messenger. He said it was delivered at the front desk by…"

"I know… a motorcycle courier."

"No, sir, by a bicycle courier."

"Well…if any more arrive I want the person delivering them detained so we can find out who is sending this stuff." He returned to his office and tore open the package. Inside was another brown envelope. He slit the flap and pulled out two more photographs and a sheet of paper.

Ms Claudia Chalon regrets that she will not be able to entertain you at her house anymore as she is otherwise detained.

He picked up the photographs. The first had a date seven weeks earlier printed on it and showed him having sexual intercourse with Claudia inside her sitting room. He was in his normal clothes and she was bending over the table. It was the day she told him everything about the investigation.

He felt breathless and his hands had started to shake again. He looked at the second photograph. It showed Claudia Chalon on a stretcher, accompanied by two police officers. He did not need to read the date stamp. She was still alive and that could spell trouble. He switched on the shredder.

His mobile phone rang.

"Yes…?"

"Mr Vandenhove, this is GFB Security, Antwerp."

Vandenhove went cold.

"Mr Vandenhove…are you there, sir?"

"Yes."

"Mr Vandenhove, the federal police are here with a warrant and they've taken over the computer centre."

Shit!

"Did you execute the emergency closedown procedure?" If they had, it would take the police months to find anything. He needed time.

"No, sir. They knew about the procedure and had disabled it earlier."

That fucks that. He would either have to bluff it out or fold and make a run for it. Perhaps he could blame it on Gärtner and save something but he needed forty-eight hours to complete his arrangements.

Later that afternoon, inside Joanna's house in Brussels, Luc stared angrily at Dirk Wauters.

"She won't see you, Luc," said Dirk sadly. "If fact, she won't see anyone except me and Dr Aziz who's with her now."

"Why?"

"According to the Doc, she needs time and space to come to terms with what happened." Dirk shook his head sadly.

"Has she told you what happened?"

"Not really. She said it was bad and that she got raped. She talks in her sleep though, something about shooting someone." Dirk looked Luc straight in the eyes. "Did she?"

"Yes. We got to her quick enough. I left her to help Benny after he got shot and went after Gärtner but he got away from me."

"Then what?" prompted Dirk.

"I heard the shots. Gärtner was kneeling just inside the doorway when I got there. He was wounded but still alive. He tried to move so she shot him between the eyes."

"And what about Benoît? Where was he?"

"Inside near the window. He was dead," answered Luc flatly.

"Jeezus. I'm sorry, Luc."

"Well, my dear Luc, that explains a lot," said Dr Aziz as she came into the room.

"In what way, Doc?"

"She's traumatised. She's been sexually abused, she's been badly beaten, she's killed her attacker and she feels guilty about Benoît."

"Why the hell does she feel guilty? That's absurd."

"Because, Luc, she feels it's all her fault. It's irrational, perhaps. But that's the way it is."

"But why won't she see me?"

Dr Aziz rested a cool hand on Luc's cheek. "She needs time and space, Luc. She cares deeply about you but she needs to come to terms with what happened in that house. She's defenceless, hurt, bewildered and she doesn't want you to see her like that."

"But I can help her." He got to his feet with an impatient gesture.

"You can help her most, young man, by giving her time. Go and finish whatever you have to do. Remove the shadows from her mind and she'll heal quicker." Dr Aziz touched his face again. "Give her time."

"I'm sorry, Doc, I can't do that." He turned away and headed out of the room, leaving the other two looking at each other.

Joanna was lying in a foetal position on the bed when Luc walked in and stood where she could see him. It was painful to see her like this and he did not relish what he had to do but there was little option.

"Jo, Vandenhove is still out there and we can take him down but I can't do it without you." It wasn't strictly true but he needed his partner back.

She rolled over and said nothing.

"Jo, do you understand? Unless you get your act together, Vandenhove will walk. Is that what you want?"

"Bastard," she replied quietly.

"You can call me whatever you want but we've got work to do."

"Leave her alone," said Dr Aziz quietly as she entered the room.

"Is that what you want, Jo?" Luc demanded coldly.

She looked at him for a moment, their eyes locked in unspoken communication, then she pushed the sheet away and swung herself into a sitting position.

"Luc Hansen, you're a bastard, but don't you dare walk out of this room without me. Understand?" She stood up. "Now give me my clothes. I can't go to work like this."

With an inward sigh of relief, Luc gave her the clothes from the chair at the end of the bed. She dressed slowly and then turned to Dr Aziz.

"Doc, don't think too harshly of him, he might just know what he's doing." She smiled sadly and then said, "Now come on, Luc Hansen, get me out of here and let's get this finished."

Wednesday 7 May, Brussels

Vandenhove knew they would be coming for him.

In the seven days since he had left the training centre, he knew he had lost. Yesterday's unwanted photographs confirmed it. With Gärtner dead, there was a chance, but with Claudia

Chalon still alive, there was none. He knew she would buckle as soon as the interrogation started, just as she had when the DER had first taken her, and she knew too much about him.

Yes, they would be coming for him soon.

He looked out of the car window at the sunlit street as his driver turned the Mercedes into the underground car park and stopped beside the security office.

He needed just another twenty-four hours to get his money safely transferred and then he'd be gone.

The security guard nodded him through and he took the lift to the eighth floor. The building seemed eerily quiet as he walked to his office, passing no one except his personal assistant on her way to god knows where.

Just another twenty-four hours to eliminate all traces. Just another twenty-four hours.

A young man with black hair and an olive-brown complexion, wearing dark-blue combat fatigues with a pistol in a holster, was standing by the window talking on a mobile phone as Vandenhove entered his office.

"Who the hell are you?"

The man finished his call and put the phone in his pocket. He turned but said nothing. It took Vandenhove only a second or two to realise he faced Hansen of the DER. Looking at the expressionless face and blank, dark eyes, Vandenhove suddenly felt sick and afraid. A nervous tick started in his right leg and he sat down heavily.

"What do you want?" he asked, but he already knew the answers.

Hansen picked up Vandenhove's telephone and quickly disassembled it. He showed the startled man the miniaturised transmitter.

"We've been listening in to all your conversations for months, Mr Vandenhove. Would you like to hear the tapes?"

"You obviously can't prove anything …"

"We don't need to, Mr Vandenhove," said Hansen softly. "You see, if you walk out of this building, you're going to stand trial for conspiracy to defraud, conspiracy to murder and for rape. Unfortunately, we will not be able to try your colleague, Gärtner, because he's dead, but your mistress, Claudia Chalon, has been most helpful and wants to negotiate."

Vandenhove started to shake. He was going to need to pull some huge political favours to get out of this. They may not be able to prove anything, but he was going to spend years in jail awaiting trial. *Godverdomme.*

And all he had needed was just another twenty-four hours. Shit!

He looked up as a second person entered the room. Despite the dark-blue combat fatigues and the holstered pistol, he recognised her immediately. He recoiled, a hunted look appearing on his face. He thought back to the scene at the training centre, of the girl's terrified face as Gärtner raped her, of his own arousal and his uncontrollable need to do the same.

"I think you know my colleague," Hansen said, his voice brittle, icy with knowledge of what they had done.

Vandenhove shrank back in his chair and huddled there. The girl had drawn her gun and he watched in horror as she approached. She laid the gun gently against his face and a feeling of uncontrollable terror gripped him. He lost control of his bladder, the warm urine seeping into his trousers.

"Oh, and by the way. Mr Vandenhove," continued Hansen quietly. "We accessed the Franco Belge computer and it appears you've been selling arms to the regime in Iraq in exchange for construction contracts. You've also been selling arms to the Kurds and the Sunnis."

The gun against his cheek moved a fraction and he shivered. Droplets of sweet formed on his upper lip.

"You know, the Americans want to talk to you, the Belgian police are cooperating, and now my colleague wants to shoot you. Frankly, I really don't think you've anywhere to go," Hansen shook his head and turned away.

Vandenhove said nothing. There was nothing to say. The girl smiled and pressed the gun to his head. He was sweating heavily, his heart was pounding and he could hardly breathe. He closed his eyes in an attempt to block out the terror.

"Goodbye, Mr Vandenhove, we won't be meeting again," said the girl quietly.

He felt the gun move slightly and there was a click as she pulled the trigger.

He lost control of his bowels.

Suddenly he was alone. He heard voices in the outer office and then there was silence.

A photograph of him leaving the training centre was on the desk beside copies of those he had received earlier. It was over.

A rapidly growing crowd had already formed around the broken body of Karel Vandenhove as Luc and Joanna emerged into the sunshine. They glanced at the dead man, much smaller in death than in life, and walked away.

www.whiteandmaclean.eu

Set up in 2009, **White & MacLean Publishing** focuses on using network technology and collaborative working practices in **a new approach to the publishing and marketing of books and documents.**

Traditional publishers have shackled themselves to a liberal-economics business model that encourages vertical integration and the pursuit of the economies of scale. The result is that they have become bound to a decision-making process in which opinions of editors are considered significantly less important than those of the marketing team and the accountants that dominate the management structure.

White & MacLean Publishing is based on the idea that this model is no longer appropriate for the modern networked world and we use a collaborative network of independent professionals who cooperate on publications on a project-by-project basis.

Each year we aim to publish between four and six works, either as hard-copy books or as electronic documents and eBooks.